BACKLANDS

BACKLANDS

A NOVEL

Victoria Shorr

W. W. NORTON & COMPANY
NEW YORK LONDON

Frontispiece courtesy of *Ricardo K Albuquerque e Sociedade do Cangaço, Foto: B. Abrahão.*

Printed in the United States of America
First Edition

Manufacturing by Courier Westford
Book design by Mary Austin Speaker
Production manager: Anna Oler

Library of Congress Cataloging-in-Publication Data

Shorr, Victoria.
Backlands : a novel / Victoria Shorr.—First edition.
pages cm
ISBN 978-0-393-24602-5 (hardcover)
1. Lampi?o, 1900–1938—Fiction. 2. Outlaws—Brazil, Northeast—Fiction. I. Title.
PS3619.H667B33 2015
813'.6—dc23

2014044314

W. W. Norton & Company, Inc.
500 Fifth Avenue, New York, N.Y. 10110
www.wwnorton.com

W. W. Norton & Company Ltd.
Castle House, 75/76 Wells Street, London W1T 3QT

1 2 3 4 5 6 7 8 9 0

To Anna Mariani, who took me there

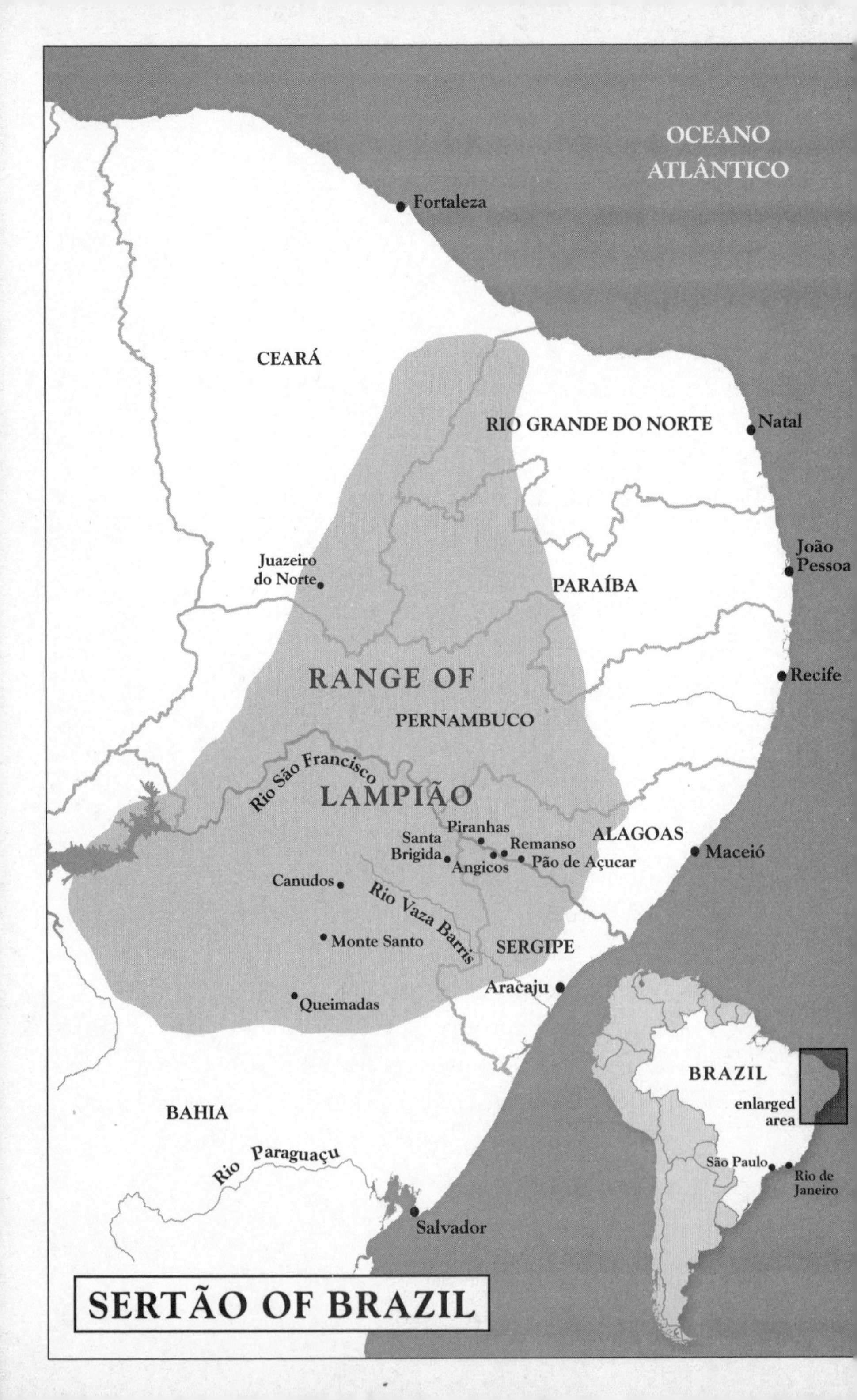
OCEANO
ATLÂNTICO
Fortaleza
CEARÁ
RIO GRANDE DO NORTE
Natal
Juazeiro
do Norte
PARAÍBA
João
Pessoa
RANGE OF
Recife
PERNAMBUCO
Rio São Francisco
LAMPIÃO
Piranhas
Santa
Brigida
Remanso
Angicos
Pão de Açucar
ALAGOAS
Maceió
Canudos
Rio Vaza Barris
Monte Santo
SERGIPE
Aracaju
Queimadas
BRAZIL
enlarged
area
BAHIA
Rio Paraguaçu
São Paulo
Rio de
Janeiro
Salvador
SERTÃO OF BRAZIL

Author's Note

Though this book is a work of fiction, it is based on fact. Every character is a real one, and most of the anecdotes come from firsthand accounts given to me on my travels through the Sertão in the late eighties and early nineties, when there were still people alive in every village and hamlet we passed through who remembered either the bandits or the "*força*" (the police), and were kind enough to tell their stories. Lampião's grandmother's remembrances of the drought of 1866 are drawn from Euclides da Cunha's *Os Sertões*. For the moment-to-moment account from Angicos, I relied as well on *Assím Morreu Lampião* by Antonio Amaury Corrêa de Araújo, and I would also like to acknowledge Frederico Pernambucano de Mello's *Quem Foi Lampião*, Leonardo Mota's *No Tempo de Lampião*, and Billy Jayne Chandler's *The Bandit King.*

Victoria Shorr

BACKLANDS

INTRODUCTION

Every January, in the city of Salvador, the ancient coastal capital of Brazil, people dress in white and throng down to the beaches, their arms filled with flowers for the goddess Yemanjah. She crossed the sea from Africa with them, and she favors white flowers, and the candles that her admirers float out to her on little wooden boats, along with their wishes. Easy wishes: "Love and money." Everything else with them is mostly fine.

Then they buy the grilled shrimp the boys sell in the street, mix their pinga with coconut milk, and dance the kind of half-samba that nobody else can do. There is music, drums, and laughter, all night, into the next day, and then maybe a little rain, a little sun. Another festival before too long. A fruit ice on the street. Light clothes, bright pink, yellow, green, on dark skin. Brazil, you think.

But get in your car and drive inland for a while, on a bad road getting worse, and you find yourself standing in the midst of the cactus and wondering if the palms of the coast were just a dream.

Or is this the dream? This vast expanse of wild rocks and thorns and tangled brush that now surrounds you. A man passes on a mule. You ask him the distance to the next village. "Three leagues," he tells you. His skin is lighter than the people's on the coast, with more of the Indian, more of the Portuguese mixed with the African. Bright blue eyes from the Dutchmen who came to conquer the place in the seventeenth century and ended up dying in their hammocks.

"Far," he says. "You should walk"—they don't say drive. They say "walk by car—for you have far to walk."

You bid him farewell and wonder, What's a league? *The map looks like it's about twenty kilometers, twelve miles, to the village, but the map's already a joke, or dreaming itself—the dirt track you're now on looks good on the map. A thick red line, like a solid highway. Three leagues to the village. "Far."*

You drive on. "Don't get caught outside a village after dark," you were warned. There are still bandits lurking about, supposedly, and jaguars, someone said. Yet, overcome by beauty, by the light coming in across the vastness, a color of light you've never quite seen, you stop the car and get out. You climb a small rocky rise and see—nothing. That is, no roads besides the one you hope you're following—or have you gone off on a goat trail? No way of knowing, no one to ask, not another car anywhere.

And no fences, as far as you can see. Instead an endless stretch of wilderness, "caatinga" *they call it, dotted with thornbush and all kinds of cactus, though it isn't quite a desert. There are trees, thick, beautiful trees, well shaped and spaced, as if planted in an English park.*

"A vast garden with no owner," the great Euclides called

it a hundred years ago, and it's still true. You listen, and hear nothing, and then goat bells in the distance, and then nothing again. You can draw a circle, like Jesus did, and sit here in the same kind of wilderness, two thousand years later, and cast your own demons out. You have come very far in a day.

THE SERTÃO. *Almost another country in the Northeast of Brazil, separated from the rest by climate, by culture, by inclination even. Its boundaries are its own—parts of seven states, the hard parts, nothing like the rest. "Semi-arid," a geographer could tell you, which means that you can raise a few cattle in a good year, goats most of the time, manioc and sisal if you're near a river, and that sooner or later a drought will send you running for your life.*

The people here know that. Every one of them has searched, first closely, then desperately, for clouds in the cloudless sky. They've gone down on their knees, whispered one-word prayers, flayed their own backs, cut off long beautiful braids, "for the Virgin." For nothing. For rains that haven't come.

And when the goats finally died, they've given up, and gone to the coast, "forever," where the sun is soft and life is easy, but they don't stay. They come back as soon as the rains do. They put on their leather, and ride out across what now seems to them the kindest of lands, with every cactus, every thorn giving fruit, in their "vast garden," and they smile and call it good.

It's a strong taste, but they'll tell you that they're "accustomed," drawn to contradiction, bred for contrast, and anything less is less. They stir great spoonfuls of sugar into the blackest coffee. The more they love someone, the farther away from them they dance. They hang the Bleeding Heart of Jesus on their walls beside the bull-god, and their hero is the violent, courteous bandit Lampião.

"FORGIVE ME," he would say as he robbed them, "you understand," and they did. His story was their story: a feud, a murder, the usual, wholesale lack of justice. But instead of turning the other cheek, as they did, he picked up a gun and joined a band of local outlaws, intending simply to kill the men who'd shot his father, and then go home to his goats.

But it turned out that he was too good at what he did to ever go home again. He was a natural leader, and his upbringing as a cowboy and mule driver had given him a sense of the land that translated into an unerring sense of strategy. When the authorities fought with him, he won. Word got out. Young men, brave and tough and mostly carrying their own torches of grievance against a system that had been killing their brothers and fathers for generations, flocked to him. By 1925, he was leading the biggest gang of bandits in Brazil.

He and his men roamed the Sertão almost at will. They could live even in the remote reaches, the badlands of the badlands, "the way thorns do, on drops of water," Lampião told a reporter. "A jaguar came up to eat me once, but he thought I was a cactus and went away."

What qualifications does a man need to join your band? the reporter asked him. "Nothing much," Lampião replied, "just so long as he's as agile as a cat, clever as a fox, can track like a snake, and disappear like the wind."

"Disappear like the wind"—yes, of course, for how else could they escape so often? More than once, the police had the gang surrounded, with no way out. Then they mapped the victory parades, called out the samba bands, and informed the press: "Lampião is dead!" Even the *New York Times* printed it, twice.

Lampião collected those clippings. "I'm used to dying," he liked to say. The people believed that he was a *corpo fechado*, a "closed body," impervious to bullets, having been blessed by Padre Cícero, the local miracle-priest.

He inducted men into his band with chivalrous ceremony, a nom de guerre—"Green Snake," "Hard Times," "Matchbox," "Come Back Dry"—a prayer, a touch on the shoulder, a new rifle. An oath of fealty to Lampião's laws and principles: no senseless killing, no harming the poor, no rape, no torture. "*If you have to kill a man, kill him fast.*" Courage in battle, high spirits. "*To die in a gunfight is to die happy.*" No low behavior unworthy of the band. Robbery, yes, but of the rich, and on a grand scale, publicly acknowledged. When he caught one of his men in a back room stealing, he shot him on the spot as a thief.

His forces swelled, thirty men, fifty men, a hundred, so many he had to form smaller bands, train other leaders. In 1929, a priest in Glória presented him with a beautifully sewn leather map of his "kingdom"—most of the Sertão, 440,000 square kilometers, 170,625 square miles. Almost the size of Spain.

When he needed something, he would head for a town. His heralds would precede him: "*My people, here comes Lampião, in love with life, and wishing you well. Receive him nicely, and he's sweet rice pudding. Betray him, and he's a rattlesnake.*"

They rarely betrayed him. They gave him what he needed—guns, money, salt, ammunition. They trailed after him as he strolled through their streets, discoursing with their mayors, offering alms to their poor, praying in their churches, getting a haircut. He would talk to them at length, tell them his life, his philosophy, his tales. They found him "shrewd and intelligent," a good listener, an accomplished speaker, and above all, "courteous." His enemies, though, had other tales to tell.

If a man helped the police in any way, as an informer, guide, or tracker, he and his family were no longer safe. The police offered protection, but everyone knew you couldn't count on the police; what you could count on was Lampião, and this was so true it became a proverb: "*The return of Lampião is cruel.*" He would burn your house, kill your father before your eyes. Make you dig your own grave before he shot you. The stories are endless. Everyone in the Sertão knows one. Courtesy, but murder. Murder and courtesy—the people comprehended both, and the oldest ones still remember his dances.

"Life is hard," he would say, "the people need a good time." And when the moon was right and the police at bay, he would invite a small town to a "ball," as they called them. He'd hire a guitarist and an accordion player, a fiddler if there was one, and with the money he'd taken from the rich, he'd pay for food and plenty to drink and send boys out through the countryside with an invitation—Come to Lampião's ball tonight—and a promise—all the girls would be "respected."

Then he and his men would deck themselves in the gold and jewels they'd stolen across the region, and splash themselves with their famous perfume. Tie red scarves around their necks, lace gold chains through their long black hair, stick jeweled knives into their sashes. The girls from these isolated places would creep in from their silent houses and dance all night with the bandits—the waltz and the courtly *xaxado*, hands behind the back, moving forward, moving back, coming closer, and then, with a swirl, away. Almost touching. Never touching.

Afterward, the street poets would sing of these girls, sitting in their windows, waiting for Lampião to come back. But he didn't, he couldn't, he was pursued, ever more relentlessly, by a chaotic combination of soldiers, police, sworn posses, and brutal irregular private forces with motives of their own. For almost twenty years, from 1921 till the end of July 1938, Lampião outfought them all, out-thought them, made them see ghosts in the night.

People said they'd never catch him. And in a way, they never did.

I

Maria Bonita

Looking up the river, she knew it would be silver. Down, toward the sea, gold. A few days ago, when they came in, it was that green that you never saw anywhere but here. The São Francisco River, the Nile of Brazil, always running, always true, even when the drought had burnt the rest of the place black.

Maria Bonita climbed up on a rock at the edge of the hideout, where you could best hear the river. Looking back, she thought she could claim to know every league of its banks by now, having, in the last eight years, either ridden, hidden, fought, or run for her life all the way from the great falls up at Paulo Afonso across into Pernambuco, then down and over into Bahia, into Alagoas, and now here in the small state of Sergipe, where they were safest, though far from safe.

Never safe. Last month it had been the police in Bahia. Two weeks ago, soldiers near Buíque. Mangueira had been shot there—one of the Vila Novas, too. They were running so hard then they couldn't even bury them properly. Best they could do was to carry the bodies out into the bush, to keep the police from getting the heads.

THE ROCK WAS at the edge of the hideout, nearest the river, farthest from camp. Lampião didn't like her to smoke. But Pedro Candido had brought them out some Jockey Clubs this afternoon, good cigarettes, the best in Brazil, and she'd found herself thinking that that's how she was going to end this evening.

This beautiful evening, by this beautiful river—not that she could even walk down there to bathe. There were too many police around, too many soldiers. If someone saw her, a fisherman or a boy with his goats, he might tell someone, and then they'd all be killed. Brutally. Horribly if the soldiers caught them alive.

The first time they came in here, she'd thought maybe she'd slip down after dark, following the dry creek that cut through the hideout, and just get her feet in the river, and splash some of that fresh water on her face, and through her hair. But the ferryman who'd brought them across had spoken of jaguars, and then she'd heard them herself, coughing in the night.

Not that that was such a bad way to die. A tracker had told her once that they shake you first, and then everything goes peaceful. You die smiling. Not the worst death. She'd seen worse, seen men stabbed. Seen men dig their own graves, and then just stand there, staring at the sun, waiting to die.

Why don't you run? she'd almost shouted to the last one—a little guy who'd sent the police after them. Taken the trouble to ride into town to betray them, and for what? For nothing, for this, his own death. Lampião had circled around the police and come back for the traitor. He was lucky that they were using a gun.

Why don't you at least die running? she'd wanted to cry as he stood there stiff and still, one tear rolling down his face.

Run!—but they never did. She ended up thinking that they'd rather take that one last minute alive, with the off-chance of a miracle, over a wild, free run with a shot in the back.

Not that there ever were any miracles. Just the shot, and then there they were. Alive one minute and in the grave the next, as dead as the first Portuguese who ever crossed the ocean, or the fleet, runaway Indian girls they'd caught and married.

STRIKE THE MATCH, breathe in, breathe out. Jockey Clubs were good, stronger than anything you could roll yourself. They gave you that double hit, *wham*, *wham*, both lungs, and then maybe you weren't worrying about how many police there were on the river. You were maybe remembering that you weren't afraid of the police.

She pulled her jacket close, and shivered. It had been

misting since they got here, and the moon was bad, too, waning, "sad," winter, July. The worst month, the cursed month—his "fatal month," Lampião called it. He always said he would die in July.

But how did he know? No one knew! All she knew was that she wanted to leave this place, everyone did. Nothing about it felt right to any of them. It was true that they'd been here before, and it had been fine—before, but then, everything had been fine before. Last time here, just a few months ago, when they'd been coming in off what the newspapers called a "triumphal swing" through the region, and in a way it had never been so easy. They'd fought with the police in Jirau, in Alagoas, run them out of town, and then fought them again out in the *caatinga*, and put them to flight out there.

"A rout," the papers called it, and right after that, Lucena, commander of the Alagoas forces, had marched out with his troops to the state border and drawn a line. "This line Lampião does not cross!" swore Lucena. He had secured his borders, he had wired the interior minister in Rio. Lampião could not get out of the state.

Though a few days later, Lucena got a present—a sack of dirt from the next state, Pernambuco. "For a pillow," wrote Lampião, since he'd always found that dirt best to sleep on. Which was why he'd broken through Lucena's police lines to get some, though Lucena was welcome to stop him, or try.

And Lucena did try. He marched into Pernambuco and chased the bandits halfway up the state, but then he was "forced" to turn back, as Lucena put it in his next wire to the interior minister. It had started raining, and his men had little food, no cigarettes, and no one in Pernambuco would extend him any credit. He blamed the governor, blamed the economy, blamed the rain, and went home.

"We're beaten up," a police lieutenant told the Recife newspaper. "Tired. We've been chasing Lampião for twenty years, and for what? For nothing. We're nowhere."

And the police were—nowhere, with nothing. And that had been just last April, three months ago. And then the outlaws came down here, same place, but everything had been different. Different stars in the sky.

The moon had been good then, too—full, rising silver, so they'd waited on the banks, till it was dark enough for them to cross, unseen. It was warm that night, just right, and they'd lain about on the banks, talking low, about nothing, really, since everything was all right then, and watching the moonlight, sparkling, on the great São Francisco. One of the boatmen told them that the old name, the Indian name, for this place was Jaci Oba, Mirror of the Moon.

And they could see it that night, all that silver, coming off the river. They could just make out an isolated hut on the opposite bank, silver-blue in the moonlight. A chapel, the boatman told them, for the ill-starred lovers, one from Sergipe, the other from Alagoas, who fell in love across the water, but for some reason weren't allowed to marry. Finally they made one last desperate pledge—to meet at midnight, in the middle of the river. They used lantern signals, he said, to jump at the same moment. When the bodies washed up, they were locked in each other's arms.

"Smiling," he claimed.

"Or not," someone said, and they started to argue, but then the moon went down and it was time to move, time to push off, into the river, under all those stars, leading toward the Southern Cross. It was black on the river, but calm, clear, so not frightening—that time—although then, right around a bend, with no warning at all, came another boat, heading down the river.

They all slammed down onto the floor of the boat, nearly tipped it, and pulled their guns, scared to death—they'd never fought on the water, never dreamed they'd meet the police at night like that, in the middle of the river. But it wasn't the police—it was the opposite of the police, cried the men in the other boat, their hands high in the air, begging them not to shoot.

"Who are you?" called Lampião as they came closer.

They were too scared at first to stammer out their own names, but it finally came out that they were a jazz band from the little town of Pão de Açucar, downriver, on their way home from playing at a dance in Piranhas.

Lampião had laughed. "Play us something," he said, "we love music." But they couldn't, their hands were shaking, but finally one of them picked up a horn and blew out, over the river.

It was a beautiful note, smoky and blue, and a beautiful song—"Tango da Vida," "Tango of Life," they said it was called, and she believed it that night. Believed that life was a tango, full of beauty and danger, mixed. Because there they were, on the São Francisco River, under the noses of Lucena and Bezerra, serious enemies, and still Lampião could make music walk upon the water.

And they played for a long time, everything they knew, going from sambas to *xotes*, and then jazz from New York, they said, and Lampião's own songs, too—and she was moved that they knew them, the bandits' marching songs, what they sang back and forth to each other as they walked through the thorns and cactus. Moved, too, to hear them here, on the water, and they all loved it, outlaws and musicians and boatmen all, and they went on until Scorpio rose, and Lampião said it was time to get across. He thanked the musicians, gave them some gold, told them he'd kill them badly if they went to the police, but they swore they wouldn't, and they hadn't, and they called out that they'd never forget this night, as Lampião sent them on down the river.

And then they'd come in here, to this very same hide-out, and the place had seemed fine then—perfect, even. Well hidden, surrounded by a serious briar patch, but with a good clearing in the middle, so there was room for everyone's tents and sleeping rolls. The weather had been good, too, and there were the "swimming pools" on top of the biggest boulders, depressions that had collected enough water so that you could take a real bath, plus plenty of level places to sleep, up and down the streambed. And she and Lampião had pitched their tent in this same grotto under this same hill, where you could hear the river, and they'd stayed for a few days, and got resupplied with what they'd needed—soap, needles, perfume, and bullets that Pedro Candido had bought for them straight from the police lieutenant Bezerra. New bullets, or at least the best they had, 1933s. The officers sold Lampião the good ones, and their men were stuck with the old ones that, like they said, "wouldn't even kill a dog."

And then they'd stayed here another day or two, barbecued some meat, drank some whiskey, danced a bit, watched the stars, and then packed up and moved on, and everything had been fine.

LAST TIME. As opposed to this time, right from the start. Even before they came in here—it was as if some bad star had risen, and suddenly what had always been easy was hard. And even if the police were "nowhere," with "nothing," there were suddenly too many of them, suddenly nothing but police in the Sertão.

And then they'd come here, but there hadn't been any jazz bands this time, and no Mirror of the Moon. No moon at all, and the river was covered with a cold mist that was somehow blacker than night, and the other side of the river looked blacker still. No one had wanted to cross that night—except Lampião.

They'd climbed into the boat in silence—it had been crowded, there were thirty-eight of them—the boatman had counted—heading out into the mist. Why? she'd wondered. To know how many he'd lose?

Still, when they got to the middle of the river, it cleared

a bit and they could see a few stars. "Nice," and "Better," they were all saying, when suddenly one of the stars, the brightest one she'd ever seen, streaked across the sky.

"*God save you, God hold you . . .*" some of the girls started to sing, for luck.

She'd turned to Lampião. "Beautiful!"

"Nah," he'd muttered, "it's the end."

"What?" she'd said to him low, fear rising. Had the others heard? She grabbed his arm. "What are you saying?"

But he'd just shrugged and turned away. "No one escapes his destiny."

"No one escapes his destiny"—except for them, all the time, it's exactly what they did. They lived escaping their destiny—how many times had they been lost, already dead, vultures circling? The real question now was less about destiny than what was wrong with Lampião. She'd come upon him yesterday when he was praying, with his eyes closed, on his knees, but leaning, and had nearly lost her breath at how tired he looked, how suddenly old.

Not that she was one to talk. She had a little mirror, she could see the changes—you don't spend eight years running through these backlands with no traces. Sometimes she even saw it in the color of her eyes, saw everything. A little line here, another there, some worse than others. A fleck where she'd given up the baby. A thin black streak where she'd been shot in the back.

Like a map of her life with Lampião, all the crossings and journeys, the battles and hideouts, she could see it all there, in the light of her eyes. Blue eyes—used to be blue. Now they were just kind of light—hard to tell. The mirrors were always small, and broken. She'd take the next nice one she saw.

When Corisco joined them with his men yesterday, he wouldn't even spend the night. He'd looked up at the steep, rocky cliffs that rose behind them and called the place "a rat trap," since the only way out was the creek to the river, and if the police came in that way, they'd be trapped, they'd never be able to climb up those steep cliffs, especially under fire—

"What fire?" Lampião had cut in. "They'll never find us here."

Which was a good point—there were no paths in here, just the goat tracks, and most of those led nowhere, just back into the thorns and cactus that surrounded the place. Lampião was the best tracker in the region, and even he still needed Pedro Candido or his brother to guide him in.

But Corisco had shaken his head impatiently. "Unless someone talks! Then the police come up from the river and shoot us like rats!"

Lampião spat. "The police."

"We've got guards on the top—" someone put in.

"Guards sleep, guards piss"—Corisco had grabbed Lampião's arm. "Look around! It's a rat trap! You're the one who taught me! 'A hideout with only one way out's the grave of a dead man!' Your words."

A murmur of assent—from everyone but Lampião. He'd never lingered before—just the opposite. They'd moved no matter how hard it was—moved in the pouring rain, moved at midnight, how many times? A hundred times, with less reason. A bad feeling someone had, a hunch, a sign. A night bird singing in the morning. A lizard crushed across a path.

Lampião murmured something about his nephew, who'd just come out to join the bandits—the boy needed a uniform. They'd gotten the cloth, and borrowed Pedro Candido's mother's sewing machine, and it was true that they wouldn't be finished with it until tomorrow.

But truer still that that never would have held Lampião before.

"Make the uniform later," said Corisco, "and come with us today!"

And she was ready, they all were. Ready to jump up right then and break camp, throw everything into the packs, and take off to the west with Corisco, head out into the Raso, and get away from the police and the soldiers for a while. They'd be safer out there, at least till July was over.

"Come on!" Corisco was urging, but she could tell that Lampião wasn't listening. She looked up then, straight into Dadá's eyes—smart eyes, worried eyes. Dadá had been thirteen when Corisco had carried her off, kicking and screaming, and the joke was that he'd had to steal dolls at first to keep her from crying. But by the time her father had come out to get her, it was too late. She wouldn't go back.

She'd fallen in love with Corisco by then—in love with the life, too. She liked sleeping under the stars, she told her father, and as an outlaw, she had nothing to fear but death. Did her father think she would come back now and make lace with the women? She showed him her dagger, three edges, forged by the best bladesman in Pernambuco, and on the handle, rings of pure gold. Plus she had a revolver, a .22, and could shoot with the best of them.

Which was saying a lot—they were all good shots. Lampião, with his one eye, could shoot anything, from anywhere. So fast you couldn't see it, and she herself was known, too, for her aim. Not long ago, they'd run into a group of farm people walking along a path to market, men, women, and children, with some goats and a donkey. She'd asked them for a drink, and they'd pulled out a tin cup and poured her some water from a leather case—splashed it, their hands were shaking, they were scared—and after she drank, she threw the cup high up in the air and shot right through it, for the children.

They'd liked that, especially when she gave them money to buy another, enough to buy ten cups, twenty. And her little iron, too, for starching collars—what was she going to do with it? Haul it around for the little ranch they were going to buy someday, where they would raise some children and make white cheese and starch collars? With every policeman and soldier in the land climbing over each other to be the one to carry their heads through the streets on a stick?

WHEN CORISCO LEFT, he didn't go by the river. Too many police around, he said. They watched in silence as he led his band slowly out through the underbrush, a solemn procession, growing smaller, then shimmering, and then turning to dust.

She'd had a thought then, just a flash really, of going with them. No good-bye, no farewell, just one step forward and then another, and no looking back until she, too, was shimmering in the distance, and that would be that, it would be over.

Because wouldn't the guns stay on him? If she left—wasn't it just possible that if she followed Corisco out of this rat trap, she'd find herself out of range? He would always be Lampião, but who would she be, if she left him? No longer Maria Bonita, just another Maria, maybe? Free to live in a house and die in her bed?

If she followed Corisco and Dadá out of here—though how would that be, after a while? Maybe for the first week she'd still be sitting by the fire, but what if food got scarce, or she got sick again, or brought them bad luck? That had happened once before in Corisco's band, with Mocinha. Her first boyfriend was shot, and her second one, too. And when it happened with the third, they decided Mocinha was a *pé frio*, a cold foot, a *caipora*, a jinx. They left her outside of a village, and the police got her and put her in jail.

Though she was probably out by now, probably alive, in a little house somewhere. Waking up in the morning and going to bed at night. Drinking coffee, eating farinha—Maria Bonita stubbed out her cigarette.

She'd been coughing blood ever since the shooting, but it was worse lately, and last week she'd actually gone to the doctor in Propriá disguised, though he probably knew. He gave her some orange blossom tea, to calm her, and told her to stay in bed for a while.

"Where?" She'd nearly jumped off the table and grabbed him. "Where?"

"Can't we leave this life?" she'd sobbed later that night to Lampião. "Go someplace far away, where no one knows us?"

And he hadn't answered, because there was no answer. No place on earth far enough away for them. No place where someone, anyone, a man, a boy, someone's son or brother, or widow even, might not step out someday from behind a doorway and shoot them down, just like that. Like dogs.

She got up off the rock. It was chilly, misty now. Time to slip into her tent, roll up in the skins and wool and get warm. Get some sleep. Try not to dream. The truth was she'd never leave. The fog had been late coming in, so maybe tomorrow would be a good day. She'd talk to Lampião first thing, and they could leave in the morning. Pull down the tents in a flash, load up the donkeys, pack their sacks, and head off, straight west, away from the river. They wouldn't even have to cross again. And they could still catch up with Corisco, either in Sergipe or out in the Raso, and then it wouldn't be July anymore.

II

Joca the Cuckold

It was the end of July 1938, and cold on the river, as cold as it gets. Joca Bernardes wondered if the moon would rise. That is, he knew it would rise—late, it was waning. But he wondered if it would come out, if he would see it. Not that it mattered to him. What he was going to do, he was going to do.

He was a boatman on the São Francisco River, and for years he'd ferried the bandits across, in silence and stealth, whenever they were moving through the region. It was a bit of a risk, granted, but good business, the best he had. The bandits paid him up front, and double what he got from anyone else—more than double sometimes, and it was what he lived on, or at least how he bought his tobacco and coffee, and even the few goats that he kept now, out at his brother's place. You could even go so far as to say that thanks to the existence of a rich and powerful band of roaming outlaws with a recurring need for conveyance back and forth across this stretch of river where the waters run green, Joca Bernardes, destined under normal circumstances to share in the general destitution, had become a relatively comfortable man.

Though you couldn't say that he was particularly happy to see them these days, because that meant that come evening, his wife would be slipping out the door.

It had been going on for a while. "Just going out for a little air," she'd told him at first, or "to see my mother," and he'd almost believed her. Tried to believe her, and even when he couldn't any longer, even when he knew who it was—Pancada, one of Corisco's band—he was still hoping that it would just go away. Hoping, too, that nobody else knew.

But then he started seeing it on all the faces, the bandits', his friends', saw the smirks. "Joca the Cuckold." They all knew. He was walking around with horns on his head.

He took another swig of the whiskey Corisco had given him yesterday. It didn't seem right to him, didn't seem fair. Joca had nearly died for the bandits last year. Someone had given the police his name, and the lieutenant, Bezerra, had dragged him into the station in Piranhas, beaten him, held a gun to his head, and said he'd kill him, right then, right there, if he didn't talk.

And he would have talked—hell, hadn't Lampião himself even told them to talk if the police got them? "Talk right away," he said, "before they hurt you, tell them everything you know, and they still won't get us." But Joca hadn't had anything to say. The bandits weren't on the river then, or if they were, they hadn't crossed, so Joca had no idea where they were.

Bezerra had almost shot him anyway, as a collaborator —wanted to shoot him, just to be doing something, was mad, hot, had his finger on the trigger. But the corporal, Aniceto, who'd grown up in the same dust as Joca, just off the river, had put his hand on Bezerra's arm, lit him a cigarette, and reminded him that Joca wasn't worth anything to them dead, not even a bullet.

And Bezerra had finally shrugged, and called one of the men to toss Joca out of the police station, where he lay in the dust for a while before he could even get to his feet.

And when he finally limped home that night, what he found was an empty bed. His wife had gone to her "mother's"—that's what she'd tell him, and that's how he'd leave it. He wouldn't have the strength for another fight that night, plus the truth was, it wasn't all bad. Joca had to admit that he hadn't minded the presents she came home with—a gold chain one time, and a bracelet another, some gold coins, too, taken from someone rich, up the river. A ring once—Joca had taken that himself and pawned it. Bought himself a dinner in Pão de Açucar, and a night in the district with the girls. He figured he deserved it. When she saw it was gone she'd turned red, but for once hadn't said a word.

And he would have let it go on like that—it wasn't as if there was much between them. She'd married him during one of the droughts because her father couldn't feed her. He'd married her not even knowing her right name. Thinking it was Cida, when it was Graça, and she hadn't even bothered to correct him. Just let him go on calling her Cida, until one of her aunts came by, and laughed. "What Cida?"

But was that his fault, and what did it matter? "Cida" or "Graça"—she was his wife, he fed her, put a roof over her head, and she swept and cooked and "received" him, as they said, when he felt like it, and wasn't that enough?

Though what she gave him back was this—but what could he do about any of it anyway? Since he wasn't the man to beat his woman, or take on one of the bandits, for that matter.

So he'd let it go, and would have kept on like that, except that now he was seeing it on all the faces—"Joca the Cuckold." He'd been drinking all afternoon, and when he saw his wife putting on her good clothes, he'd walked over and grabbed her arm.

She'd looked good tonight—when had she last put on her striped skirt for him, or combed out her long dark hair? He didn't even know how long it was, almost down to her waist. She kept it wrapped in a scarf at home all the time these days, even when she was sleeping. No one would call her beautiful, with her small eyes and no chin, but she had that hair, and she could dance like an angel, not that they'd danced in a long time. When had they last danced?

"It's Pancada, isn't it?" He'd grabbed her arm.

"Let go of me!"

"You're not going!"

She tried to twist away. "Leave me alone!"

"Tonight you don't go!"

"Says who?"

That was the question—says who? Joca the Cuckold, even with a bottle of the bandits' whiskey in his hand? A skinny little boatman with a slant in one eye and thinning hair? Against a bandit with two guns and a ten-inch knife?

"Quiet!" he whispered. The houses were small, made of mud. They shared a wall with the neighbors.

Her voice rose. "Try and stop me! Just try! I'll tell him, and he'll come straight over here and tear you limb from limb!"

It was true. "Shut up!" he said, and, "Daughter of a whore!" but he dropped her arm, and she ran out the door and slammed it as she left, so the neighbors would hear.

And laugh. Joca the Cuckold, the biggest joke in town. He took another drink. Cavalinho, what Lampião himself drank. Not that he ever saw Lampião—Lampião didn't work with him anymore, maybe didn't trust him. But Corisco, one of Lampião's lieutenants, did, and Lampião had probably given this very bottle to Corisco, who'd passed it on, easy come, easy go, to Joca. He'd stood there for a while, bottle in hand, staring at the door his wife had walked out; and when he finally lay down, it wasn't to sleep.

He counted the cocks' crowing, and got up at the third one. He didn't get dressed, since he hadn't undressed. It was still dark outside, and cold, the end of July, winter on the river. The mist was heavy, so no moon, which was probably good. He saddled his donkey, and strapped on his spur. One spur, all he had, he would look ridiculous—"Joca the Cuckold." But it would get him into town faster, and it had come to him that since they'd cast him anyway as the fool, he might as well amplify his role.

IT WAS STILL gray when he rode up to the police station. Piranhas was right on the river, and the station was just up from the banks, on the little square. The door was locked for the night, but there was a bench out front. Joca tied up his donkey and sat down.

An hour passed, two. The town was coming to life, but from the police station, nothing. Joca got up and walked down to the river. The boys were taking the boats out, the fishermen unknotting their nets, and when he'd seen enough of that, he walked back, and now the door was open. Joca walked in.

Everyone glanced up, and then away. Joca the Cuckold. He asked for Bezerra.

"Bezerra's not here," one of them said, and Joca walked back out again, and stood by his donkey. Then he turned and went back inside.

"Who I'm really looking for is Aniceto."

A shrug, a shout into a back room, and then the corporal, Aniceto, came out and nodded when he saw Joca. "So. You've come to repay me for saving your life?"

"Could be," said Joca.

"What have you got?"

"Not much, but maybe enough."

Aniceto liked the look of it already. Joca was here early—he must have left his house downriver before dawn. So, a man who hadn't slept. Tormented, you could see it, and still half-drunk—good. If it ever happened, it would be like this.

He motioned for Joca to follow him into the back room. Even before he'd closed the door, Joca started.

"I dreamt I was the cause of Lampião's death," he said solemnly.

There were some who would have laughed at Joca, but Aniceto knew about Joca's wife and the bandit, and he could see that Joca knew, too. And must have known, as well, that if this didn't work, he was a dead man. Plenty of people had tried to betray Lampião before—no, plenty of people had betrayed him. They'd gone to the police, the army, the government. Given details, led them right to him, moved in complete secrecy, under cover of darkness, to exactly the spot where Lampião was, only he wasn't there—ever. And then he came back and killed them. Always.

"*The return of Lampião is cruel.*" A young man in Pernambuco had recently set the police after him, and he'd circled around them, and cut the informer into very small pieces. Joca Bernardes must have heard about that.

But Aniceto could see that Joca had something stronger than fear in his heart that morning.

"Twice now I dreamt it," said Joca.

Aniceto put his arm around Joca's shoulder, led him over to a chair. "He's around here, isn't he?" he asked.

"I took Corisco across the river yesterday to meet him."

"Did you see him?"

"No, but Corisco did."

"Where's the hideout?"

"Just across the river from Remanso."

"Can you take us in there?"

"No, but I know who can."

"Who?"

A pause. Aniceto could almost see the good from the whiskey draining out of Joca's face, giving way to a hangover, and Joca starting to remember how well the bandits had always treated him.

"I'll kill you myself, Joca, if you back out now," said Aniceto. "You know that, don't you?"

Joca knew.

"These dice are thrown," Aniceto said.

Joca nodded. "Go step on Pedro Candido. They're on his mother's place."

Aniceto wasn't entirely surprised—everyone knew that the local merchant Pedro Candido was one of Lampião's suppliers, they just didn't know how key he was. His mother had a sprawling ranch where they ran goats, right across the river, in the wild uncleared bush, a good place for Lampião to hole up, Aniceto could see that. And if he was there, there was a chance they could get him, or at least try. It wasn't like the last time he was in the region—camped safely on lands belonging to the governor's father. No way they could touch him there.

But Pedro Candido's mother's ranch was another story.

"Where's Pedro Candido now?" asked Aniceto.

"At home."

Good. That meant Entremontes, just down the river. "You're sure?"

"I saw him last night."

Good. Aniceto called for coffee, and gave Joca a cigarette. Lit it for him, and told him to wait while he went out for a few minutes, told his men to keep him there, "no matter what," if he tried to run. Told them, twice, that he'd have them all stood up against the wall and shot if Joca wasn't there when he got back.

Then he walked out of the station—didn't run. He didn't want any of the infinite spying eyes in that or any town to notice a policeman running and wonder why. He strolled over to the little bar, had a coffee, and then made his way to the telegraph office, and talked to the man there about the weather.

"Cold."

"This time of year."

"July."

Then he mentioned that he might send a short wire to his chief, Bezerra, who was downriver, in Pedra.

The telegraph man was an old friend of Aniceto's, not that he could trust him or anyone else with news about Lampião. You never knew people's loyalties. It was always complicated and often secret, a matter of blood and old ties, which was precisely why Aniceto and Bezerra had settled on a code, should something like this ever come to pass. Should they ever chance upon this kind of significant betrayal that would give them a shot at capturing or killing the most wanted man in Brazil.

The date on the telegraph was July 27, 1938. *Bull in pasture*, Aniceto wired Bezerra. *Come with urgency*. That was all. They'd already set a meeting spot—the last cornfield just south of Piranhas.

Aniceto handed the message to the man and said he thought there was more fog than usual, but agreed that the sun might come out later that morning. He then walked out of the office, hoping he looked more like a man on his way back to a desk job than one bound for either death or real glory, the most there was in all Brazil.

He'd been chasing Lampião and the bandits all his life—they all had, every policeman and soldier up there. Plenty had died, more had failed, some had come close, but no one had gotten him. It was almost a law of nature out there. "*The man to catch Lampião has never been born.*" That had been the saying for twenty years now.

But twenty years is a long time, Aniceto was thinking as he walked back toward the station.

III

She awoke at dawn, peeked outside, saw the first light, and thought, *Already?* She had the feeling that she hadn't slept, although she must have, since he'd been there for a while, though was gone now. He was probably up on the ridge, watching, praying. All that praying—she could have married a *beato*, a pilgrim, even a priest, for all the good it did her.

He hadn't even looked at her for days—hard to believe he was the same man she used to lie with, face-to-face, his hair wrapped around her fingers, hers in his. When did that stop? When she cut her hair?

She shouldn't have, though—he hated it. It was after one of their fights, and she had done it to show him. But it was growing—couldn't he see that? If he looked?

The first ones were up, making coffee, she could hear them. Which would be good, great even, after a cigarette. The best, the first one of the morning. She picked up her basin—she would wash her face after. First was to get back to the rock and clear herself. Purify. Have her smoke.

She struck a match, breathed in, breathed out. Tobacco was sacred to the bull god, some places. She remembered when Gato was hit, not too long ago, he lay in the dust, calling not for God or even water, but for a cigarette. "Roll me one, Nenê, *bem fininho*, a really thin one," he'd gasped, and then died.

Just like that. Dead. Shot, the best they could hope for. "*To die in a gunfight's to die happy*"—she used to think that meant it was good to die in action. Now she thought that maybe it was just that you were glad to be shot instead of stabbed.

The sun looked like it might be trying to come out, for the first time in days, and some buzzards were already circling. Someone must have left out a calf, and it had been eaten by a jaguar, half-eaten. She used to hate buzzards, but she'd come to see that they were just doing their job. Cleaning up the place.

She watched the circles getting lower—any one of those birds could have flown in this very morning from the trees around her home. It wasn't much more than ten leagues away, if you went straight overland. Lately, she'd been imagining doing it herself, turning her face to the sun and heading west, over that beautiful stretch of gray and green, thorn trees and cactus, no fences, no clearings, all of it exactly like the day it was made, heading for the blue peak she'd soon see in the distance, that would get her to the path she knew better than any in the country, that led to the mud house with the old tile roof at the end of a dusty road that she used to call hers.

And, "Come into the house!" her grandmother would be standing on the porch and calling. Just the way she used to—"Maria, come into the house!" Long before she was a bandit with the highest price in Brazil on her head, when she was just a girl among girls, on a hardscrabble ranch like the rest of them, in the backlands of Bahia.

That life seemed almost miraculous to her now, the one she'd lived day by day, and each of them absolutely, miraculously, the same, with nothing extraordinary about them, nothing to run or hide from. It had occurred to her lately that her mother and grandmother, her father even, had probably never been scared in their lives, not really scared, not of being shot, anyway. What they feared was what everyone feared—God and the devil, drought and starvation, disease.

Though less that, since the vaccine for smallpox had come out from the coast. She remembered that her grandmother had been against it—"Leave it in the hands of God," she'd advised her mother. There were eleven children—too many.

"Leave it to God," counseled her grandmother, let Him collect some of them back from where He'd sent them, and leave to this hard, dry land the few it could sustain.

But her mother couldn't see letting them die such a

death, once you could help it. The pocks, the mad wild prayers, and then the fever. A blessing, almost, when the crying finally stopped.

So she took them into town for the prick in the arm, and then there they were, alive and well, growing and eating, wearing clothes, needing shoes, all eleven. Too many, though her father could still feed them, as long as everything else went well. As long as it rained even a little, as long as proper relations were maintained with the neighbors—they couldn't afford any feuds, no stolen goats or cattle. "Unless you boys want to join the bandits," her father had joked.

But he was joking. Maria Bonita's father was a man of peace, born on the right side of the law, which was to say on the same side of the divide as the local powers, and there were no feuds, and no big droughts for a while, just life flowing along.

Which meant goats, and a few cows, so cheese and milk, and a small crop of cotton. Her grandfather had made money with that cotton in the days when buyers would come in from the coast with big wagons and take everything they could grow. But that was before she was born, and it had been years since her father got a good price for his cotton, even when by all the blessings they had out there he could grow it, which was to say, even when it rained, and not only rained but rained enough, and at the right time.

"It's too rough"—the local Colonel João Sá used to shake his head with her father—"too brown." The Portuguese wouldn't buy it anymore, he said, not when they could buy smooth white cotton from North America.

And her father had shrugged—what else could he do? Anyway, he was happy enough just to be talking to Colonel Sá, the biggest landowner in that part of Bahia, the richest, and so the boss, the king, the law. "João Sá commands the rain," people would say, and if he was talking to you, stopping and shaking his head over your cotton crop, if he then bought you a shot of *pinga* at the fair and asked after your wife, your mother, then that meant all was going to be fine with you, whether you sold your cotton high or low. All was going to continue, that is to say, just as it was.

A simple life, the country life, just as it had been led, more or less, in the Bible. Up at dawn, the animals, the cooking, the sweeping, a bit of wash, and then down at dark. There were kerosene lamps by then, but kerosene was expensive, a luxury for a feast or disaster, and most days they were asleep as night fell, just as her father was barring the door.

Though occasionally there'd be a feast day or a goat fair when they'd go into town, to church, or to the square, to dance under the moon and eat little cakes filled with guava paste and run wild with the other children. And once in a while they'd have a visitor, like the time her cousin came out with the newspaper, and they saw their first picture of Lampião.

It must have been around 1922 or so, when she was already thirteen or fourteen. "Look at this!" Her father whistled. "They've got the Colonel Gurgel and his wife," two of the regional gentry.

She and her sister had looked up from their sweeping. "Who's got them?"

"Lampião—'The most dangerous bandit in Brazil,' it says."

"I'm not afraid of him!" one of the boys shouted, and it was true, why should they be? He was one of them, a small rancher who'd been drawn into one of those terrible feuds through no fault of his own. Bad neighbors—the state of Pernambuco was "famous" for that, her grandmother had said. Famous for the blood feuds that come from bad fences.

In Lampião's case, the neighbors were the powerful Nogueira clan, and when things got tough, during the drought of 1918, they started stealing Lampião's father's goats and moving in on his water.

Bad business, that, but the Nogueiras were a bad lot. Still, they had the local police in their pocket, and ended up killing his father, which was why Lampião and his brothers were bandits, which was only fair, Maria's mother and father agreed.

They crowded around, all of them, to get a look at the picture—a band of young men in leather, some kneeling in front, some standing behind, rifles in hand, and gunbelts strapped across their chests. Their captives standing among them, formal and absurd, the colonel in his white suit, his wife in her hat.

But he wouldn't kill them, her father said. Lampião was known not to be "perverse." He only killed when he had to, when a man betrayed him, or was part of the police, a sworn enemy, which was more than they could say for the police.

There was a general murmur of assent—that part of Bahia was partial to the bandits. Even the colonel, João Sá, was said to be their ally.

"Which one is he?" she asked, moving closer. She'd never seen such a picture, all those boys, some dark-skinned, some light, some handsome and posing for the camera, and others staring as if they'd just run off from their fathers' goats.

"This one"—her father pointed to one in front. He was kneeling, awkward, and you could see he was gangly, and she already knew that he had only one eye.

But there was a story, too, that went with the picture. There'd been a bad skirmish, in which the police had shot Lampião, in the foot—killed him, they claimed.

"Lampião's dead!" announced the police, not that anyone was inclined to believe them, except that this time the story had come down through the people, too. A cowboy had seen the trail of blood. Which meant that they hadn't killed him in action—he'd gotten away. But his horse had been killed, and his men had had to keep fighting, to cover his retreat, and then they'd been chased off in another direction, so he was alone and on foot—crawling, actually, he told her later. All the police had to do was follow the blood of a crawling man.

"He's dead," the major in the field concluded, and wired the governor. "We're looking for his body, day and night," though that was a lie. They managed to lose the trail as night was falling, and then they'd retreated back to whatever village was closest, and huddled by their fires and drank their rough sugarcane liquor, scared of even the half-dead Lampião, who took the chance to crawl off to a little draw beneath a fallen tree trunk, where he lay for twelve days.

"Lampião's dead," the governor told the press, and it was almost true that time, as good as true for twelve days. He'd had some dried meat and a little water on him, but that hadn't lasted long, plus his ankle had swollen and turned black, so that he was thinking he probably should die. He couldn't live as a cripple, they wouldn't let him.

Twelve days. The police weren't even bothering anymore. "He's dead," said the papers. They started giving details: "Major Teófanes Torres killed him, the governor of Paraíba saw the body"—though the bandits kept looking, "following the buzzards," his brother said afterward. And he himself was falling away from life as he lay there, already more lizard than man, as he put it, breathing in and breathing out, hot in the day, cold at night, no longer thinking, when a woman passed nearby, singing low.

He thought she was Santa Luzia at first, his grandmother's patron saint. So he called to her gently, not really expecting her to turn, but when she did, scared, he saw she was a real woman. She narrowed her eyes, and peered from a distance through the thorns and briars to where he lay, frightened equally of man or ghost.

But the people of the Sertão, his people, had all prayed themselves at one time or another for an open hand and an outstretched arm, and they understood pity. The woman had looked from his black lips to his black ankle, fed him, drop by drop, the little water she had, then went for her husband, a scrawny little man in rags, who lifted the terror of seven states onto his back and carried him down to their mud hut.

And from there Lampião sent word to his brothers, who came out with sixty men and carried him to the hills of Paraíba, to a ranch belonging to one of the big landowners in the region, whose borders the police didn't cross. Lampião had recently sprung the landowner's son from the local jail, and now the landowner returned the favor and brought out his cousin, a doctor from town, who somehow managed to save the black foot.

He didn't even limp after that, though he should have, he told the reporters, and as soon as he was better, he traveled to the village of Sousa to take on the police who'd "killed" him. He led them into an ambush where they started shooting each other in the cross fire, and then he raided a few of the big houses around there, took Colonel Gurgel and his wife hostage, and sat down with his men for a photograph, with that half-smile Maria and her sister saw in the photo that day.

That *Dead, eh?* smile. That smile that she could practically hear saying, *Where'd you say you saw the body?* In a teasing, mocking voice that made her knees feel weak and her heart beat in places she hadn't felt before.

Later that afternoon, she and her sister sneaked the paper out to the wispy trees near the fence.

"Would you marry him?" her sister asked. She didn't say *Lampião,* but they both knew who she meant, and knew, too, that that wasn't really the question. That was like asking if you'd marry the emperor of Brazil, if he came back to life and would have you.

"Would you marry any one of them?"

That was the question. Would a backland girl step into the dark with absolutely any one of them at all? Give up a settled life for a life of passion? The kind that comes with a ticket to the graveyard, though maybe not for a while.

She studied the faces of the gang—hard to make them out, now that she looked closely. It didn't matter, though. They were all young, all free, and not afraid to die—boys who had broken away from all that held them and were laughing right in the face of Colonel Gurgel. She'd never seen that before. Even the toughest cowboys she knew took off their hats to João Sá.

"Yeah," she said.

"Even the ugly one? Even the short one?"

"Yeah," but she was thinking it wouldn't be that way. Her eyes were blue, her skin the color of honey, her hair long and thick, hanging down her back. The boys in the village were starting to follow her through the streets on market day, starting to hand her little leather bands they'd made themselves.

She would marry one of them, a cowboy. A good one, though. Someone who could dance.

From inside came the call: "Come into the house, Maria!"

She'd put down the paper and run inside, and helped serve the beans and manioc that night, and even sat and ate as always, but found herself strangely riled and, later, unable to sleep. She'd lain in bed, wondering. Trying to lie still so as not to wake the others, trying to keep her hands off herself. Was it really true that Lampião had only one eye? What did the other one look like? He had on glasses, and anyway, you couldn't tell much from the picture. Just that some of the other boys were better-looking, better posers. Lampião wasn't posing. He was looking at you straight.

At who, though? Her, maybe? But that was impossible, it was just a picture, she knew that. But still, she'd fallen asleep wondering.

AND WOKEN UP the next day to the drought. Or maybe it was the next year, when she turned fifteen, that people started looking up at the sky. It was blue all the time now, and bluer every day, a hard blue, with no white, nothing that could turn to a cloud anywhere on the horizon, and all the signs were bad as well. The frogs were gone, and the worker ants had disappeared, "and are the ants ever wrong?" people were saying. Drought was coming, and drought would come.

The poets were already singing it in the square—"God, look down at our Sertão! A tragedy without a name!" and the oldest ones were reminiscing about the Drought of the Double Sevens, in 1877, when every cow out there died of thirst, and a million people, too.

And compared to that, it wasn't such a bad one, the drought of 1924. It didn't kill people or put them off their land, but her father had to separate some of the goats and sell them early. He couldn't wait for the fair, when he'd get a better price, because there wasn't enough for them to eat, he said, and it wasn't just the goats. There was less on the table—some meat still, from the goats, but no cheese, and their manioc crop had failed, so there was first only a little grain and then none. They couldn't afford to buy anything, so no sugar, and no coffee.

And there was nothing they or anyone else could do about it, except stand and watch the sky, or follow their neighbors into town, for a mass repentance, when they all got down on their knees and begged God to forgive them the sins that had brought this, His just punishment, down on their heads.

And they beat their breasts and even flayed the skin off their own backs, but to no avail. The sun rose hotter every day, in a sky first heartless blue, then white. They started hearing tales of wandering desperate bands who were looting the grain depots in the market towns. And then her father came back from town one day with the news that the farmers were lining up outside the barracks with their weeping daughters, to give them to the soldiers, marriage or no marriage, just so they wouldn't starve to death at home.

And it was shortly after that that she heard her mother crying. "No! You can't! He's too old! And she's beautiful!" or actually, "starting to be beautiful." Those were her mother's exact words—"starting to be beautiful." Funny, she could still hear them, exactly in her mother's voice.

"All the more reason to get her out of the house!" her

father had shouted back. She could hear that, too, and still remembered the fear.

She and her sister had looked up from their lace. She was sixteen then, and not bad with a needle, though her sister was the good one.

"Tell him to wait a bit," her mother was pleading. "Talk to him!"

But her father wasn't doing any more talking. He'd already "spoken the thing" to the shoemaker, given his word. It was done. They were "lucky," he shouted, that he was taking her off their hands.

The girls exchanged a look. Who?

He didn't say, just stomped out the door and past them, through the dust, which swirled around his cracked boots. But when they crept inside, her mother raised her red eyes to her.

THERE WAS NEVER anything anyone could ever do about anything in the Sertão, just bear what came and hope for the best. That's how she'd been raised, and that's what she did. She'd heard her father say, "Saturday," so she could hope and pray, first of all, that Saturday wouldn't come. She was just sixteen and "starting to be beautiful," and she felt somehow that this couldn't be her fate, to have her life shut down before it had properly begun. To be married off to an old man, the town shoemaker, who would, after all, have taken anyone, her older cousin with the limp, or one of the other girls. And she could sense that even her father felt that he'd make a mistake, acted in haste, in fear—from seeing the farmers and their girls, all that misery. He'd panicked and made a bad deal, and would maybe now figure out a way to withdraw, or "respeak" it.

There were ways. They all knew that—even in the Bible, there'd been the marriage swindle, one veiled sister substituted for the promised one. Not that she'd want her sister taken in her place, but something, maybe some goats. A promise of money when the rains came.

So she hoped, and her mother did, too, she knew, though they didn't speak a word about it, because what was there to say? It would either happen or it wouldn't, and there was no point in making it worse by talking about it, too—but she heard the pleading, the tears, and then the harsh words, which led to more slammed doors, and finally to her father swearing on his own father's bones that he was doing the thing and was going to do it, and by Friday a silence had descended on the house, and on Saturday morning he went out without a word and hitched the last horse to the cart.

Her mother clung to her, sobbing, as she wrapped a long cotton scarf around her head for the dust, and gave her a small sack to take with her, with a comb, a few underthings, a blouse, and her bridal nightgown. The one she'd made for her when she was a girl—what all their mothers made for their daughters, white lace, their best work. It was the sight of this that suddenly brought the whole thing out of the haze, and set it all right there in front of her.

"No! Please!" She started crying, for the first time, into her mother's shoulder, but her father had come to the door by then.

"My daughter, you must receive your husband willingly," her mother whispered into her hair. These were less words than an incantation that could be said, just like the nightgown could be given. Not much, though still everything. *You are trapped, but such is life. Here is the lace—see, it is beautiful.*

"Let's go," said her father, and she walked out the door and climbed into the cart, and never spent another night at home.

Actually, there was one, but that was a long time coming. What came first, what had to come first, was the desert of her life with the shoemaker that started that day in the church in Santa Brígida.

Even before, on the ride in that morning—she could still remember the silence, the feeling, as she and her father drove off, that they were driving not only into heat and dust, but into silence. Neither of them said a word. She had loved her father—the way they did, quietly, distantly—and respected him, always. Thought he was smart, and that he did things right, kept them safe. Protected them, and if there were going to be people starving, it wouldn't be them, or at least not at first. They'd be among the last to go.

And she'd loved him for that, as a child, but that was over, that intensive love that was itself half-gratitude, half-joy, at just being safe, under his tent. But she was outside now—he'd put her out, not because he had to, as he'd insisted to her mother, but because he'd misjudged, he'd made a mistake. She'd looked up at the sky that morning, on the way into town, and knew that though it hadn't rained yet, it had gentled up already, and would rain soon, in a week, maybe two, and this drought wouldn't kill them. And she knew he knew it, too, and that he should admit it and turn the horse around and send the shoemaker his apology.

But his word, his name, was worth more to him than her life, or at least her happiness, so he kept on driving, through the dust that came up and half-choked the horse, and she knew that the best thing for her, the only thing, would be if he were struck down and died on the road to Santa Brígida that morning.

And she kissed her tin medallion and made that sinful wish, with all her heart and soul, sinful, yes, but in response to his sin. Sin for sin, and looking back, she couldn't remember ever speaking to him after that. Whatever there had been between them ended that day, and she might have said hello or good-bye to him those few times when she went out home to see her mother, but she might not have. She couldn't remember. Anyway, she never really looked at him again.

WHEN THEY PULLED UP in front of the church in Santa Brígida, her blood went cold, and she had a momentary thought to throw herself from the cart and fall, kicking and screaming in the dust. Maybe her black-hearted father would take pity, or the shoemaker would take her for crazy and back off, but she didn't do it. She knew it wouldn't work anyway, that her father would drag her into the church by the hair if he had to, and that no one would give it a second thought. It wasn't as if these things didn't happen out here. Sixteen-year-old girls, "starting to be beautiful," married kicking and screaming to old or even young men, men they didn't want, men they hated—it happened all the time.

So she climbed down out of the cart and followed her father into the church, not because of him but because of her own pride. Before he could say anything more to her. Before she had to hear his voice one more time.

IT WAS DARK inside the church, and they stood at the door, half-blinded at first. And as her eyes were getting accustomed, she made out a young man standing at the altar, and took it, for one wild moment, for a miracle. But he turned out to be the shoemaker's nephew, who'd come in as witness. Her husband was the old man at his side.

Older than she'd remembered, older even than her father, with gray hair and gray whiskers—so, a man who hadn't even shaved for his wedding day. She saw that all at once, saw everything, and it nearly knocked her over, and she couldn't look up after that, just kept her eyes fastened on her shoes.

Her old sandals, open-toes, closed back, same as everyone's, but shaped to her feet in a way they all recognized at home—"Maria's shoes." As opposed to Dondon's shoes, or their mother's, funny how your things took on so much of you. She observed the clumsy boots across from hers—flat-footed, heavy. Clearly the shoemaker's. Strong rawhide, homemade, by him, to last a hundred years, but not a jot of grace about them. No tooling, not an extra stitch for style.

And then she looked across to what must have been the priest's—black, shiny, like nothing she'd ever seen before. Smooth leather, sewn with tiny stitches, long, sleek, and pointed with thin laces—they must have come from the coast, or even the capital, so beautiful were they. Priests always had money, drought or no drought, she was just thinking, when the book slammed shut.

Was it over? Already? She didn't remember saying, "I do." Had they? She hadn't, anyway—she couldn't have, couldn't have said a word. At least there had been no kiss. They had all turned and were walking out of the church and into the square, where they were blinded again, this time by the sun. And as she stood there, in a kind of daze, wanting to ask if they had said, "I do," and if they hadn't, had something happened? Had the shoemaker changed his mind?

But then her father was shaking hands with the shoemaker, and then, strangely enough, with her—"Obey your husband"—and then he climbed back into the cart and turned the horse toward home.

"Get up," he said, and the horse started, and she stood watching until all that was left of them was the dust, sparkling behind them in the noonday sun. Dancing, that dust was, and she could have stood there watching forever, but finally the shoemaker said, "*Vamos*," and started down the cobbled street.

She followed. It was hot, high noon, and the streets were deserted, silent, with everyone inside, waiting for the evening cool. She was clutching her small packet to her chest, walking in and out of black and white, deep shade and bright sunlight—the nice trees that grew along the shoemaker's street she would realize later, but that day she couldn't look up. Just followed along, over the cobblestones—as long as they were walking it was okay, she figured. As long as he didn't stop. There was a sort of grunting, and a troop of pigs came snuffling by, little black ones, skinny, half-starved. They'd eat anything, she knew, and thought of her nightgown. They'd gobble it in a flash, or if not, at least tear it to shreds, trample it underfoot, if she could just slip it out of her pack to them. But just then, the shoemaker stopped at a door.

Run! a voice whispered.

She looked up.

Run now! Fast!

But run where? The voice didn't say. She looked around—they were standing in a quiet street lined with houses, filled with people she didn't know, who'd never think of taking in a bride on the run from their neighbor, and who wouldn't have any extra food to give her if they did.

The shoemaker had out his big key and was fiddling with his lock.

Right now!

But unless she was ready to run all the way out to the caves under the mountain where the *desordeiros* took shelter, unless she was prepared to live as a madwoman or an outcast, there was nothing for her to do but follow the shoemaker inside.

SHE STOOD IN the doorway.

"Eh?" said the shoemaker. He peered at her through narrowed eyes, as if studying to make sure he'd got the right daughter, then nodded and disappeared inside. Nearby she could hear a bird beating its wings against the sides of a cage, probably a little cardinal, with its red hood, that some boy had brought in from the *caatinga*. At home, they sang all day in the thornbush.

The shutters were closed against the heat, and it was cool inside, and so dark that she could hardly see at first. Not that she needed to see to know the place—she knew it without even looking. Knew the front room would be half-empty as they all were, with beaten earth floors and polished mud walls. Knew there'd be a hammock either strung or unstrung, and maybe a homemade leather chair, and a small table. A little altar, or maybe not, since it was the women who saw to that. Knew his bedroom would be off to the side and his kitchen at the back of the house, with his stove, his firewood, his brooms. A privy in the yard, and a stone basin for washing. His cooking pot hanging on the wall, just like her mother's, beside his pictures of Padre Cícero and the Bleeding Heart. There would be manioc flour in a sack, and maybe some coffee, maybe some beans. A piece of sun-dried meat hanging in the larder, if he ate it. No cheese, since he didn't keep goats.

He came walking out of the gloom, in her direction. Terror rose in her throat, but all he did was tell her to go in and make his dinner. She moved swiftly toward the kitchen, her pack still clutched to her chest. She didn't know what to do with it, wasn't sure if she could put it down. She'd never been in a stranger's house before.

She looked around hastily in the kitchen for a place to stow it—she didn't want him to see it and maybe ask to see what she'd brought, and then there would be the nightgown. Although it came to her that she'd die, choke and die, before she put on that nightgown for the shoemaker. Her mother's white lace.

But why had her mother sat there, day after day, working on it anyway, since chances were always good, she saw now, that it would come to this? All those needles, the bobbins, the whitest cloth and best thread, all bought instead of coffee or sugar from the peddler who came out specially from Feira de Santana—and then all that work, the best lace these lace-making women could make for their daughters. Complicated treasures, she saw now, works twinned like the thread, of passion and regret, and worn as often as not in panic and revulsion. Why did they do it? Why hadn't they told her? Why didn't anyone say anything?

On the other hand, what was there to say? The convents weren't taking any girls these days, especially not drought-stricken farm girls, and there were no schools, no work, not even a rich family needing a maid anywhere around there. Nothing but this, and now that she thought about it, her mother, too, had probably worn her own nightgown in fear and trembling before the dreadful stranger who was now her father.

What was life, then? Why had she ever been born? She steadied her shaking fingers, and lit the fire under the shoemaker's stove.

Then she took down his clay pot and poured out a little water from the cistern. What would he want? He hadn't said. She looked around frantically, and found the manioc flour and poured some into the pot. There didn't seem to be much else, no sun-dried meat, no beans—was that all he ate, then? Porridge? Like her grandmother? So he was toothless, as well?

And did he want it sweet or salty? He hadn't said, but she couldn't find any sugar, so she put in the salt, and prayed that it wouldn't anger him. She found his bowl and poured out the porridge, and then tried to figure out how to call him in without reminding him that she was there.

Though she didn't want to risk angering him, either, by letting his food get cold, since that, too, could turn to something—"Lust hard by hate." The tiger's eye on the lamb. But just as she was weighing the evils before her, the shoemaker came in, sat down, and started eating without a word.

She pressed herself into the corner. "My *daughter, you must receive your husband willingly.*" The shoemaker belched, then pushed back his chair, and she barely kept herself from crying out. But he just turned and walked outside, and then she heard a splash of water. A tear rolled down her nose. "Mother of God, protect me!" she begged, though she knew She wouldn't. Knew that God's mother didn't intervene with the lawfully wed.

She was just sixteen. She studied the shoemaker's floor of beaten dirt. Clean. At least there was that. The door opened, he walked in. She would try an excuse—she was sick, she was bleeding, though she'd heard that didn't work. She turned to the wall, in the far corner where she was standing, and picked up something, a broom. Started to sweep. She was as far from the door as possible. If he was planning to grab her, he'd have to cross the room.

But he just walked through and out again. Did he expect her to follow? If he called her, she'd have to go.

She bit her lip, and waited. She wouldn't go, even if he called. He'd have to drag her in, and maybe he couldn't because he was old. She could hit him with the broom, drive him off, though then he'd go to her father, which would be bad, but better than anything else that could happen right then. So, fine, she wasn't going, no matter what, she was just deciding, making up the argument in her head, to her father, to the judge, to anyone—when she heard the sound of low, steady snoring coming from the shoemaker's bedroom.

Was he asleep? Was it possible? She crossed herself. Was it a nap, though, or his night's rest? It wasn't dark out yet. What did it mean? Would he get up later, refreshed, strengthened, and come after her? Or had the holy Virgin looked down and heard her prayers?

SHE REALIZED, thinking back, that she didn't move from her corner in the kitchen that night. Not to take a sip of water, not to eat, not to wash. She didn't want to risk the slightest noise, anything that might wake him. She spent her wedding night scarcely breathing, huddled in the corner of the shoemaker's kitchen, wrapped in her own arms.

And the next night, too, but by the end of the first week she felt safe enough to string up a hammock. Her husband wouldn't mind, she was thinking, wouldn't even notice. He hadn't touched her. Couldn't, it turned out.

She thought at first that he was tired or just being respectful, but finally she walked out to see her mother. She'd never seen a man naked before.

"A withered little seed there, between two dried-up coconuts," she whispered. "Is that what it's supposed to be?"

"YOU'RE LUCKY," her friends told her.

"Maybe."

"No, lucky!" They were already chasing babies, a new one every year. Their husbands would come home drunk on a Saturday night, and there'd be some scuffling, and then that would be it. Another. The whole thing all over again.

"Lucky," they assured her.

Maybe, she said.

HER LIFE STARTED to take form at the shoemaker's, as lives take form anywhere. She rose at dawn, lit the shoemaker's fire, made the shoemaker's coffee, and then combed out her long hair—or didn't. Her hair didn't need combing, she was starting to figure, to sweep the shoemaker's floor.

Her husband was a man of little family and no father, a "son of the weeds," as they put it nicely out there, and he hadn't been brought up to conversation—not even "Good morning," not even "Good night." Days would pass without a word between them. He ate the gruels she made him, the various tapiocas, sweet or salty, hammered at his bench all day, and then slept "one sleep all night," she told her mother, "snoring like a pig."

She herself slept alone, in the hammock. A year or two went by, and then another. "She's getting thin!" said her mother.

"She's not starving," was her father's answer.

And it was true, you don't starve married to the local shoemaker, though you spend a lot of time watching the lizards at night, she told her mother. They had dances, just like people—

Her mother gave her a strange look. "Lizards?" Was she

herself looking strange? She suddenly couldn't remember when she'd last washed her hair—or her clothes.

But that wasn't as important as the lizards. "They line up, late at night, for a *xaxado*, and just when you think they've turned to stone, *zup*, up go their tails!"

Her mother stared.

She laughed and walked across the yard to where the boys were. She was nearly twenty now, but had nothing to talk about with the women. Didn't bother to make lace anymore, since there would be no babies.

LATER THAT NIGHT, alone in her hammock, she wondered when you go from being a virgin to an old maid. She ran her hands up her arms, down her legs. They'd told her about the werewolf who'd come to their cousins' house, about a week ago. Her aunt and uncle had walked out, "to a funeral," and hadn't made it back by dark. The children were there alone, but they were old enough to feed the chickens, bring in the goats, and the oldest girl remembered, when they were already in bed, to get up and heft the heavy bar across the door, and she had to wake one of the boys to help her, and they were barely strong enough together to get it done. And even so, it almost didn't matter. He almost broke it down anyway.

They'd woken to the sound of his howling, his clawing, and crawled together into the farthest corner, where they'd huddled, clutching their mother's cross and medallions, and watching the door heave. All night long it went on, the howling and clawing, though once in a while it would let up, and they'd hear a commotion among the chickens.

But then he'd come back, and the only question was whether the door would hold till dawn. The oldest girl had heard that he couldn't stand even one ray of sunshine, and it must have been true because he was no longer there when their parents came back the next morning, hooting and shouting, into the yard with the dead chickens scattered all around it, and the house still barred and the children still in the corner, but safe. Alive.

The priest came out afterward, her brothers said, with holy water, and everyone came by to stare at the gashes in the door. One old tracker said it was the work of a jaguar, but the children were adamant. It was the *lobishomem*, the wolf man, they'd heard him clearly, even if they hadn't had to look him in his terrible face.

What would have happened next? she wondered. Not to the children, but to her, if he came in here? What would he do? Would there be love before the murder? He was a wolf—but he was a man, too. Which was he more? Wolf or man?

She walked over to the shutters, closed tight, as everyone's were, every door and shutter in the whole Sertão, shut and barred before nightfall. The nights were filled with danger, werewolves, bandits, terrors all, to be shut out. But what, she wondered, was she afraid of? Really, what she was afraid of anymore?

. . .

ANOTHER YEAR PASSED and then one more. "Time is a river," someone was singing at a wedding.

"Want to dance?" a cowboy asked her. He wasn't from around here.

She shook her head. She was twenty-two, but she didn't dance. She was the shoemaker's wife.

"Time is a river," the man sang.

But it didn't seem that way to her. To her, time was more like one of those endless days in a drought year, when the sun rises already hot, already noon in what should have been the soft cool part of the morning. One of those days that is born old, one blinding spell under the noonday sun.

She'd been married six years now, but between her and her husband, it was still the first day. To her, he was still "the shoemaker," not "my husband," nor did he have much call to use her name, either, why would he? She brought him his coffee in the morning, his porridge noon and night. No one was sick, no one was dying—so what was there to talk about? Now and then there was cheese on the table, if someone came by selling it, but that was nothing to talk about, either—they came or they didn't.

"She's like a field dove singing in a cage!" her mother cried to her father.

"She's not starving."

True, but what if you weren't hungry anymore, or tired, either? What if you were waking more and more in the night, climbing from your hammock, stumbling over to the window, and throwing open the shutters to the darkness, to whatever demons and rippers were out there? Whispering to the night, "I want—"

But want what? She didn't know, until the day she saw gun belts on her husband's workbench, and knife sheaths, twenty inches long.

THE SHOEMAKER HAD done work in the past for Lampião's great band of outlaws when they'd been roaming in this part of Bahia. Now they were back. One of the bandits had brought in some gear from the outback where they were camping. There was a lot to fix—sandals, hats, harnesses, bridles, along with the gun belts.

"It'll take a while," the shoemaker told him.

"He told me to wait," the bandit, Luis Pedro, had said with a shrug.

He lounged in the doorway. Rolled and smoked a cigarette.

"No police in this town, right?" he asked.

"Nah," said the shoemaker, nothing to worry about. João Sá commanded the rain here, and he was Lampião's friend.

Luis Pedro ventured out a little way, gun at his side, and came back. The sun was crossing the sky. The shoemaker's work wasn't fast, but it was strong.

"Guaranteed," he promised his customers. The bandit rolled another cigarette and pulled up a bench.

He told the shoemaker about how they'd taken over the town of Capela, not too far from here, a couple of months ago. They'd gone first, as always, to shut down the telegraph office, but the office was closed. The telegraph man was in the town hall, along with everyone else, watching an American cowboy film.

The bandits had never seen a movie before. Lampião left two of them to guard the door, and the rest crept in, and stood watching, silent, spellbound—until one of them was jostled in front of the projector, and the shadow of his hat—that distinctive bandit half-moon, molded, people said, on the breast of a virgin—was thrown up onto the screen, "as big as the cowboy's horse," Luis Pedro said, laughing.

And then, sheer pandemonium. The fiddle screeched, the piano thudded to a stop, and the projectionist burnt the film. Everyone ran for the doors, but Lampião's guards stopped them. "Everybody calm!" he shouted. "Back to your seats. I'm crazy to see this movie!" And they all went and sat back down, but the projectionist couldn't get it going again. His hands were shaking too hard.

"*Bicho danado!*" the shoemaker grunted. His one expression. "Holy cow."

Not that it ended badly in Capela, said Luis Pedro. The police had decamped when they heard Lampião was approaching, so the bandits hung around for a day or two, long enough for a sort of carnival spirit to take hold. They collected some money from the rich, then bought what they needed—salt, khaki, perfume, and every gun and bullet in town—got shaves and haircuts, heard mass in the little church, where Lampião left his usual sizable donation, and then had dinner with the mayor in the town hotel, "all very friendly," said Luis Pedro, though Lampião had the mayor taste everything first.

And later that night they threw a dance for the people, the poor. The country girls were shy at first—they crept into town in twos and threes, clutching each other's hands, but once those girls started dancing, one by one, it turned out they had something special, they were magic, those girls, they had "feet of gold!" Knew all the steps, and some dances so old they must have come straight from the court of the great Sebastião, of Portugal, and they danced with the bandits all night, their hands behind their backs, moving in, moving out, turning, swirling, till the sun rose and their fathers came to drag them home.

"And Lampião?"

The bandit whirled and pulled his gun. A young woman stepped from behind the door. She didn't flinch. The shoemaker glanced up, then back at his work. So. The shoemaker's wife. Luis Pedro put his gun back.

"Did Lampião dance?" she asked him.

"No. They didn't give him a chance. The mayor and the judge and the rest of them kept him talking all night, asking how they should do this, what he thought of that."

She nodded. Not bad-looking, Luis Pedro saw, now that he looked at her. Pretty, even. Very, maybe, if she let down her hair.

"And the girls threw flowers after us when we left," he said. She nodded. What was her name?

"And the mayor gave Lampião a picture book—*The Life of Jesus*. 'To remember our town,' he inscribed it!" Luis Pedro laughed.

"*Bicho danado*," from the shoemaker. From her, a smile—half-smile. Nice, though, good teeth. Wasted on this old guy. Too bad.

"The mayor said Lampião was a prince, since he had everything—brains, money, power, and good luck."

"Good luck." She repeated it: "*Uma boa estrela*"—that's how the bandit had put it. "A good star."

"But his life is hard," Luis Pedro said, not that she needed to be told. She'd been watching the shoemaker pounding new soles onto worn-out sandals, restitching leather shirts that had been torn by thorns, resewing bullet holders that'd been ripped out in haste, or maybe panic.

"He suffers," Luis Pedro went on, "but then he's happy. He says that that's what life is: suffering and happiness."

Suffering she knew. But happiness?

Luis Pedro lay down on the bench and took a little nap, then woke up and rolled another cigarette. Tried to teach the bird to sing. Lampião's marching song, to the women of the badlands: "*You teach me to make lace, and I'll teach you to make love.*"

She listened. "*To make love*"—so there really was such a thing? Not only that, but someone who did it? Not only that, but someone who taught it?

WHEN LUIS PEDRO left that night, she followed him out. "Tell your captain if he'll have me for his wife, I'll go with him."

"You mean that?"

"Tell him I'll be at my mother's house tomorrow—Caysara Malhada. You know the place?"

"Yeah, sure." How many times had they crisscrossed this part of Bahia? They knew every homestead and goat path out here.

"Tell him I'll be waiting."

Luis Pedro nodded and went off.

"HER EYES ARE BLUE," Luis Pedro said to Lampião that night.

"She's married," Lampião replied.

"She might as well not be. He's never touched her."

Maybe yes, maybe no. Lampião wasn't sure that was even the point here. He had lived almost ascetically till now. Padre Cícero, the great mystic priest of the region, had told him that he'd be protected, a *corpo fechado*, a "closed body," impervious to bullets, as long as he didn't have a woman.

"GOOD ADVICE FOR priests and hermits, but not for men of flesh and blood," Maria's mother said to him the next day, when he and some of his bandits appeared in her yard. She'd lost her breath when she first saw them—a band of armed men suddenly there, out of nowhere—but then he smiled, and she wasn't afraid.

Not of him, anyway She'd been horrified, though, when her daughter had shown up early that morning and announced that she was running off with Lampião.

"You're crazy! Dreaming!"

No, Maria told her, he was coming—maybe. And if he did, she was going—definitely.

"But—"

But, "No buts," she'd said to her mother, no more "buts." The shoemaker was a "but," her life for the past six years had been one long "but," and now she would have no more of them. No *But the danger*, nothing of the early death, or even the police brutality that would surely fall upon the heads of her family, who would overnight become the home address for the most avidly sought fugitive in all Brazil.

She faced her mother. "Help me or not!"

Her tone was harsh, almost cold. Her mother hadn't heard that from her before. As a girl, she'd always tended toward the headstrong, though not enough to prevent the wrong of her own marriage. But she'd been only sixteen then. Her mother could see how six years of lying alone in the shoemaker's hammock had been enough to harden whatever was still soft.

"Yes or no?"

Her mother had shrugged. She'd watched her daughter grow thin, grow sad in her bloodless marriage. She knew that Lampião had burnt towns, murdered policemen, come back and wiped out whole families, anyone who'd ever betrayed him—but only if they betrayed him. He was known to be fair, strictly and always. He was, in fact, the closest thing to justice they had out here. Plus she'd been to one of his dances, the best dances in the Sertão.

She looked into her daughter's eyes. She might die young with the bandits, but wouldn't she die anyway, at the shoemaker's? Of "sickness," they'd call it, of utter lack?

So she crossed herself, and went with her out to the well. Helped her bathe and comb scent through her long dark hair. They'd done none of this for her wedding to the shoemaker. Neither of them had had the heart.

They pulled the dotted gingham dress over her head, the one she wouldn't wear to her wedding. It fit her perfectly, better even, since she was thinner now, more elegant, with her long hair, and her blue eyes sparkling—so bright that her mother almost couldn't look.

She was beautiful, especially with that wet hair hanging down, wetting the front of her dress. "Come on, I'll put it up," her mother said, but as they turned toward the house, there he was, standing at the edge of the yard, under the acacias, with a few of his men.

They'd heard nothing, no footsteps, not the crackling of a twig, and they'd both started at the sight of the bandits—long-haired desperadoes, glittering with gold chains and medallions, and armed with knives and guns. Lampião himself was taller and thinner than she'd expected, and darker, too, with long wild hair and the dark glasses, because of his eye, she knew. He had on a blue-and-white-striped shirt, a red scarf around his neck, rings on his fingers, and a jeweled dagger at his waist.

Dazzling, but shocking, too. Her mother made a panicked grab for her hand, but she had already moved away, toward him. He was smiling at her in a way that would keep a woman who'd slept alone for six years from dwelling on the details.

I'll teach you to make love, his smile was saying, and she walked straight out to meet him, with a smile of her own that was saying, *Yes*, before she'd even said hello.

Maybe they never said hello, maybe they were both beyond it—both lonely, both isolated, though you'd have to look to know it. She lived with a husband, he lived with a group of men, yet they were both still essentially alone, still untouched. That was what had come to her, listening to Luis Pedro's tales—that Lampião gave dances, but didn't dance.

So maybe they didn't say hello, she couldn't remember afterward. What she remembered was walking with him, out into the pasture, and sitting down under the big *ipê* tree that was famous around there—a landmark for pilgrims on their way to Monte Santo, and Lampião, too, used it in that part of Bahia, he told her. It was in bloom then, "starry," as they said, with white flowers, and it was there, under that tree, that he took her in his arms and kissed her.

And, true, she'd been married for six years, but truer still was that she'd never been kissed by a man before, and after that kiss, he didn't have to be King of the Bandits. He could have been anyone.

He turned to her. "Do you have the courage to tell me what you told Luis Pedro yesterday?"

She nodded. "I'll go with you if you'll have me."

"But you're married."

"It's like I wasn't."

And then he kissed her again, and then, somehow, after that, they were all sitting around her mother's table, eating the best meal in the whole world. Sun-dried meat, fried manioc, tapioca in butter, sweet potatoes, and fresh white cheese, from their own goats, that only her mother could make, so much taste that it didn't need salt. And good coffee, too, strong and sweet, and everyone was laughing and talking, except for her, who couldn't say a word.

The sun moved across the sky. He got up, nodded to his boys, and they took their leave, thanked her mother, moved across the yard to the fence. She got to her feet, too, suddenly not sure. Should she get her bag? Leave without it? She would. She was ready.

"Let's talk," he said to her low, and walked away from the others, to the acacias, where she'd first studied his picture all those years ago. The dust had that smell, half-sweet, that you never got in town.

"Sometimes it's hard with me," he said.

"Yes." She smiled, thinking what was hard was life at the shoemaker's.

"You might be shot at."

Smiling, "Yes." Because what was that to one more night at the shoemaker's?

"Maybe shot."

Which could not be worse than another spell of silent days.

"And run through the night . . ."

Yes.

" . . . never sleep in a bed . . . "

But she didn't sleep in a bed anyway.

" . . . you'll die young."

She smiled at him. She'd already died young, she was thinking then—though she knew now that that wasn't true. That moping through life at the shoemaker's wasn't the same as being shot at or, worse, being shot.

But that's the sort of thing you only know when you know it, so she'd just smiled that day, and said, "We all die."

That's when he stopped smiling. "You don't know what you're saying! You've got to *think* about it!" he said.

But she *had* thought, she told him, she'd been thinking for six years, and she was ready to go, right then, right there, but he fell silent then, and looked away.

He told her he had to go, and they walked in silence to the stick fence at the edge of the yard. She searched his face, but couldn't read it anymore. He kissed her again, but this time she wasn't sure what it meant. An hour before, it had been, *I'm yours, you're mine, we found each other and we're riding off together.* But if it wasn't—since it wasn't—then what was it?

Luis Pedro and the other boys were waiting at the gap.

"Think *hard!*" he said to her again. "Think *well!*" He'd be back tomorrow to get her if she still wanted to go. And then he stepped through the fence, out into the wild *caatinga*, and was gone.

. . .

SHE'D WALKED SLOWLY back toward the house. Was this it, then—her life? One silk ribbon tied to an old shoe? One short bright afternoon with Lampião, in the midst of a long stretch of endless days and nights with the shoemaker? That happened, she knew, happened all the time—there was no shortage of windbags to repeat their one story. "The time that such-and-such colonel danced with me." "The time the Conselheiro passed through, and we roasted a goat." "The time it rained," "The time it didn't"—how many people lived their lives on that?

"Think well," Lampião had said to her, and the first thing she thought was that she wasn't going back to the shoemaker's, whether he came back for her or not. She'd meant what she'd said. If he didn't come back, she'd stay here for a while, just to catch her breath. She could pick up the needle again, and maybe sell her lace to the people at the market who came through from the coast. And if that didn't work, there were other paths, plenty of paths, all of them better than the one that led back to the shoemaker. She could dress herself in blue and follow the next wave of pilgrims up to Padre Cícero in Juazeiro do Norte. Let life carry her along from there.

If he didn't come back.

And then she stopped thinking, and started praying, one prayer, all night, to Maria Aparecida, the Virgin of Lost Causes: *Let him come back!*

He almost didn't, Luis Pedro told her. He sat with his men, and had someone play his favorite song over and over, "Never Love Without Being Loved." He wasn't going back for her, he announced.

Women were complicated, and he wanted no complications.

He wanted to be free, *had* to be free.

That was his life, like it or not.

He couldn't change now. He wasn't going back.

And then, at dawn, he threw down his hat with a curse and went.

SHE'D BEEN KEEPING watch from the first light, just inside the stick fence, and her heart leapt when she saw him coming out of the vast infinite thornbush and cactus that stretched out all around him. He didn't come inside this time, just stayed outside the fence on his horse, as if to show her the choice, stark and simple.

Inside was house, garden, family. Chickens, goats, and cheese. Lace and children, and a bed to die in. Outside was none of these. Her roof would be the heartless sky, her garden would grow cactus, her bed would be made of leaves. There would be no door to bar against the night.

But she wouldn't need a door, since she would be the night—if she rode away that day with the man who claimed he would teach her to make love, and which she felt from his kiss might be true.

HER MOTHER CRIED when she left, and whispered a blessing, not that she had much thought for her mother that day. She was on a horse with Lampião, riding away from all she knew through the morning sunshine, with everything in her life changed forever.

They rode through the village, past her husband's mud house, the little shop that was suddenly no longer a prison. It was just a place, now, where she'd lived for a while, a house on a nice cobbled street with trees and songbirds, painted, she thought, a very pretty blue.

The shoemaker was sitting in the window, hammering.

"Farewell, Zé!" she called out to him, gaily, to this stranger whose floors she'd thought she was destined to sweep forever.

He glanced up once—"Are you really leaving me, Maria?" She heard these days that he'd moved west, to the Mato Grosso, to fix the boots of the tin miners there. He didn't remarry, just found some Indian woman to make his porridge. That was all the wife he needed.

"Farewell, and all the best to you!" she cried as she rode away from him, and from every man, woman, and goat in that town. *Good-bye and good luck to you all, from Maria, formerly wife of Zé Nenem, the shoemaker, and whom you all pitied with good reason till this morning.* This same Maria who, by some bizarre twist of fate that must happen, since it had, was riding out of her miserable life as the shoemaker's wife in Santa Brígida, into the grand blue with Lampião.

THEY DIDN'T SPEAK as they rode—where they'd gone, there seemed to be no words. She listened, and heard nothing, and then bells in the distance, soft goat bells, and then nothing again. When they sat under a tree to drink some water, everything around them, the very ground, the land, smelled like the cinnamon buns they baked at home once a year, for the Feast of Saint João.

They rode on, following a *riacho*, a dry streambed, rocky, with tough wispy trees on both sides. The sun was getting higher, and she was starting to think that maybe the whole world had gone away and they were the only two left, but then he guided his horse around a bend, and though there hadn't been any signs of anyone—no tents, no fires, no noise—now there were men coming out on all sides, shooting off small rockets. They had reached the bandits' camp.

The rockets were for her, he said, as he helped her down from the horse. The camp was by the side of a dry, rocky stream, and there was a small tent, and must have been a campfire, but she couldn't quite call it back, or much of the landscape, even. They were still in her own state, Bahia, but someplace far and different, deep in the *caatinga*, the real wilderness, remote and empty, with no sign of ranch life anywhere around them. No farmhouse in the distance, no sheds or fences, or even goat trails.

There were some trees, though, and thornbush and cactus, coming straight out of the dusty ground and blooming all around her, round barrel cactus with red flowers, and tall standing "spears" covered with delicate white buds. Someone brought her water to splash on her burning face, and sweet coffee, and there were more rockets, for this was a wedding feast.

The men had roasted a wild turkey for her, and there were toasts as they sat on the rocks, eating. Luis Pedro, her first friend among them, brought her a cup of what they called "cognac," cane whiskey. She'd never really drunk before, maybe a sip or two at someone's wedding, but not a cup of her own, nothing like this, and slowly the purest enchantment took over, there amid the rocks and cactus. She still wasn't sure if it had really happened, or how. How she'd woken up that morning the wife of the shoemaker, with nothing to hope for, not even the standard consolation of a baby's head to sniff, and now found herself, by lunchtime, the queen of a band of merry men.

For that was how they were treating her. Lampião presented them to her one by one. Proper names first—Jose Vicente, Manoel, Virginio—and then their bandit names—Windstorm, Midnight, the Kid. They walked up and saluted her, and she nodded to each one in turn. Kept her eyes level, even though she'd never looked a man in the face before. But she had a sense that this was what was expected of her, and then one of them took out a guitar and started playing, and Lampião took her hand to dance.

She was a bit unsteady when they first stood up, but she took a breath and he held her, formally, for a *forró*, the first dance. Which was good, she needed it, but soon she found her balance and was able to take a turn with each of the boys one by one.

And then they started dancing with each other, and she danced with Lampião again, really danced. The *xote*, apart, close but not touching, the real thing. When you really want someone.

"*She*," sang one of the men, to a small guitar, "*is like a thought, a feeling . . .*" The kind of song that sways you back and forth, and someone passed her another cup of whiskey. "*She*," the song went on, "*lights the square when she passes*"—she moved closer, had to move closer, her head was spinning again. And he was smiling at her now, smiling down from up there where his beautiful head was, his mouth, his nose, his one eye, and then she was in his arms, and dancing like that, and then somehow they got to his tent, a little ways away from where the boys slept, white canvas, trimmed with yellow silk. Yellow silk—was it possible?—and strewn with desert flowers. The bandits must have done it. Wildcat or Sharpshooter or Rattlesnake must have put down their knives and guns, and gone out collecting little flowers for Lampião's bride.

He took her hand, and held open the flap of the tent and looked at her with a smile and a question—yes or no? Would she like to go in?

She paused for a moment, didn't change her mind, but just paused, before the enormity of the thing. She looked up at the stars, each one a clear fire. *Life is a mystery, life is entirely strange*, she was thinking. *Life is*— But then he kissed her, and there wasn't anything to think about anymore. They went into the tent, and then it turned out that he'd meant it, the part about teaching her to make love. He taught her so well that she didn't let him out of that tent for a month.

. . .

OR THAT'S THE WAY she remembered it. Nothing but love in a yellow silk-trimmed tent. No eating, drinking, or washing, even. Just love.

Not that it could have been that way. Of course they'd have crawled from their tent every day, for food and water and even coffee; and they must have broken camp and moved, even, more than once, lots of times. They could never have stayed in one place, the way she remembered. Surely they'd have pulled down the tent, loaded the horses and the donkeys, and crossed into other states, and run from the police and soldiers, fought with them, even. But she remembered that time as a simple long delirium, one silken thread, all of one piece.

And that's when he started calling her "Maria Bonita," his beautiful Maria, and gave her the first necklace she'd ever owned—gold, with two hearts interlocking, brought all the way from Italy, he told her, and taken from the *baronesa* of Água Branca.

And he wrote a song about her eyes, her skin, her hair:

> He who doesn't love them
> Dies young and sees nothing.

"Maria Bonita." She blew the smoke from her gun she was learning to shoot, and she was good at it. She hit the target, again and again. When they went into a village, she would stroll into any shop and out again with whatever her heart desired—a small mirror, a new perfume. Silken cloth so luxurious, so impractical that no farm girl could ever buy it, and then she'd make herself a dress of it, just for fun, in her spare time—spare time! Since the men did the cooking, and there was nothing to sweep, nothing to hoe, no goats to milk or chickens to feed. No babies.

"Maria Bonita!" In one of the villages, a photographer called her by name. She turned with a smile, and he sent the photo to the newspapers, which printed it—"Maria Bonita, the Fiercest Woman in Brazil."

IV

Two weeks earlier, João Lucena, captain of the Alagoas Forces, had paid an unexpected visit to the police station in Piranhas. He invited Bezerra into the back room and closed the door.

"Choose," Lucena had said to Bezerra that morning. "Catch Lampião, or go to jail."

Lucena didn't specify charges, but he didn't have to. Bezerra had sold bullets to Lampião; they all did it, how else would they feed their families on a policeman's salary? Nor was it any secret—how else would Lampião have the best ammunition in Brazil, better than the police, much better? Even the bandits joked about it, publicly, to press: "The police bullets are so old they won't kill a dog."

So, yes, he'd done it, as recently as a few months ago, even, when Lampião was last in the area, and someone must have given his name to Lucena—though, now that he thought about it, it didn't even have to be that. Lucena could just have figured it out for himself. Hell, the truth was Lucena himself had sold Lampião bullets, more than once, but now someone was putting the heat on Lucena, and he was passing it along to Bezerra.

"Choose," Lucena had said—but choose what? To catch Lampião? As if Lucena himself hadn't tried—hadn't tried so hard that he himself had unleashed a reign of terror on the region that had proved far worse than anything the bandits had ever done. In his official campaign to "finish with banditism," Lucena had depopulated entire villages, beaten, maimed, and blinded workingmen, fathers of families, suspected of even unwilling, and minor, complicity with the bandits, and then finally dug giant, unholy pits by the side of local jails in which he'd had the prisoners—"potential bandits"—buried alive, and for what? For nothing. "The only one completely and utterly untouched by all this," as the papers put it, "is, as always, Lampião."

And here was Lucena, sitting in the police station in Piranhas, getting tough with Bezerra.

"I could denounce you," Lucena had said. "Arrest you. Your life would be over. They'd put you in a little cell with no window. You'd stand in excrement up to your knees."

And that would be the least of it, Bezerra had thought. He knew what happened to policemen who got locked in on the other side.

"Well?" said Lucena.

Apparently the new president, Getúlio Vargas, wanted a new Brazil. Modern. Disciplined, like the new Italy of

Mussolini, or Hitler's growing Germany, masculine and strong. Brazil, too, could be part of this brotherhood, should be, why not? Getúlio canceled civil liberties, centralized the government, and rededicated himself to the motto, "Order and Progress"—hard, however, to apply to a country with a defiant, active bandit-state within its borders, or, more to the point, a powerful class of landowners, the colonels, who functioned as regional potentates and supported the bandits for reasons of their own. Getúlio Vargas didn't know if he could neutralize the colonels completely, but he knew how to start.

"Kill Lampião." The order had come down from Getúlio to Lucena, and Lucena was passing it along to Bezerra.

And, "Yes, of course, right away," Bezerra had answered—what else was there to say? Certainly not, *How?* though he hadn't a clue, but neither did Lucena, or Getúlio, or the king of Portugal or the Pope in Rome. Lampião was invincible. Both Bezerra and Lucena knew it. Knew that meant they'd get him only when they did.

THOUGH AS HE stood outside the little bar in Pedra that morning two weeks later, Aniceto's telegram in his hand, Bezerra realized that he'd never really expected it to happen. He'd come down to Pedra two days ago, looking for Lampião—on another bad tip, he realized now.

He reread the coded message. *Bull in pasture*—Lampião, who else? There were no other "bulls" to be sending telegrams about, not along that part of the river.

Not anywhere in the Sertão, now that he thought about it. Aside from Lampião—plenty of people said because of him—there wasn't much crime around. It was funny, the way Lampião kept the place safe, kept a certain strange but real order. Once he and his band had run into some horse thieves, out near the Raso, over in Bahia. He shot the leaders as "worthless," and sent the horses back to their owners, with his compliments. Or at least, that's what he'd heard. What people said, and believed.

Lampião. "The governor of the Sertão," they called him—for a long time now, twenty years, almost. But maybe times were changing, maybe they already had.

So: *Bull in pasture*—but whose pasture? Everyone knew that Lampião was in the region, but, as always, no one knew quite where. Had someone talked, finally? Meaningfully?

Come, Aniceto had wired. Bezerra would come. Pedra wasn't far from Piranhas. There was a truck leaving shortly. He'd be on it.

With urgency, yes, though not with haste. The kind of haste that makes waste, that spills milk—not this time. Bezerra wasn't about to be the next verse in Lampião's mocking song. They all knew it, they all sang it—hell, hadn't he even caught himself singing it the other day? "*All I wanted* mesmo / *was to pay back Mané Neto . . .*"

A good joke, that one had been, the way Lampião had made monkeys of every policeman and soldier who'd ever come his way. But maybe it would be different this time—though for it to be different, Bezerra would have to do everything right. Would have to do it just like Lampião, in fact.

Fine. Maybe he'd play Lampião this time, and let Lampião play the policeman, the fool. Then there'd be a new song to sing in the Sertão. He walked to the square and asked the truck driver which way he was going.

"North," the guy said. The wrong direction. Perfect, Bezerra realized Lampião would think.

"I'm going north," Bezerra announced in the square, "to Moxotó. I hear Lampião's up there."

Odilon Flor, leader of a crack posse who'd followed the bandits over from Bahia, raised an eyebrow. His spies had been consistent—Lampião was somewhere to the south.

"You want to come with me?" Bezerra asked him.

Odilon mumbled an excuse.

"Could you lend me your machine guns, then?" Bezerra asked.

Sure, why not? Odilon was willing to oblige his colleague. Let Bezerra haul those heavy bastards up to Moxotó, and when he limped back empty-handed, Odilon Flor would take some of his men and ammunition in return and go after Lampião south of the river.

Bezerra loaded the machine guns into the truck, head bowed under Odilon's mocking smile. Knowing now what Lampião must have known all along: that the last laugh was the only one that counted.

"North to Moxotó," he shouted to the driver, and to whatever spies, Lampião's "eyes and ears," were lurking around the place. Bezerra had eight men with him from Piranhas—one of them had a girlfriend in Moxotó. She had pretty friends. Even if Bezerra's soldiers knew that Lampião was nowhere near there, that didn't mean they weren't happy enough to be going.

The truck started off north, up the only road out of the village. The driver was carrying dry goods, mostly cotton and sugar, to the various little towns along the way. It was an easy enough drive, the dirt road was well packed, he could do it in his sleep. The only thing was that he should have bought more tobacco in Pedra, but with any luck they'd be in Água Branca for lunch. He lit his last cigarette. They rolled along.

But then Bezerra put his hand on the man's arm. "Will you be so kind, friend, as to turn off here?"

"Here?" The startled driver looked up. They weren't more than a league outside of the village. "You want to go back? You forgot something?"

"It's not exactly that," Bezerra told the driver. "It's more that we're going south instead of north."

It took the driver a minute to get his meaning. He stared at Bezerra—but you didn't argue with the police, or even discuss. And Bezerra himself offered no explanation, just pointed to a track that led off, overland, to the south.

"That's our road, my friend," he said.

The driver shrugged. His cargo was dry, it would keep. So would the plans he'd laid for this evening, away from his wife. Everything except his lack of tobacco, which would have to take care of itself. He turned the heavy truck off the road onto the track.

"Hey!" The soldiers in the back pounded on the window. "What about Moxotó?"

"Moxotó can wait!" Bezerra shouted back to them. He didn't tell them that they were headed south, to a cornfield outside Piranhas, where he would meet Aniceto, who might have in his hands exactly the kind of traitor this case required. One of Lampião's spies, one of his countless agents, who for some reason—times change!—had decided to talk. Bezerra pulled out his own cigarettes, store-bought, Jockey Clubs, and offered one to the driver.

Just so, thought the driver, as he took it and drove on.

V

She walked over to the fire, sat down on a rock, and stretched her feet toward the warmth of it. It was still quiet—hardly anyone out, just one or two of the younger boys, who would hand her some coffee but wouldn't bother her with conversation. Which was good, since what she needed was to sit and sip and pull herself together. Before she got up and went to find Lampião and shake him into moving.

Which would take some doing, all the strength she could muster, plus whatever coin she had left with him. Not like the old days, when she could get anything she wanted from him, anytime, all the time. Although back then all she wanted was whatever he wanted, since she'd thought he was a true prince then, in the beginning. A new kind of man who'd found a whole new way of living. A man who had it all worked out.

Only she'd been wrong—although she hadn't, really, not then. It was more that he'd changed. Or she had. Or it had—whatever it was that had been working. In those days, the good days, her first years—years and years, who knew how many, impossible to know—who cared, when it was all good, those years when even July was no problem. When no one was talking about dying in July, so no one was worried about what month it was, or counting the days.

Like now, when they all knew there were four days left, or five, maybe—four or five, and then maybe he'd smile again at her, lie in the tent with her, run his fingers through her hair which was growing. Like before, and maybe then they'd get back to the old days, when the police were not much more than poor players in a game Lampião was winning, always won.

It wasn't that she hadn't been scared, in those years, in the beginning, but not like now. Then it was more like excitement, like being even more alive than ever, those first brushes with the troops. One game after another—she remembered "the Chevalier," as they called him, from Rio, an aviator who made news by announcing that he was going to go after Lampião with his new airplane, a thousand soldiers, and a film crew to record the whole thing for posterity.

And there'd been pictures in the papers, the Chevalier in his boots and goggles, talking to the press in Rio, and a confetti parade up Avenida Atlântica to celebrate in advance, and pictures in the papers—that was right after she'd come out with him, and she'd been frightened. Lampião's only comment was something about always wanting a ride in an airplane, not that he got one, though, since what with Carnival, followed by Easter, and then rains, and then drought, the Chevalier never made it up there with his plane at all.

And then came Luis Mariano, with his troop from Glória, not too far from her home, who told the papers that "Lampião may burn bright in Pernambuco, but in Bahia, we snuff him out!" He himself would "finish with the bandits, easily," since the Bahia police were neither "incompetents," like the Pernambuco forces, "nor armadillos, to fall into a hole."

Allowing Lampião to point out afterward that he, for his part, had never found armadillos "incompetent," nor were they the only ones to fall into a hole.

That might have been during those early days in his tent—if she remembered it right, they didn't even have to break camp for Mariano. Didn't even cost them a bullet, Lampião told the press. All he did was send out a decoy party, who led Mariano and his men into a small box canyon, then circled back and took the entrance, trapping them inside.

And then it would have gone better for Mariano if he *had* been an armadillo. He could have burrowed into the dust, curled up, and slept till something changed, got better. But as it was, his water ran out the first day, and his food the second. And it was hot in that canyon, with that wind blowing through it, but there was nothing for Mariano to do, except wait or die, or maybe wait and die. He and his men were starving and half-mad from thirst, but they could hear the bandits at the mouth of the canyon, whistling back and forth, whistling constantly, maddeningly, for three whole days.

Though on the fourth morning the wind died down and the whistling stopped. What did it mean? Was it a trick? Finally, one of the soldiers, opting for one quick bullet over any more death-by-thirst, staggered out into the blinding sunlight and stood there, croaking, "Go ahead, you sons of the plague! Shoot!"

But there was no shooting, since there were no bandits. No traces of bandits, even, no old fires, no signs of the men who'd been whistling out there for three days. But what there was was one little bird lure, rigged up just outside the canyon, the kind that whistles when it catches the wind. It was silent now that the wind had stopped.

The soldiers filed out and looked at it one by one, but no one said a word. Just turned and headed back to Glória, "crawling" by the time they got there, they told the press.

"He's a dog from hell," was Mariano's official statement, but the newspapers called it "Lampion-esque," and so was their next brush with the police, though that one touched on another aspect of it all—Lampião's luck.

This time they were deep in the Raso da Catarina, a no-man's-land in western Bahia that the papers called "Lampião's mysterious hideout," a trackless wasteland, an empty quarter, with few wells and no rivers, even when it rained. There were no villages out there, or even any ranches, which also meant no police.

They'd never tracked the bandits out there before.

There was nothing to eat, nowhere to sleep, and no water—you had to carry in your water, which was hard work and dangerous, since you could get lost easily and run out of water unless you knew the place well. Which no one did, except for the rattlesnakes, people said, the last few Indians, and Lampião.

And one tracker, it turned out—Antonio Cassiano. But Cassiano had never worked for the police before, which was why the bandits had gotten used to "walking carefree" out there. And even more than usual this time, because more girls had joined the band by then.

Which Lampião had been against, for just this reason. But once he'd taken her in, how could he stop the others? And it wasn't as if the girls who joined weren't good bandits. They'd all grown up in the same heat and dust and hardship as their boyfriends and brothers, and were just as tough and almost as strong.

But they were women, and the night before, there in the Raso, Corisco had met up with them, and it had turned into a real party, with more drinking than usual and dancing almost till dawn. And then, the next morning, when they should have been halfway to the next state, they were stumbling out of their tents, rubbing their eyes, and making late coffee, when out of nowhere came a shot.

She'd turned, terrified, to Lampião, who'd already leapt into action—everyone had. She and the other girls grabbed their guns and crawled to cover, as each man ran to the defensive position that Lampião had given him as soon as they'd gotten there that first night, in the small hills around the camp. There were always preassigned defensive positions, and always hills around their camps, and now she knew why, as the bandits started shooting down on the government soldiers, who'd spent next year's budget and more force and energy than they'd ever have again to almost get the bandits out there in the Raso that day.

And they'd almost done it that time, those soldiers. As they were moving silently through the thick underbrush around the camp that day, hearing the bandits' laughter, smelling their coffee, they'd probably figured they had done it—caught Lampião "in his underwear," every policeman's and soldier's dream.

And those soldiers had done everything right: they'd hired and paid the great tracker Antonio Cassiano, and followed him through the Raso on their bellies, under the blazing sun. And some had died of snakebite along the way and a few more had fallen to thirst and sunstroke, but the rest were poised that day for real glory, not to mention the serious riches, in both jewels and money, that the bandits carried in their packs—when, just as they were creeping into final position, one of their guns had misfired, and that was that.

"Lampião's good star," his famous luck, the newspapers had called it. Lampião, shooting at the front, recognized Cassiano—"the only one who could have done it"—and shot him first, though just in the leg, since he didn't begrudge the man his living. And then they shot the lieutenant and the sergeant, and enough soldiers to give themselves a safe retreat out of there, though in their haste they had to leave most of their supplies and the horses, and take off on foot, though it didn't end up mattering, because the soldiers didn't follow.

They claimed to have been unnerved by the girls' voices, but what really happened, one of them told a reporter later, was that they'd come to blows over the silk stockings and bits of lace the women had left behind.

THOUGH WHAT LAMPIÃO regretted losing was his book, his *Life of Jesus*, from the mayor of Capela. When he realized he'd left it, he actually thought of going back, for that and the horses, but his brother said there were other books, and "horses all over the Sertão," and he was right.

Horses they mostly "borrowed," with an old man or a boy to lead them back when they were tired, since "we're bandits, not thieves," as Lampião said, and hardly outlaws, since as often as not they found themselves guests of those who constituted the law up there.

She'd been surprised at first by Lampião's close association with the rich and powerful—those with whom he shared familial and territorial bonds. The fact that he lived outside the law was no problem for them, since they did, too, when they had to. Mostly they didn't have to, since mostly they were the law and always had been, ever since the first Portuguese married the first Indians, marched west from the coast, and staked claim to as much land as they could control. And here were their descendants, still appointing judges and mayors, assessing taxes, rewriting titles, redrawing land deeds—still "commanding the rain," as far as the people who lived on their lands were concerned.

In the Chapada Diamantina, it was Colonel Horácio de Matos, the biggest landowner out there. He and Lampião had one of those understandings: the bandits could camp on the colonel's lands, he'd supply them with food, money, and bullets, and Lampião, for his part, would leave Matos's cowboys and diamond miners alone. Better still, he offered a sort of de facto protection, since no one laid hands on anyone he called his friends.

Which was more than the government could claim. "The government!" Matos had snorted one night when he brought them out a side of beef and stayed for dinner. He'd let the government worry about Lampião, he said, but as for himself, he'd brought him out some of his own cane whiskey, made on his ranch, in special barrels from Portugal.

He poured Lampião a cup. "To your health, and"—he turned and smiled—"to the lovely Maria Bonita!"

And she'd smiled, though she saw that Lampião let the colonel drink first, and then drank carefully, always, from the same bottle. But that was just the way it was, even among friends, or rather allies who felt like friends on nights like that one. They'd pitched their camp on one of the colonel's farthest pastures, rolling land, with some trees and blue hills in the distance. They roasted the meat, and then ate under the trees, laughing and joking, and drinking the whiskey, as the stars came out one by one, first the false Southern Cross, and then the true one.

And then someone picked up a guitar, and they'd all

lined up for a *baião*, two lines, men and women, moving in, moving back, swirling, turning, closer then, and back again. And then someone played a samba, and the colonel asked her to dance—and she glanced briefly at Lampião. She had never danced with a colonel, never thought to dance with a colonel. He had been rich the full five hundred years she'd been poor.

On the other hand, that was where life had led her, and Lampião nodded, and she took his hand, his equal, at least that night. Lampião's woman, and beautiful, the one he'd chosen from all the rest.

She felt she was dancing for her mother, too, and her grandmother, her aunts and cousins, especially the ones who'd died young. Died of old age at thirty—the poor. Whose lives and deaths colonels like this one would never know.

Except through them, through her and Lampião. Later that night, when the rest of them lay sleeping under the trees, Lampião and the colonel stayed up talking. It was 1931, and the news was that a group of farmers, run off their land by the drought and starving, had invaded the grain market at Caruaru.

But it didn't look like that would spread—the Vaza-Barris River still had water, it wasn't one of the worst years, so the talk had moved on to other topics of interest, politics, bullets: who was selling good ones, whose were old, worthless. Lampião had recently gotten hold of a good supply from a captain of the Alagoas forces. He'd had to pay in gold, but for that had got the best bullets in Brazil, sent out by the federal government for the troops, new ones, stamped "1930," while the police were still using "1911s."

"The government." And had he heard, asked the colonel, that there'd been a revolution in Rio, and now the governors were called "interventors"?

Lampião had heard, but wasn't sure what it meant to them.

"Nothing," said the colonel. The poets were already singing in the streets:

My name is Virgulino,
My nickname, Lampião,
My job, since Revolution,
Interventor of the Sertão.

WHICH WAS FINE with both of them that night, those two men of two worlds who'd made their peace with life as it was. Found their places at the top, though their paths had been different.

But she fell asleep thinking that Lampião was a fighter, not a dreamer. Revolution, with its dream of fundamentally changing the system, with its entrenched oligarchy and helpless masses, didn't cross his mind. What he did for his people, the poor, the simple, the powerless, was to descend now and then like a thunder god, take over a rich man's pastures, drink his whiskey, and sit at the table for the ones who never would.

And the next day, the sun had risen, and they'd walked away from the colonel and back into their own lives—hot in the sun, wet in the rain, eating when hungry, sleeping when tired, though cautious, yes, sentries always. And of course there were nights on the run, with no moon, in the rain, but the next day there'd be a campfire, and everyone sitting around, laughing, joking, rhyming, wrestling, and the music, the dancing, bandit nights.

And golden days, especially between her and him, and then at night they would lie face-to-face in their tent, her hands twined in his long hair. And it was shortly after that that they went into the town of Tucano. The police had fled, and all the people turned out to greet them.

She saw the eyes of the girls on her—her uniform, her gun belt slung across her chest, the seven chains of solid gold around her neck. They rode through the streets that day on the back of a truck, laughing and singing songs, firing shots in the air, shouting cheers to Padre Cícero and the Sertão, "while the people," a reporter wrote afterward, "looked on, amazed, as if they were watching an impossible dream."

AND THAT HAD felt like who they were, heroes, golden, living a life of gold, as they said out there, blessed by the first light of morning, by the very rocks and thorns of the place, smart and lucky, beloved of the stars, until one day, no different from any other, the whole thing reversed itself and she found herself running through the heat and the dust for her life, less daughter of the land than renegade outcast, worth nothing but the price on her head.

Hardest for her was how it had come out of nowhere.

They were moving through a part of the land, not far from her home, in fact, where they'd never had real trouble before. They weren't even planning any action, and had hidden in some underbrush outside the village of Canindé, waiting for dark to move on. But then the village police came marching out, to cheers and a trumpet, and passed right by them, heading off into the wilderness, to "get Lampião." The bandits watched them go by through the sights of their rifles.

Lampião told them not to shoot, but once the police had disappeared around a bend, the bandits had crawled out of the draw and strolled into the village, freed the prisoners in the local jail, robbed the houses of the police chief and mayor, and then set them on fire and roasted a cow over the flames.

The usual, but the mayor had gone crying to the governor, and the governor had gone crying to his friends, and then suddenly there was a united campaign against them, with too many of their enemies coming together and smelling their blood.

And not just local soldiers, but the three fiercest *volantes* in the Sertão, brutal roaming militias, coming across Bahia, in from Alagoas, down from Pernambuco, on bad pay and worse rations, just for the chance of killing them all.

Worst was the troop led by Mané Neto, from the village of Nazaré, in Pernambuco, where the men lived and died to chase bandits. Lampião had been born and raised near there, and his fight with Mané Neto, and every man and boy in that village, was older than any of them, had started with their fathers or their grandfathers, over something none of them remembered but all of them believed in—land, livestock—and were willing to die for. And what those men lived for was to kill Lampião.

And they were going to do it this time. They had the numbers, and the government had just issued them radios to replace the long horns and whistles they'd used to communicate in the field until then.

One of Lampião's spies came into their camp before dawn, riding fast. Mané Neto had stopped just long enough to hold a press conference in Pedra. He told the reporters that the samba bands had been ordered and the parade routes mapped out. It was just a matter of days before he'd be back with Lampião's head on a stick, said Mané Neto.

Hers, too, why not? Three forces were said to be converging: Liberato's troop from Alagoas, Germiniano's from Bahia, and Mané Neto's. Together they had at least two hundred soldiers—maybe twice that, the spy had heard. Lampião had only thirty-two men with him. The rest were scattered throughout the region, working in small groups. They couldn't get back in time to help him now.

The spy, clearly nervous, galloped off. Lampião tossed away the rest of his coffee. "Let's go."

They started breaking camp, packing their gear—"Leave it," he said. That's when she got scared. Someone reached for the liquor—"Leave it!" he ordered. Even the dried meat, even their perfume—"Nothing but guns and water," and then they set off, straight into the bush, moving faster than she'd ever known them to move till then.

They were in the middle of nowhere, outside Maranduba, in the wrong part of the country, with badlands all around them, and no draws, no canyons, just low scrub stretching as far as the eye could see. It was bad country, with nowhere to hide, and no water.

It was January 1932, summer, as hot as it gets. She was twenty-four and had been with Lampião two years, or not quite—not long enough, anyway, to die that day.

How bad was it? She glanced sideways at Luis Pedro, but he didn't meet her eye—no one did. Were they scared, too, or was it always this way? Had they run like this before, or was this time different, and were they all going to die out there near Maranduba?

The sun had never been hotter—was that a sign? The devil in the place of God? Lampião wasn't talking—was he scared? That, she realized, was the question. He didn't look scared, but how would she know? He stopped suddenly—they all stopped. They were on foot, with no horses. She watched him scanning the horizon.

But for what? There was nothing to see there, just low scrub, nothing but the worst kind of thornbush stretching across the flatland, where two hundred police could move in easily, flank them on all sides, and shoot them all—the lucky ones, it occurred to her. She'd heard about the ones who didn't die, who fell into their hands still alive. Heard about throats slit, skin flayed.

And of course for a woman it would be worse. Lampião

had some fast-working poison that he always carried on him, with enough for her, too. This had sounded good in the abstract, though now she wondered, how fast was fast? And what was it, something magic or prussic acid? Strychnine? Where you lie there foaming at the mouth? And if it was that, wouldn't it be better to be shot? To shoot herself, even, to put her gun to her head?

She wanted to ask him. She ran forward. "My love," she said to him.

No answer.

"Virgulino"—his Christian name. What they called each other in bed.

Still nothing. Did he hear her? She realized he was concentrated, totally concentrated—she followed his eyes. What was he seeing? There was nothing out there to see, nowhere to run, nowhere to hide, but he signaled a change of direction, and they set off on a slightly different course. But would it matter in this wretched wilderness? Everything was low and open, and silent to boot. Before, they'd always managed to hear the soldiers' horns and whistles, but they couldn't hear the new radios, pulling in all those soldiers, all those forces, in silence. Where were they, the hundreds of soldiers?

Not that they hadn't beaten these same soldiers before—didn't they always beat them? In fact, when the federal army was called to account recently, asked why, with the resources of the entire nation at its command, it could do nothing against a force of indigenous nomadic bandits with rarely more than a hundred or so men, the commander explained that the blame wasn't his but

Lampião's, "since he always takes for himself the best locations, and his men are better shots."

Lampião had half-smiled when he read that. Now he stopped again, and swept the horizon with his spyglass. "Leave the tracks uncovered," he said.

She turned to him in alarm—they all did. They always covered their tracks, went to great lengths to leave no traces. It was what they did, always, all the time, everywhere—dragged bushes behind them, walked backward, even drove cattle over their trail. Leapt off to the side, climbed up over rocks, but not this morning?

She looked around and saw her own hesitation on all the faces. They all trusted him—with their lives, in fact, it was how they lived, although it came to her that morning, maybe it came to everyone, that there would come a day, sometime, someplace, where they wouldn't escape one more time but die. She could sense the doubt—was Lampião ill, or out of his mind with the heat?

Or doing something that only he could understand?

"This way," he said, low, and no one dared question him, no one said a word, just left their tracks there in the dust for the world to see. She slipped a rosary from her pack, a nice one, silver, that she'd taken from an old woman near Patamuté, in exchange for leaving her horses.

But they'd have left the horses anyway, or sent them back! They were bandits, not horse thieves. They took what they had to, that was all.

From the people. The rich were another matter. They started up a hill that turned out to be higher than it had looked, a sort of escarpment. The path wasn't much wider than a goat trail, rocky and steep. Narrow. "Strait," she remembered a priest saying, "strait is the gate." But the gate to where? Heaven or hell? She couldn't remember. There was dust in their faces, the sun beating on their heads. Heat, dust, and blazing sun, and it came to her that noon, not midnight, was the devil's hour.

A thorn caught her skirt. She jumped, tears in her eyes. She had sinned, she knew it, and she was on the road to hell already, there just over the border from home in Sergipe, not too far from Maranduba.

Pray for us poor sinners—she tried to picture the Virgin, the one in the church in Santa Brígida, where she was married to the shoemaker. *Now and at the hour of our death*—but what she kept seeing were the goats, the way they knew, even before you took out the knife, when you walked out to kill them. The way they looked at you, with those strange striped eyes, full of pleading, in vain. And the chickens, too, the way they ran off to the sides, clucking and scolding. They knew. Anyone who said they didn't just didn't know animals.

The path got steeper toward the top, and the dust worse, and the silence. The whole world nothing but heat, dust, and silence.

Her mother had cried when she rode off with Lampião. *Now and at the hour or our death.* They weren't that far, as the vulture flies, from home. Didn't she have some cousins in the force there? Maybe they wouldn't kill her if she begged them. Though maybe they would. The price on her head.

And, she realized now, too, that there'd be no grave.

No blessing of the bones, no "ashes to ashes"—she hadn't thought about that, that she'd die like a dog out here, unblessed, in the wilderness.

The hill leveled out at the top, and to her amazement, she saw there was a small clearing with two *umbu* trees in the middle. Was it possible that Lampião had known they were there, those trees—didn't he know every *umbu* tree in the region? With their fruit and shade, they were the difference sometimes between dying of thirst and living, and if he knew these trees, then he knew this place, had been here before, and maybe he'd brought them here with a plan.

Which would have included for some reason leaving their tracks uncovered for all the soldiers to see. She turned to him, but he wasn't looking at the trees. He was studying the path they'd just struggled up, and then he walked away, toward the steep sides leading down the other side. He walked along the entire escarpment, twice. Once he disappeared, behind a small rise. Volta Seca, the boy, licked his finger and held it up. "They'll smell us," he muttered.

It was true. They were upwind from the police. The scent the bandits practically bathed in would bring the troops right to them.

"They won't have to smell us"—Quinquim pointed down to their tracks, there on the dry plain below them. Leading the police straight up.

She looked at the faces around her—they were scared, all of them. It was usually easy with Lampião, easy to trust him, to follow him, put your life in his hands. You could usually see what he was doing, and it made sense. But this was something else, and she could see the same question clouding every eye: had Lampião made the one mistake that would be all it took to kill them? Leading them here, where the police could smell them? Leaving their tracks uncovered, where the police could see?

HE CAME BACK, and all heads turned to him as one. No one said it, but you could see the question: *Are we going to die out here today?*

He took out his new pocket watch, a gold Patek Philippe—the only kind worth stealing, he always said. He'd taken this one from the mayor of Canindé.

"Nearly noon," he said. "Good." They'd been informed that Mané Neto had taken the fast train to Piranhas. He'd still have to march out from there, several leagues at least. "There's still time."

He started with his brother—"Ezekiel, over here." He positioned him, their best shot, at the top of the path, and then called to the others one by one and gave them their positions around the escarpment, under little rises, behind rocks. Pointed out the escape routes, "in case we decide to leave in a hurry." He didn't smile when he said that, but she noticed their faces lighten up a bit.

Then he turned to them. "There's nothing to worry about here," he said. "Everyone calm, and shoot straight and sure. Don't waste any bullets, not one. Pay close attention to my orders. God willing, we'll walk away from this one, too."

He sent Bananeira out as a sentinel, and hung his watch on one of the trees. "Time to pray," he said. "Bring your guns. Keep them cocked," and he knelt, they all knelt, under the trees.

"*Eternal King, our Father divine . . .*" Lampião led the prayer, head bowed, eyes closed. All eyes closed, except for hers, watching him. He looked to her like a holy man then, and the rest of them, the worst bandits in Brazil, pilgrims in a sacred grove, praying for one more miracle.

" . . . *Holy Mary, Mother of God*"—would She do it? Maria Bonita wondered. Would She preserve them from the hundreds of soldiers closing in around them? Would God's Mother see beyond the government's accusations to the essential justice of the bandits' stance? They had grown up, all of them, in a land with no justice, a land so far, so profoundly isolated, from the rest of Brazil, the seacoasts from where justice issued, that they'd found themselves, all of them, the people of the Sertão, beyond the reach of any earthly law and order. Wholly at the mercy of whoever was bigger or stronger or better armed.

But perhaps She had noticed as Lampião's family had first their few goats and cattle stolen, and then their poor, dry land usurped by neighbors who were, as it happened, enemies by both blood and marriage in one of those typical, endless regional feuds, made worse by the unfenced land, and growing boys on both sides of the uncertain boundaries.

The neighbors were wrong, but they were stronger, and Lampião's father had nine children to raise, three of them boys old enough to be shot, and he'd made his deal.

He sold off his goats, gave up his ranch, and in exchange for a pledge of peace, "witnessed and shaken on," had moved away from the land they had called home for as long as anyone could remember.

They tried one place and then another, and Lampião's mother sickened and died in all the moving, and his father finally settled with a cousin in the next state. Far enough away from the neighbors, he figured, but he was wrong. And was the Mother of God watching that bad day when the enemy-neighbors' gunmen—who also happened to be policemen—came riding up to the quiet house where Lampião's father was sitting on the porch with his cousin, peaceably shelling corn, and shot them both down in cold blood?

"My father didn't even own a gun!" a distraught Lampião had sobbed to the district judge. Though he wasn't Lampião then, he was still Virgulino Ferreira da Silva, a law-abiding cowboy who'd gone into court seeking justice. He was twenty-one years old, and except for the one eye he must have looked pretty much like everyone else in that courtroom that day. A little taller, maybe, and thinner, but with the same cinnamon skin and straight dark hair as the rest of them.

Though afterward, when the press dug around and found him, the judge said what he remembered were the glasses—they made him look like a schoolteacher, the judge said. Which of course he knew he wasn't, though you could see, too, that his people weren't destitute, at least not until the neighbors had moved in on their ranch.

"My father wasn't armed, he didn't know how to

shoot!" Lampião had cried to the judge, who didn't doubt it.

"I'm here for justice!" he'd cried.

Had ridden, the judge knew, many leagues for justice, hot dusty leagues. The judge could only sigh and pass down the usual verdict.

"Your father is dead," he said. "There's nothing we can do for him now. But the men who killed him are alive, and they can come back and kill us both. I'm afraid we'll have to leave justice to God."

The young man had just stood there, the judge remembered, or claimed he did, staring at him, or maybe past him, with that one eye, even as his uncles and cousins got to their feet and moved toward the door, with that half-smile of resignation they all kept ready, those true sons of the Sertão. They'd walk out now, heads down, and have a drink or two, maybe more, maybe shoot it up a bit through the town, but not too much, not enough to bring trouble down on their heads. The devil was bigger than they were, they all knew that.

Still the young man had lingered, still staring, but what he was seeing, he told her, wasn't the judge but his own life, passing before his eyes, like a boat cut loose, floating away down the river. There was the house where he lived, with his sisters and brothers, there was his bed and his beans and coffee, and a pot full of goat meat, cooked the way he liked it, at home. And there were his mule trains, the work he did then, which he liked. It wasn't ranching but it was all right, going from ranch to ranch to market, and doing well, delivering both ways, never losing any livestock, any produce, and making a name for himself as one of the best.

There were his dreams, too, his plans for a ranch of his own again someday, maybe in a different part of the state, and the other kind of dreams, himself standing beside a pretty girl in a little church on a dusty town square somewhere. And a family—boys he'd teach to be cowboys, girls she'd teach to make cheese and lace. Them living all together, him with his pipe, her with a small guitar, living and growing older, and, one day, dying in his bed.

Life—normal, nice, real. Floating away, just behind that judge's head. Because when the judge said, "Leave justice to God," he knew right then that he wasn't the man to do that.

He'd followed his family out into the blinding sunlight of the little town square that day. Had a drink with his cousins at one of the little stalls set up in the shade, under the wispy trees. The young ones spoke of vengeance, the old ones of resignation. One of them told him how their grandfather had killed an enemy in the state of Paraíba, and then fled to Pernambuco to get away from it all.

But his son, Lampião's father, had always hated fighting, hated conflict, and even changed his name, from Feitosa to Ferreira da Silva, to put more distance between the family and that feud. He'd been a man of peace all his life. They raised another glass, and everyone drank with tears in their eyes, except for his son, Virgulino.

He'd done his crying. The town, as he remembered, was small, but nice. There was the sandy square, with small mud houses around it on three sides, attached one to the other, and nicely painted, those beautiful watercolors you only get here, pink, blue, green. One half-green, half-yellow—they were changing the color for the next holiday. Funny, what a difference that made. Changed the "*astral*," people said, the feel, the luck.

Anyway, he drank and then put down his cup that day, and went into the church at the far end of the square. It was dark inside, and cool, despite the heat. He knelt before the blue-robed Virgin. "*Ave Maria*," he whispered, and the tears came again, unexpected tears, for his dead father, his lost land, and the life that had floated away from him that morning—a beautiful life, he realized, the life of a rancher. He hung his head and cried for all the beautiful red goats he'd never drive to the fair, and the drinks he'd never have in the open town squares. The cows he wouldn't brand, and the horses he wouldn't break. The wife, the children—He got to his feet.

He begged the Virgin for both protection and indulgence, and asked Her to bless his quest. And then he'd walked back out to his uncle's, where they were staying, kissed his sisters, shook hands with his brothers, packed one shirt and two rifles, and rode out to Vila Bela, to join Sinhô Pereira's bandits, where he went from being Virgulino to Lampião.

And from then on he made his own justice, and it occurred to Maria Bonita that day outside Maranduba that God's Mother must have had at least some sympathy for him. He'd faced four hundred soldiers at Macambeira, and three hundred at Serra Grande. And here he was, still kneeling in the noonday sun, under this perfect *umbu* tree, beautifully shaped, like a tree in a park or a dream.

Lampião got to his feet. "Let's rest a bit," he said, and she still remembered the smell of the ground there, the dirt, that cinnamon smell, in the shade where it was still so hot you could almost see it, where they all stretched out and where she hoped they would leave her if she fell.

TIME STOPPED FOR a while, and then the sentinel ran up to Lampião. "They're coming!"

He sprang to his feet. "Everyone to your places!"

She took cover behind one of the trees, as he'd told her, and watched as Lampião ran up to the front.

"No one shoots until I tell you!" he commanded, low. They were ready, waiting, crouching down. She closed her eyes with one last prayer. *Preserve me! And him. All of us . . .*

Her gun was cocked, safety off. She'd never been in a fight like this before, but their position looked good. They were up above, hidden, and the soldiers were down there below them, in the open.

She heard a voice then, one of the police, ordering the attack. "The Sour Dog," someone whispered, Mané Neto, Lampião's mortal enemy. She'd given him that nickname, but this would be the first time they met. If they met. *Let us not meet.*

Lampião remained watching, motionless, spyglass to his eye.

"Attack!" shouted the Sour Dog. He was excited. He'd followed their trail, right to where Lampião wanted him, it came to her. He was right underneath them, with no cover, smelling their perfume and shouting, "Attack!"

With his radio turned off, for the trail had been so clear that he'd decided that maybe he'd follow it alone, with only his own men. It was looking suddenly easy to Mané Neto—why hadn't that scared him? He'd been chasing Lampião for ten years—hadn't he learned anything at all? He should have known, or at least should have paused for a moment and scratched his head, beginning to suspect, beginning to figure, and then he should have turned on his costly, much-vaunted new radio, and shared his reconnaissance with his colleagues and their hundred soldiers, who might then have come in and flanked the bandits, and Mané Neto might in fact have killed Lampião that day.

But Sour Dog that he was, he stood below there, right where Lampião wanted him, thinking less of strategy than of treasure, the bandits' gold and jewels, counting it up, and figuring that maybe he wouldn't share it after all, or the glory, either. It would be his alone, both treasure and glory, the most and the best in all Brazil.

So Mané Neto stood there that day in Maranduba, richer than he'd ever be in this life again, and shouted, "Attack!" And Lampião just sat and waited as the troops who'd trekked all the way from Nazaré to kill him charged up a narrow path with no cover, and no way to make their superior numbers or technology mean anything at all.

"Fire!" cried Mané Neto. There was a burst of gunfire, and then much smoke down below, where the soldiers were essentially shooting their bullets into the air. From up where the bandits sat ensconced, well positioned, hidden—nothing. Not a shot. Not even a whisper.

Lampião passed his finger before his lips and held up his hand. "Wait."

The soldiers were encouraged. Excited. They'd done it, they were thinking. Lampião! Why had they ever been scared?

They ran forward, up the hill, shooting and shouting.

"Let's see if Lampião's more man than I am!"

"Come out if you've got any balls, you pestilent bandits!"

"Led by a one-eyed blind man!"

"Come on, blind man, if you're a man at all!"

Lampião gave them no answer. He didn't take his one eye from their faces. Familiar faces, he saw now. Personal enemies. Old enemies. Getting close enough, finally.

At last he saw the son of a man closely associated with the murder of his father. He got to his feet. "No one shoot this *sujeito*," this creep, he ordered. "He's mine!"

And he stepped out directly in front of Hercílio Nogueira, who froze at the sight of the one-eyed blind man, then ran like a rabbit.

Too late. Lampião shot him in the back of the head. His blood gushed out on top of his brother, whom Lampião shot next. "Two dogs already at the gates of hell!" he shouted.

"How many are there?" she called to one of the bandits as he ran by.

"Not so many! The Sour Dog forgot to wait for his friends!"

Now it was the bandits' turn for shouting.

"Come on, monkeys! Don't be afraid! Don't stay so far away! We've been waiting for you!"

"Don't try to run, Sour Dog! Did you think fighting us would be as easy as stealing your neighbors' goats in Nazaré?"

Lampião's brother Ezekiel, known as "Ponto Fino," Sharpshooter, took aim at Vicentão—another one from home, with years of enmity between them. "Let's see if I can hit you where I want to," he shouted.

Ping—the first bullet, straight through the left buttock. Vicentão wheeled. "Now turn to the right, monkey!" Ponto Fino instructed. "Point your *mucumbu* over here!" Second shot, into the right buttock.

Vicentão fell: "I'm dead!"

Though they found out later he wasn't. Just as their grandmother used to say—"The worst pots don't break."

But Vicentão was finished for that day. They all were, all the troop from Nazaré, finished pretty much forever. Mané Neto buried seven of his best men in Maranduba, and had to carry twelve others, seriously wounded, back up to the river.

As for the bandits, no one was thinking about dying anymore, at least not that day. And when Lampião led them away from Maranduba a little while later, it was laughing and singing a new verse in his long, mocking song: "*All I wanted* mesmo," he rhymed, "*Was to pay back Mané Neto.*"

And they knew that all the other soldiers in the area, the hundreds that had marched out to kill them that morning, could hear them shouting and firing shots of pure defiance into the air. But they weren't running anymore then, or hiding, and though this was both challenge and insult to the soldiers, it remained unanswered.

Lampião had just had his way with Mané Neto and the Nazarés, the toughest, most ferocious—the worst, which is to say, the best of them all, and she heard later that the soldiers who came after them had started seeing ghosts even before it got dark that night. They were, after all, just backwoodsmen with no real quarrel with the bandits. They'd joined the forces for the money, but were seldom paid and poorly fed. Worse led.

And that night they refused, point-blank, to give chase to the bandits. Which was all right with their officers, too. That campaign was over. Everyone went home with the same story—Lampião was invincible. They'd never get him.

ALTHOUGH A FEW nights after that, the dreams started. She'd awake in a sweat, in tears—some soldiers were after her with their knives—and Lampião would put his arms around her, tell her that would never happen, and to go back to sleep. But one night Lampião wasn't in the tent when she woke, and she was too shaken, it had been too vivid, too real, her heart was pounding, and she pulled a skin around her shoulders and crawled outside.

It was still dark, and the camp was quiet, but Luis Pedro was sitting by the fire. Good. He had the last watch, which meant that the night was almost over.

She walked over and sat beside him. "I had a dream—"

He looked up at her, smiled. "Yeah, the dreams."

Which meant what? She wasn't sure. She picked up a stick and poked at the embers—glowing red, with a little flame now and then.

What it didn't mean, though, was, *Tell me*, since the last things Luis Pedro needed were her bad dreams.

Or her confession—that she had been badly frightened out there in Maranduba, but what could that mean to him? That she'd been a child till now, a poser, strutting through towns with her gun belt, but so scared the first time it came to it that she was ready to beg for her life, beg and bargain, if the soldiers gave her a chance to talk?

And what of it, now, anyway? It wasn't as if she could quit and go home. Explain to the police and the judges that it had all been very nice when it was singing and dancing and looting, but now that she'd seen the other side of it—smelled it, lived it, and now dreamt it—she'd come to understand that perhaps she'd made a mistake.

And had she? Wasn't she alive and well that day, that night, that early morning? Hadn't she and Lampião fallen back into each other's arms after Maranduba, with more passion than ever? And if she was in fact unworthy, if she'd betrayed him in her heart that day, in her fear, her thoughts were hidden, and who knew what anyone else was ever thinking? Dreaming? Who knew their secret fears?

She looked up at Luis Pedro. "Roll me a cigarette?" She'd never smoked before, but as soon as she said it, she knew it was the thing.

He hesitated. "The captain won't like it."

It was true. Lampião didn't like women to smoke.

But truer still that if the monkeys hadn't been just that—monkeys—if Mané Neto hadn't played such a perfect fool, then not even Lampião could have saved her out there under the sun in Maranduba. There would have come that moment when she would have found herself facing it all absolutely alone.

"Come on," she said to Luis Pedro, and he shrugged and took out his tobacco—what could he do? She was Maria Bonita. Because there was that, too. She was queen out here. While she lived, she was queen.

Luis Pedro rolled her a cigarette in a corn husk, lit it, and handed it to her. She inhaled too hard and coughed.

Laughed. He laughed. She took another puff—easier this time. *So that's how you do it. Like that.* How funny, how crazy—and what would Lampião say?

What could he say, though? Because the truth was if she was going to die young out there anyway, the least she could do was smoke.

VI

Time in a truck passes its own way, the driver knew, especially when the passengers are policemen and the road isn't much more than a goat track. The sun had come out and was in his eyes. No one was talking but someone had pulled out a harmonica, and there had been more cigarettes offered and smoked.

And then they came out on the river, the São Francisco, almost back where they'd started, nearly back at the town—they could have taken the road. They must be up to something, and the driver figured they wouldn't even pay him. The gasoline would come out of his own pocket, and he might have his pay docked for being late. On the other hand, they weren't beating him up or even threatening. And with the police, that was at least something.

Bezerra was studying now, out the window. "This way." He pointed up a small hill, away from the river.

They drove up—nothing up there but a cornfield. "Here," said Bezerra.

Good, thought the driver, it could have been worse for him. If they let him go now, he'd get back to the road before dark, and maybe even sleep in a bed that night. He pulled up. The men in the back were jolted awake by the sudden stop.

Bezerra jumped out, looked around. Nothing. Corn—and then, men, soldiers, sitting on the ground, eating the corn raw, poor guys. No fires—good. Aniceto was doing it right, too, though his men didn't look happy.

"Everyone out," Bezerra called to his own men in the back of the truck, who climbed out in silence, worried now that something was afoot.

Aniceto came across the field to Bezerra, pushing a man in front of him. When Bezerra saw who it was, his first thought was, *Him?* He'd had Joca in before, the guy knew nothing, he was worthless.

"You brought me back here for this?" he began to Aniceto, who took his arm and walked him off to the side, and told him, low, about the bandit and Joca's wife, and that Joca was ready to talk, and he'd taken Corisco's group across the river yesterday to meet Lampião.

Bezerra looked back at Joca—Joca Bernardes, "Joca the Cuckold"—he'd heard those whispers, too. Funny, it wasn't like Lampião. To let one of his guys move in on the wife of a boatman, someone he depended on for discretion. Was he slipping? Enough for this to be a real chance?

Probably not, although if anyone would do it, it would

be Joca—someone like Joca. He could see the guy was enjoying the attention. Talking big—a man who couldn't control his woman. "Let's see," he said to Aniceto.

He walked back to Joca and took his arm. "So, my man," said Bezerra, "you've got something to tell me?"

Joca nodded. "I dreamt that I was the cause of Lampião's death."

Did Joca Bernardes really think that Lieutenant João Bezerra would stand here listening to his dreams? A man like Joca, with no loyalty, no human decency, and conjuring excuses for betraying Lampião, the best friend he had in the world, and no wonder his wife had put horns on his head.

On the other hand, Joca might be in a position to know something—though he shouldn't have been, clearly, so maybe Lampião *was* slipping? Which was the only reason Bezerra restrained an impulse to kick Joca around the cornfield, and instead nodded solemnly back.

"You know where he is?" asked Bezerra.

A pause. "Maybe I know who does."

But this was too much for Bezerra. He flew at Joca, knocked him into the dirt, then fell on top of him and grabbed his shirt. "This time I'm not playing!"

"It's Pedro Candido! He's hiding Lampião, across the river!"

Bezerra got to his feet, brushed off his hands. Pedro Candido—that part wasn't news. Bezerra knew that he was one of Lampião's suppliers, suspected it first when he opened a little store of his own. How else could he have done it, without Lampião's money? Which was why, a few months back, when he himself was in a small fix and needing some ready money, he had approached Pedro Candido about selling some bullets. No questions asked, although he was well paid in gold coin.

But dealing with Lampião when he passed through, as Pedro Candido and hundreds of others up and down this river and throughout the whole Sertão did, and knowing where he was—hiding him, in fact—were two different things.

And was it possible that Pedro Candido was hiding Lampião? It came over Bezerra like a warm rain that it might be. He remembered that Pedro Candido's mother had a place across the river, and he had a flash for a moment, a feeling he hadn't had since he was a boy, of everything suddenly making sense. Everything falling into place all around him.

"Where's Pedro Candido now?" he asked Joca.

"At home, in Entremontes."

Just down the river, not far from here. Bezerra knew the place. "When did you last see him?"

"Yesterday. When we took Corisco over."

Fresh news, then. His soldiers finished pulling Odilon Flor's machine guns out of the truck. He turned to the driver, elation rising.

"Thanks for your service."

"*Sím, senhor,*" said the driver.

Bezerra handed him a little money, which was more than he'd expected, plus the rest of the cigarettes. Good, thought the driver, that would get him to back to Pedra, anyway.

"You'll be stopping at the little towns on your route?" Bezerra somehow couldn't stop himself.

"*Sím, senhor.*"

"Well, you can tell them that after tomorrow, Lampião's story will have a different ending."

"May I ask how you know?" the driver ventured.

"Because I'm going to step on him tonight," Bezerra said.

"*Sím, senhor.*" The driver nodded. Adding, "Or not," but low, as he climbed back into his truck, lit one of Bezerra's cigarettes, and drove off.

VII

The sun was coming up, cutting through the trees, and starting to feel warm now on her back. She should get up and try to stir Lampião if they were going to leave that day—and they should, she knew it. But on the other hand, the sun hadn't been out since they'd been here, and maybe he was right after all. Maybe there was nothing to fear.

Or would be, once they were through with July. The worst month, the cursed month, when all they should do is crawl into a hole somewhere—yeah, like armadillos—and wait it out. Take a long sleep somewhere, if there was somewhere, but there wasn't, that was the problem, there was no place on earth where they could sleep out July.

Although if it weren't for Julys, she'd have no sense at all of the year passing, since there were no children getting taller or goats to kill in season. For a while, in the beginning, this had given her a sense of being outside not just the laws of the state but the laws of nature. But then one day she'd stopped in the middle of the path, fingers to her lips, and realized she was just one of the women after all.

She tried all the remedies, the barks and the teas, but none of them worked, and then there she was, mad as hell at life, at the same world that had been her garden till then, and that had now reduced her, "the fiercest woman in Brazil," to common misery, as, growing bigger by the day, she straggled behind the group, or sat, heavy, beside the fire, longing for a bed, a chair, and sewing little shirts trimmed with lace for a baby she'd never see grow to wear them.

She knew what she had to do, she wasn't the first one. Other girls had had babies when there was no chance of keeping them. They turned them over to foster parents, ranchers usually, or occasionally a priest, to be raised as one of their own, along with a good sum of money for the baby's keep.

And so it would be with hers. She refused to acknowledge any needs, any changes, cursed her condition, refused to feel the kicks, though once, caught off guard, she'd gasped, awestricken, and moved her hand to her belly. But Lampião saw, and a look of such sadness crossed his face that it hurt her, and though there hadn't been much said between them—for what was there to say?—she saw how much he felt it, too.

Not that it helped, just made it worse. He started drinking at night, and then cursing "this life that won't let me live with my child!" But what could they do, run away somewhere? Turn into a nice little couple, Virgulino and Maria, on a farm in the backlands with a couple of goats?

Not that she wouldn't if she could have then. Not that she hadn't weakened and started begging. But he told her what she always knew—there was no place they could run, nowhere far enough away in all Brazil where they'd be safe from their enemies. Because there were so many enemies. Which she knew all along. It was why she couldn't have a child, never wanted to anyway.

When her time came, Lampião himself delivered the baby. He'd grown up delivering cows and goats, and was a good midwife—he'd delivered all the other babies of the girls in the band, and never lost one. But this time he got scared and made a desperate vow to Saint Expedita, the patron saint of childbirth. He swore if they lived, she and the baby, he'd name the child after the saint.

So that's what they'd named her, Expedita. "Tita," she'd found herself whispering into the baby's hair, despite having hardened her heart. Tried to harden her heart.

He'd arranged for a rancher he trusted to take the baby, whose wife was due to give birth right then as well. It was agreed that the man would put out the word that his wife had had twins, so no one would stop and wonder. Since if anyone knew whose daughter the girl really was, her life wouldn't be worth a damn.

On the day planned, they met him at his ranch and handed over the little bundle—"Tita"—and enough money for ten babies. Lampião told the man he'd kill him the worst way possible if he mistreated her, but the man didn't take offense, just told them not to worry, they would love the child like their own.

"Do you promise?" she had whispered, and the man had promised. His name was Zé Severo Mamede—"Expedita Mamede," the girl would be called. Though her real name, the name she should have had, Expedita Ferriera Silva, was more beautiful, and didn't "Severo" mean cruel? Harsh? But the rancher had a nice face, and so did his wife, who came out to take the baby.

"Tita," Maria Bonita told the rancher's wife, searching her face for kindness, as she smiled down at the baby and kissed her.

"Here are her clothes"—the woman admired them, said they were beautiful, and the baby was beautiful, and Maria Bonita said, yes, the baby was beautiful.

"So beautiful," tears coming to her eyes, milk rising to her breasts. Bind them, the girls had told her, but she'd thought maybe to nurse her one last time.

But it turned out she couldn't, there were police around, they had to move on, and Lampião gave their daughter one last blessing, and the rancher and his wife swore again to love her, and she believed them.

Why wouldn't they love her? She was lovable, she was lovely. She smelled like heaven, with beautiful little hands that closed on her finger. A rosebud mouth—perfect, all of it.

And then they said good-bye and walked away, back to their old life, free again. Fine. Done. Over.

But milk was dripping from her rock-hard breasts,

and that's when she and Lampião started fighting, and it wasn't long after that that they'd ridden into Serrinha.

ANOTHER JULY, three years back, and what were they doing in the state of Pernambuco, where "even the leaves on the trees are my enemies," as Lampião always said? It was where he'd been born, and grown up and started fighting, and for every lifelong friend there, he swore he had three blood enemies.

It wasn't as if they didn't have men who hated them in other states, too, men who chased them not for their pay but out of passion, but there was an edge to it in Pernambuco. Something personal, something mean and treacherous. Where they'd murdered his father, and would have murdered him, too, when he was young, just because they could. She hated the place, hated the red rocks and even the way they made their *imbuzada*, that one time when they were there for the feast of São João. Too much sugar, because the *umbus* weren't ripe. They'd pick them green, they couldn't wait, couldn't separate them out, those greedy Pernambucanos.

But Pernambuco was "nothing but money," too, and every once in a while Lampião would make a foray into the state—in and out, as fast as possible. That year, 1935, Lampião had sent out letters to isolated ranchers requesting payment, and then divided the men into small groups of six or eight to make the collections, all of them following zigzag routes to confuse the police. And everywhere they went, Lampião was sighted, sometimes at opposite ends of the state simultaneously—"Proof," one of the newspapers had concluded, "of his taboo of invincibility."

Which was fine with him—let them think he was magic. As far as he was concerned, things had gone all right. There'd been one incident with his own group—a farmer, a hothead, trying to stop them from cutting across his land, had pulled a gun, and they'd shot him. But that was all, and now they were on their way down to Bahia, as well supplied with food and horses as they could be, plus a new supply of bullets and all the paper money they could carry, so much that they were handing it out in the streets and leaving bundles in the small churches they passed.

And they were almost out of Pernambuco, just eight of them, on their way to meet up with the others in Bahia. It had been raining and was chilly—it was the twentieth of July—and they had stopped in a barn, just north of the village of Serrinha, to sleep a bit and warm up.

They wanted to get out of the state before dawn, though, so they'd started off again at the second crowing, when it was still pitch-dark and quiet, before the birds. And nothing had felt wrong that night when they rode into Serrinha. No signs, no falling stars, no night birds calling. It was late—close to four in the morning, but no light in the sky yet. The town was deserted, but that happened. People heard they were coming and ran into the bush. There were four men, though, standing in the road, outside one of the houses.

"Don't move!" Lampião called to them. He had only five boys with him that night, plus her and Maria Ema. But that was all they'd need in Serrinha.

"Hands in the air!" Lampião had shouted to the men.

Their hands had flown up. "We're not armed!" they'd shouted back.

Good, she remembered thinking. She hadn't wanted to see them shot. Lampião rode up to them. "You've been waiting for me? You know who I am?"

"Yes, *senhor*." Smiles—she could still see them. She'd recognize those smiles at the gates of hell.

"How many police have you got here?"

"No police. They've all run."

A laugh all around. "Where are your guns?"

"We don't have any guns," those men had replied, and they'd seemed so well disposed, and at the same time so humble and unprotected, like every true soul in the Sertão, that Lampião had believed them, though if a cock had crowed then or a cat had crossed the road, maybe he'd have stopped and looked a little harder at those smiles.

But, "We mean no harm," they said, and, "Then we mean no harm," Lampião had answered, and said good night and started off again, instead of shooting them down on the spot like he should have.

And those sons of the beast had crept into a house where they had a gun after all—one rifle and four bullets, she learned later—and then out of the silence there came a blast that slammed into her back.

She screamed, spun, and fell—"I'm dying, Virgulino!"—and then lay down her head in the dirt and died.

Or thought she had. Not that it was so bad—just that it was over. He told her afterward that he himself was so stunned, so shocked, so horrified, that he'd stood stock-still at first, a perfect target himself for those four men with their smiles, so confused was he, so uncomprehending. Not that those treacherous dogs had shot her—but that he'd let it happen, hadn't seen the shifting eyes behind those smiles, or heard the lie in "We have no guns."

But then, "Virgulino!" she cried out again, his Christian name. Beautiful, he always found it on her lips—"I'm dying, Virgulino!" *And I'll die with her*, had been his first thought. But when he ran to her, he found she wasn't dead, though shot in a tricky place, and bleeding badly.

"Out of here!" he screamed to his men. A wave of panic had come over him, and he no longer knew what he was up against—the armies of the night, or four lying hotshots with a gun? They retreated back down the street, shooting blindly. He grabbed a hammock hanging from a porch, to wrap her in, picked her up, and then led the group off into the *caatinga* in such panic and confusion that they left everything behind—horses, dried meat, salt, everything but the money he didn't even remember he had, in the pack over his shoulder, and just lit out, headlong, with her moaning, and him shrieking, "Vengeance without limits!" to the stars.

He could hardly run straight at first, he told her, could barely make out the path in front of him. All he could see was that street in Serrinha, those smiles, and all he could hear was that shot.

He played it over and over in his mind, as if that could change it, undo it, but then he'd feel another gush of warm blood sticky on his shirt, her blood, and know he had to keep running.

They found a deserted barn, and laid her gently on the straw. The one thing he hadn't left behind in Serrinha was his medical kit, a good one he'd taken recently from a doctor in Jirau. He bent over her. He knew wounds better than most doctors, and he opened the iodine and phenic acid, and cleaned this one meticulously. Then he made a compress of the shredded bark of a *quixabeira* tree to stanch the bleeding, and wrapped her wound carefully in clean gauze. There was a chance that it wouldn't be fatal, he told his men, depending on what came next.

Not that it would be easy—he didn't have to tell them that. They all knew that the word would already be going out to every policeman and soldier in the godforsaken state of Pernambuco that Lampião was on the run with only five men and a wounded woman, and there'd never be a better chance to get him than now.

He sponged her forehead. "Pick her up," he said to one of the men. He himself wouldn't look at her for a while, he decided. Her only chance now would be if he did what he did best the best way he could, with no distractions—and if his luck came back.

It was July, his fatal month. He got to his knees and made a promise to the patron saint of the whole Sertão, São Antônio: he would fast every July for the rest of his life—serious fasting, no meat, no music, no dancing, no lovemaking even, ever again in July, if she lived. "Let her live!" he begged.

Then he got to his feet. "Let's go, quick."

She cried out when they picked her up, but he didn't turn around. Just scanned the lightening sky, and then led them back to the ranch where they'd shot the man the day before. What had the guy been thinking, to pull a gun on them? They wouldn't have hurt him, and now he was dead, and as they approached the farmhouse, they could hear the wailing and praying of the funeral, which was just what Lampião was hoping for.

He sent two of the bandits in, guns drawn, to grab the pallbearers to carry her hammock, which would free his own men to serve as rear guard. And then they took off, heading north, then a quick turn south, running as fast as they could for their lives. Her life.

Afterward the pallbearers had their own tales to tell, of sandals worn backward, branches dragged behind, of twists and turns off the path. And still they couldn't manage to hide the blood. It left a trail wherever they went.

Once, they told the reporters, they'd hidden in the bush near Lagoa. They could hear the police coming right behind them. Lampião had them lay down the hammock, and motioned them to the front, between his men and the soldiers, guns to their heads. One word, one sign, and they'd be the first to go.

And as they crouched there, barely breathing, bandits at their backs, guns cocked, the soldiers passed by "so close we could have touched them," the pallbearers told the press—which was a slight exaggeration, Lampião pointed out afterward.

Still, he wouldn't say he wasn't as relieved as he'd ever been in his life when the troop passed by and continued on in the wrong direction, and he started wondering, guardedly then, if his luck was coming back. What was the date? Time was passing. It was nearly August. From the hammock, more blood.

They paused at a hut near Riacho, to eat quickly and change her bandage. He poured a few drops of water though her cracked lips.

"Let me rest," she begged, but they couldn't rest. There were more police behind him, following the blood. They ran on, and just before midnight they reached a ranch on the edge of a steep ridge, near Águas Belas. Lampião himself went in and pulled the rancher out of bed.

"Take us down the ridge," he ordered.

The rancher, Mané Belo, short and fat, a bon vivant with a hangover that would have kicked in had it not been trumped by terror, had tried to reason. "There's no way down that ridge, you have to go around, it's too steep—"

"Get dressed."

"It's not possible, especially at night, there's no path, even the goats barely make it down in the daylight—"

The police were coming closer every minute. She herself, wrapped in the hammock, falling in and out of consciousness, was begging him to leave her there. "Let me die in peace!" she whispered.

And he was considering it. It was true that if the police

got any closer, he'd have to shoot her. Couldn't leave any chance for her to fall into their hands, their butchery.

He put his gun to Mané Belo's head: "Choose," he said. "*Ou desce ou morre.* Take us down or die."

Everyone who knew Mané Belo said that nothing short of mortal fear could have gotten him down that cliff that night, or ever. His short fat legs buckled at first, but he steadied himself and led them down, step by step, and the bandits followed, guns drawn, as they clambered, slid, clung to cactus, fell over rocks and into thornbush, and somehow made it down, with her moaning in the hammock, and the police up above, staring down the slope.

Which was just what Lampião had counted on, his first break. But this one was far from over. One of their spies met them with the news that more troops were coming after them from the west, so they headed north again, and then east, to the hills around Tará. He didn't have a sense yet if she was going to live or die, though the bleeding seemed to be lessening, except when she was jolted around. When they were flat-out running, or moving up and down through steep terrain, then she'd lose some blood. But when she was left to lie still for a bit, it seemed to be holding—no hemorrhages, no infection. He was starting to think that if they survived this, maybe she would, too.

ANOTHER IF. He had an old friend, a trusted ally, in the region, just outside Curral Novo. They stopped at his barn to eat and rest up a bit. She didn't remember this part, just remembered that she was no longer afraid of dying. She'd made friends with death somewhere between there and Serrinha, and if she died, she died, and anyway, that would be better than more pain.

"Put me down," she was begging them, "leave me in this bed," by which she meant the barn floor, which seemed like a bed to her, compared to being dragged through the night. "Let me die here." This bed. So nice, so safe and calm.

That barn was feeling like a haven to him, too, but then one of their spies came thundering out with word that Mané Neto himself had just gotten to Curral Novo, not much more than a quarter league away, with two hundred and fifty soldiers.

And then Lampião was faced with it again—should he shoot her? There was a hill nearby, where they might hold out if they could get to the top, which they could do only if Mané Neto's soldiers stopped to eat and rest before they came for him.

"Grab your guns," he said to his men—when had they last slept or eaten? He couldn't remember. They hoisted her hammock onto their shoulders and took off again, headed for the only real hill in the region.

The terrain was broken and steep, cut by deep gullies and rock faces that made it close to impassable. But he'd fought here once before, in his days with Sinhô Pereira, and he remembered a path, overgrown now and lost in the briars at the bottom, but more open higher up; and he found it, and they pushed up in silence, leaving no trace, no tracks, no cuttings, and entrenched themselves at the top of the hill.

WHEN MANÉ NETO got there, he tried at first to take the hill, but his men couldn't get across the gullies or up the rock face, not with the bandits shooting at them from above, and after he lost a few men, Mané Neto called off the charge and pronounced the place "insurmountable."

On the other hand, he pointed out to his colleagues, Captain Miguel Calmon, Lieutenant José Joaquim, and Sergeant Jorge Percílio, the best and the brightest in the Sertão, who'd converged around that hill, everything else was on their side. They had all the food and water in the world, and two hundred men. All they had to do was close the circle around seven exhausted bandits and a half-dead woman, and wait.

"The very last hour of Lampião!" Mané Neto exulted to a reporter from Riacho, adding that he always knew it would happen like this one day. Not only was he doing it, but he was doing it the best way, the way he'd always wanted. He'd cornered Lampião, outsmarted him, and proved himself "more man" in the end.

Though as the second morning dawned on Lampião's "last hour," Mané Neto started wondering when he'd last heard any shots, noting that it had been some time since there'd been any activity from the bandits' "last hour" up there. Were they out of ammunition? Sleeping? Sick?

Mané Neto stared through his field glasses. Nothing. He sent up some scouts, who didn't draw fire. Were the bandits dead, then? Mané Neto had wanted the pleasure of killing them, Lampião in particular. Had he died of thirst up there already, or exhaustion, or maybe shot them all, her, too, and then himself, in despair?

But then the scouts came back with the incredible news—the bandits were gone.

"What?" Mané Neto grabbed the guy by his tough leather shirt, ripped it, actually, and then ran up the path himself, jumped the gullies, scaled the rocks, to no avail. The bandits remained gone.

WHEN MANÉ NETO was besieged by the press afterward, his best explanation—"The only explanation!" he insisted—was that Lampião had escaped through occult means. He'd been trapped on the top of that mountain, inside a "closed circle," with all paths blocked and guarded, and even so, "he vanished into thin air," Mané Neto declared solemnly. Proof that he was "Satan in the flesh."

Maybe so, Lampião had retorted, but when it came to closing the circle, Mané Neto hadn't quite done his job. There'd been that one small path through the briars that he hadn't noticed and so didn't guard—and not only did Lampião not blame Mané Neto for this oversight, he'd been counting on it, praying for it, praying, on the way up, that this would be his way down.

And sure enough, as soon as it got dark that first night, he and his men had picked up the hammock and crept silently down through those unguarded briars, down a hillside so steep not even the goats would have liked it. But they were bandits, not goats, and every one of them had wanted to live to see the morning. They'd seen worse, done worse, even in the last few days. So down they went, in the perfect silence of sure-footed children of the land, and out past Mané Neto's two hundred sleeping soldiers—"We could hear them snoring!"—and away.

THEY HEADED NORTHWEST then, to the least populous part of the state, over by Buíque, where one of Lampião's colonel friends had a ranch, and that's when he took his first breath. He put Maria Bonita in a clean hammock, got out his kit again, and took off her bandages. The bleeding had stopped. He kissed her, and then examined her back and re-dressed the wounds, but without the bark now. He sent to town for some fireworks, and held a feast of thanksgiving. She would live.

But he wasn't done with Serrinha yet. He sent out word to the rest of his men, Corisco and Sereno, called them together, and they went out from their refuge near Buíque, back to Serrinha where she'd been shot, and shut down that part of the Sertão in vengeance—shut it down! Raided, burnt, spread such terror that the town of Serrinha became a desert, without even a market, and every man and boy who lived there went looking for the grandstanders who'd shot her, to lynch them, to cut off their heads and put them on fence posts for the bandits to see.

But they were gone, those dogs, long gone, running for their lives somewhere. Ever farther—he heard that no village in the Sertão would take them in. Good. Let them run themselves to death.

And when was that, now? Three years ago, three Julys. And it had been hard with her at first, even after she was up and around, sitting by the fire, looking all right again, looking better every day. Still she couldn't stop jumping like a cat at everything, and at nothing—because there had been nothing, it had come out of nowhere. No warning, and then a shot in the back.

And that's when she started plaguing Lampião, especially when her back hurt, to "leave this life, go far away, where no one knows us—"

And at first he humored her. "Like where?"

"Anywhere! Somewhere far, the Mato Grosso, the Amazon."

He was willing to joke with her a bit—"The Mato Grosso's snakes and fever, and the Amazon's nothing but rain."

And sometimes he'd explain—again—that there was no place far enough, no corner so remote or city so far that people didn't know his face, his name—hers, too. No place where some old enemy or the son or even widow of an enemy might not step out from behind a door and shoot them down like dogs in the street.

This she knew. This she agreed. He was right. Of course. But then she'd find herself saying, "What about way out in Minas, with the Pereiras?" until he'd push out of the tent, saying that Padre Cícero had been right, he never should have taken a woman.

And she never should have come, she'd shout after

him, but there came a day when she faced the truth, that even if he could escape, get out the way some of the others had, how would it be for him somewhere else? Wasn't he made of Sertão dirt, and wouldn't he die of high wild melancholy if he found himself a stranger, away from this land, this dust and cactus—wouldn't they all?

She took out her gun again after that, cleaned it, and started practicing her shooting. It felt good—she had forgotten how good. She was still a good shot, "Maria Bonita," and the first one, always, to spot the moon rising.

"Beautiful!" she started saying again at night, to Lampião.

Because when wasn't it beautiful?

VIII

The police sat in the cornfield outside of town that day, watching the sun move as slowly as it ever had across the sky. They had to get back to town, just to take the first step, which was to get a boat to take them downriver, to Pedro Candido's house. With each hour that passed, the likelihood of finding Pedro Candido at home lessened, but on the other hand, Bezerra knew better than to rush it now. His only chance of success depended on getting in and out of town absolutely undetected, so as not to contradict any of Lampião's spies, who were, unwittingly, working for Bezerra now, spreading the word that he'd gone chasing like a monkey up to Moxotó. Lampião would be hearing it anytime now and laughing. Telling his men they could "sleep in your underwear" tonight.

Though the thought of Lampião, Lampião himself, in the flesh, across the river sent a cold chill down Bezerra's back. The truth was that no one had ever come close to killing Lampião. The closest they'd come was to die trying.

Bezerra had a wife at home, and a child. He lived well in Piranhas—a beautiful life, now that it was passing before his eyes. Some of the boys were playing cards, Thirty-one. He walked over to them and sat down. Threw in a few centavos, nothing much. Didn't want to use up his luck in a card game.

Anyway, it was complicated, winning at Thirty-one. If you hit it right on the nose, you won, true enough, though on the other hand, sometimes it also foretold imminent death.

He'd go after Lampião tonight, sure, why not? Just to get Lucena off his back for a while. He'd follow up on the tip, go down to Entremontes, and see what they could get out of Pedro Candido. He'd even take his men across the river if it came to that, but if it did, they wouldn't catch him. One of the bandits had said it plainly enough—"The man to capture Lampião has never been born. To pick up the pieces, maybe, but to capture him, never."

Who was that? Volta Seca, maybe. The police had made a big deal out of it a few years back when they caught the boy, who for his part had been happy to talk. He'd joined the bandits when he was eleven—he didn't have any parents, and he'd begged Lampião to take him in. And Lampião had done what he could and tried to teach him—"If you have to kill a man, kill him fast, don't hurt him"—but Volta Seca couldn't be taught.

Despite all of Lampião's efforts, he still "liked blood,"

Volta Seca told the flurry of reporters, "liked killing." Whenever there was a man to be killed, Volta Seca pulled out his knife. This made Lampião mad, but he had a soft spot for the boy, the son he'd never have, and Volta Seca took good care of his horses, and for this Lampião forgave him his trespasses—for eight years, until that day outside Jatobá.

The bandits were skirmishing with the police, who outnumbered them but were still shooting high, shooting scared, over the bandits' heads, the way scared men do. This was fine with Lampião—he counted on it—but Volta Seca couldn't resist a dig.

"Lower your guns, you monkeys!" he'd shouted in jest. "Your fight is with us, not God!"

And the police had lowered their guns then, and shot two of the bandits, and that was the end of Volta Seca, too. Lampião turned him out of the band, and the police picked him up and took him down to Salvador, where people lined the streets to see him, and girls brought him little cakes and cigarettes in prison. Bezerra had seen the photos—Volta Seca smiling like an angel among schoolgirls whose throats he'd have cut for their glass earrings or a piece of candy in their hand.

"Thirty," said one of the men. Bezerra threw in his cards. They took his money—fine. The truth was, he felt lucky. And if Pedro Candido was still at home and knew where the bandits were, and if the bandits were over there, "sleeping in their underwear," and if by some strange twist of fate he had the luck now instead of Lampião, then maybe instead of being dead in the morning he'd be a very rich man. The bandits' loot was legendary. He didn't expect to be "the man to take Lampião," but maybe he and his men would run the bandits off, and if they did, there'd be some pieces to pick up, and he wouldn't mind being the one to do it.

One of the guys cut the cards. They still had plenty of time left in the cornfield before they could move. Bezerra put out some more money.

"Let me lose," he whispered to whatever angels might be hovering around his shoulders just then.

IX

"If they catch me in Alagoas, they might not kill me," Zé Sereno overheard Dulce saying. She and Cila were already out, sitting on some flat rocks, taking turns with the sewing machine, working to finish Lampião's nephew's uniform.

"Same for me in Sergipe," Sereno's girlfriend, Cila, had answered. "I've got cousins on the force there, I don't think they'd kill me. They've known me ever since I was a little kid."

And Sereno backed away, so as not to have to explain to his own true love that it had been a long time since she was a little kid in Sergipe, as opposed to one of the most-wanted bandits in all Brazil, worth her deadweight in gold to every policeman out there, including distant cousins on the Sergipe force.

Who might not kill her, but how much better would it be for her to be taken alive anyway? Gangbang on the way to prison, where they'd lock her in the deepest cell they had and lose the key till her teeth fell out.

And why was he even listening to this kind of talk, when what he should be doing was folding his tent and leaving, now, today? Everything he'd ever learned as a bandit, everything Lampião had taught him, was telling him to get out of there—yesterday, but since they hadn't, then today.

He told Maria that he'd go over and try once more to get Lampião to come, too, but if he still wasn't moving, then Sereno would leave anyway with Cila and his own group of boys. They wouldn't have to go far, just off the river, where he wouldn't have to listen to his woman wondering which police would or wouldn't kill her.

He didn't blame her. It was the place, this river—too many police around, and too many players. Too many tongues to wag, or even half-wag. Even if someone told only a little, it could be too much.

And there was something else wrong, too, that no one was talking about, which was Lampião himself.

Sereno figured he was up there praying, on the Morro dos Perdidos, Hill of the Damned, or Lost—some said one, some the other, but either way, it wasn't good. Sereno even knew the prayer: *With the light of day, I see my Lord, Jesus Christ, and the Virgin Maria. I walk with the Lord and nothing can touch me.*

And it used to be true. Every morning for Sereno's whole life in the band, Lampião would open his one eye and "see the Lord," one way or another, in the clouds, the birds, even in the blazing sun. And it was nothing but that, that clear vision, that they'd lived on for all these years, but it turned out to be enough.

But if he didn't have it, and Sereno was thinking maybe he didn't, and so were the boys—he'd seen it on all those worried faces around the fire this morning, everyone shifting around, standing, sitting, and no one looking anyone else in the eye. Christ, someone had forgotten to put the sugar in the coffee, and no one even noticed it at first. They were all just drinking it down like dogs.

The worst part was that Sereno wasn't sure there was any real solution here. July was always bad, granted, but would it get better come August? Once a pot is broken, does it mend?

Because Sereno had begun to think that Lampião's trouble was that he was no longer seeing what came next. Not just today—which was bad enough—but overall, where they were going. Or where they fit anymore. Not just as bandits—anyone can rob and ride and fight the police—but as another force out there, that came from the people and acted like them, too. Just a braver, tougher, richer, stronger version.

But had something changed? Behind their backs, while they were doing what they always did? He himself had started to wonder a couple of weeks ago, when they came up on the new road, outside of Pesqueíra—where they hadn't been for a while, but still, it was land they knew, just as they knew all the land out there, and it was—or had been—a stretch that they could more or less call their own. Land where they knew the landmarks, knew the trees along the way, and which goat trails led to water in season, and knew where the knife-cactus stood like brothers in arms, which *riacho* they'd follow to some rocks they could sleep behind, and what it would smell like when they got there.

But in the distance, they could see something they didn't know, a break in the brush in front of them, as if there were a river. But there was no river there, there'd never been a river. They crept forward in silence, almost in combat mode—that's how strange it was to them—creeping, guns drawn, though against what they didn't know. But then they walked out of the underbrush and stood silent on a new road, wide and straight, smooth pounded dirt, that ran from Pesqueira toward Rio Branco.

It was flat and as wide as a river—wider, and straight. Nothing out here was straight, and nothing was flat like this dirt, pounded hard by machines that had nothing to do with anything that lived there. Cutting right through the land, right across a piece where they used to follow a curving rise over a creek that flowed every few years, when the rains were good. Flattened now.

Lampião had always been able to stop those roads till now. He ran the first workmen off with a warning and an explanation: "They're building these roads to chase me!" Told them he'd kill them or anyone else he caught working on that or any road in the Sertão, and he did. Killed any number of road crews, generally leaving the youngest one alive, to "tell the tale": that Lampião would show no further mercy. Anyone who worked on the roads would be shot—and were.

And for ten years the government couldn't get men to build those roads at any pay level, even combat. But there was a new president, Sereno had heard, Getúlio Vargas, a southerner, from the south of Brazil, so far from here that they were a different breed of men and spoke a Portuguese you couldn't understand. This foreign president had sent up soldiers, and convicts even, from the south, too many to stop. Men who hadn't heard of Lampião, and now here was the road, built. And all Lampião's work, his strategy, and the lives and deaths of those workers, innocents after all—killed for a reason, though, killed to stop the road—were nothing but dust. History.

Which seemed to be moving away from them.

LAMPIÃO HAD STOOD there that day, not saying a word.

"It doesn't go far—" Sereno had pointed out.

"Yet," Lampião cut in, and everyone fell silent again. The worst part was people were using the road. An old man came by with his oxcart on his way to market.

"What have you got in there?" asked one of the boys, teasing. "Guns? Money?"

The old man pulled back the tarp. "Fifty *jaca* fruits, six watermelons, and a heart without malice toward anyone." Then he cut them a watermelon, and the best *jacas* any of them had ever eaten, and when Lampião asked him what he thought about the road, he said it was easier now for him to get to market.

AND SERENO ENDED UP thinking that that was the real problem, more than the road—the fact that Lampião was split off now from the people. He'd always been their man, dedicated in his way to their Sertão. It was true he scared them, true he took what he took, but he had been essentially one with them, till now.

Not long ago, Sereno had overheard a boy they'd come upon, running back home through the underbrush, singing to himself, in awestruck tones, "*I saw Lampião, Lampião, Lampião! I saw Lampião, Lampião, Lampião!*" And in the songs, too, the ballads sung in the town squares, he was their governor, their justifier, their laugher of last laughs in the face of entrenched power.

> My name is Virgulino
> my nickname Lampião . . .

That's how they sang about him—"My." "I." He was them—till the road. And now there were dams, too, across some of the rivers—who would dam a river? What kind of a man, with what kind of god? Different, anyway, from Lampião, who loved the land and the waters just as they'd been given.

He'd stood there on the road that day, looking almost lost, a stranger in his own land. And then they'd made their way back here, and he wasn't moving. They should have followed Corisco out yesterday—Sereno himself almost did. He'd held back out of sheer loyalty, nothing else.

And that was the first time that had happened, too. He'd always wanted to be with Lampião before, always looked forward to coming back to him when he'd been off with Corisco, or with a group on his own. It was with Lampião that they had their fun, all together, and where he got his ideas, his strength, his education, you might say. Lampião had taught him everything he knew, and now he knew it was time to leave.

PAST TIME. Last night he'd dreamt of Nenê again, Luis Pedro's girlfriend, though he wasn't sure afterward if he'd even been asleep. Maybe it was more a visitation. "Nenê of Gold," they used to call her, because of the solid gold medallion she wore around her neck. She loved it and never took it off, even though they joked that it weighed as much as she did. One day when they were marching along, he'd sung to her, playfully, "*Oh, Nenê of Oro, who gave you that medallion?*"

And she'd rhymed right back at him, "*My true love, Luis Pedro, who beat a whole battalion . . .*"

She was like that, Nenê, sharp and quick. From the same part of Bahia as Maria Bonita, though no one knew her people, or even her real name. Not even her—she told them she'd never been called anything other than Nenê, "Baby," except once at the baptismal font, and after that not even her parents could remember what name they'd given her. "Something from the Bible," was all they could recall.

So Nenê she lived, and Nenê she died—last year, at Mucambo, not far from here. They were sleeping in the corral of one of their suppliers, and a troop surprised them there, just at dawn. It was going all right, they were shooting their way out of it, when Nenê's skirt got caught on a piece of barbed wire as she was climbing over the fence.

And that was all it took—one false move, and you were dead. You could get away from the police most of the time, even if they caught you sleeping, but you couldn't trip. Couldn't look back, but that day Nenê must have woken up in a kind of fog, and didn't gather up her skirt right when they were hopping the fence, and when she was caught for just that one moment, that was all the police needed to shoot her in the side.

He himself had been right there, right in front of her, and he turned and pulled her off the fence when she screamed, ripped her skirt right off—but she was already bleeding like the devil, shot in the wrong place. He and Luis Pedro had carried her off, and Lampião had bandaged her carefully, but even he couldn't stop the bleeding. And she never opened her eyes again, just drifted off that night without a word, the small, light, golden Nenê.

And it seemed like she'd come back to him last night, to tell him something, though it wasn't clear what, and he must have been talking in his sleep, because Cila had woken up and asked him if he was all right, and he'd said yes, but he was shaken, and couldn't get back to sleep. So he'd crawled out of his tent and walked over to the edge of the hideout, and felt again how closed in the place was.

Corisco was right. There were too many rocks, it was hard to move around, especially at night—and then he'd seen Lampião, over beside a rock, praying.

He'd had a thought to go over and kneel down beside him, add his own prayers, but then he decided that better would be for him walk up over the top and reconnoiter. It wouldn't hurt to have an exit plan of his own.

X

Bezerra threw in his cards and walked down to the river. It was particularly beautiful, this stretch where the waters of the São Francisco ran green. Strange to think that right across there somewhere was Lampião. The river was broad, but Bezerra could swim across this part, right to them, if he knew which one of the countless little dry streambeds led up to their hideout. If they were still there. Who knew? If Bezerra was a betting man, he'd bet against it. Lampião had an instinct for betrayal.

He was probably heading out over the far hills away from the river even now, as Bezerra stood there scanning, not that there was anything to see. That side of the river was completely closed in with underbrush, thorn trees and cactus, and you couldn't see in more than a foot or two. There were no small clearings, or even any little houses, not till the cashew plantings started farther down. But that was where the land flattened out a bit, gentled up. Here there was no possibility of a garden. The banks were too steep, and the land rough and rocky.

Bandit country. His, too; he, too, was a man of the backlands, and could just as easily have been over there with Lampião, instead of here, hoping to kill him. If he'd been born in a different place, with different cousins.

Not that it made much difference either way. You were bound to fight out here, on one side or the other, ever since the Portuguese mistook the land for someplace else, maybe where they'd come from, across the sea. And they soon found out that their guns could never be far from hand, even after the boundaries were drawn, because the disputes never stopped. How could they, when you're trying to live off a land that doesn't feed you?

The Indians who'd been here first had it right. Their nomadic lifestyle was perfectly suited to these dry, grand expanses. When it rained they set up a nice camp by a bend in a river, strung their hammocks between the palm trees, shot the small deer that came to drink, clubbed an anteater or armadillo now and again, and life was good.

But when the frogs stopped singing, and the joão-de-barro birds built their nests facing south, when the sky was already burning white before midmorning, the Indians would roll up their hammocks and follow the drying creeks back to the one river that kept flowing, this same São Francisco, as the Portuguese would rename it. There was no point in lingering, those Indians knew; drought was coming, and drought would come. They would live by the river and fish for as long as it took, a year, two, sometimes longer, for the rains to come again.

And they were fine, those Indians, and didn't leave much of a trace upon the land. But their Portuguese successors, or Brazilian by then, the new people soon made of Indian and African blood mixed with the Portuguese, came out here as ranchers with their cattle and goats, and built stout houses before they'd properly looked around.

The lessons they learned straight off were the easy ones: that you needed twice the land for half the livestock. Not only that, but with ranches that big, the animals had to be left to roam, to scavenge, so there was no possibility of fences out here. The first thing a rancher had to do was devise his own brand, distinctive always, artistic now and then, harking back to the Portuguese heraldry, if there was culture in the blood. But most importantly, legible to the illiterate, so that your neighbor's cowboys could give back your goats.

Which was the way it was supposed to work, and did, in the good years, just as the notion of extensive ranches in a land that wouldn't sustain smaller ones seemed to function at first. During the roundups in a good year, neighbors would sort the herds and return each other's animals, and then they would kill and roast a cow, pull out their best *cachaça*, and dance with each other's sisters and daughters into the night.

But these new sons of the Sertão didn't know the drought god's irreversible advent like the Indians did, and they'd stay on in their fixed abodes, praying to Santa Luzia and São Antônio, long after the Indians would have decamped to the river.

And then, when the drought had settled in and misery descended upon the region, there they'd be, starving in their houses, these settled folk, watching their water holes turn from brown to gray, and their cows and goats stagger and finally drop.

It was during those famine roundups that if a rancher found a neighbor's brand on some of the cows among his own, cows who had after all eaten his own sparse grass and drunk what was left of his water, there was the temptation, even tendency, not to give them back.

And then the armed bands would form, and men would kill each other, never once stopping to ask themselves the bigger why, never once considering that it was the land itself that was the fundamental problem—but it was too late for that anyway, because they loved the place by then.

Loved the very distances, the great broad vistas with nothing to break them, loved the fact that it wouldn't be tamed, couldn't be trusted, and loved even what it took from them to survive. Let the dandies stroll around their plazas in town—they, the people of the Sertão, would stand with their guns and wait for rain.

Because in the end it would come, and when it did, the carts would rumble back from the coast with the rich who'd fled, the colonels' wives and children, and the dirt roads would fill with the poor walking back from wherever they'd got to, and herds would swell, neighbors would honor each other's brands, and their guns would go back into their packs, till the next time.

. . .

SO IT HAD BEEN, for two hundred years. But by the early 1920s, things were changing—getting worse. For one thing, there were more people, and the great ranches were being cut up among too many heirs. You could watch the big houses falling into ruin, whole wings turning to rubble, while the inhabitants, counts and *baronesas* who'd studied French in Recife in their fathers' day, now stooped in silk rags beside their ruins, trying to scratch up beans and manioc in land too dry for cactus.

Not only were there too many rich among them—the poor were worse, putting untold pressure on the land. Smallpox had served till then as a sort of demon goddess, killing off enough of them, rich and poor, to preserve the place for the rest. But by the late 1800s the vaccine had made its way first to the cities on the coast, and then out to the backlands, and there were suddenly too many mouths to feed. Ten or twelve of the fifteen children that made up these families were surviving, but what were they supposed to live on? Who was going to feed them?

Stakes got higher. Personal feuds became regional, as people needed more from the government, deeper wells, bigger property claims, jobs for younger brothers who'd been pushed off their ranches. This meant the feuding lasted beyond the drought years, and that it mattered more to a cowboy who controlled the nearest town, and which side of a fight he'd been born on.

In the state of Pernambuco, the families were the Pereiras and Carvalhos. In the confusion around the Revolution in the 1880s, when Brazil was moving first toward independence, they called themselves "Liberals" and

"Conservatives," and killed each other for that. But once the emperor and the princess had been shipped back to Portugal and political parties were no longer tolerated, they went back to being Pereiras and Carvalhos again.

By the early 1900s, the whole state of Pernambuco was involved. Every child out there, rich or poor, was born either a godchild or blood enemy to one of them, depending on who owned the land where their parents lived, or who was mayor of the closest town. Lampião had been taken to the baptismal font by a Pereira. Bezerra had been blessed by a Carvalho, which was why he was over here, chasing bandits, rather than across the river in Lampião's camp, training his gun on the police.

Not that he wasn't sympathetic to the bandits. He knew Lampião's story, everyone did. It was the usual feud, with the usual components—bad neighbors, half-wild goats on unfenced land, and growing boys on both sides of uncertain boundaries. And the people who lived among the red rocks in that part of Pernambuco pretty much agreed that the neighbors were at fault there, and everyone knew that Lampião had sought justice first in the courtroom.

Bezerra wondered, in retrospect, what Lampião had expected in the courtroom that day. He was still young then, eighteen or nineteen, but didn't he know that justice in Brazil existed to serve power? There'd been no Magna Carta anywhere in their history, no Rights of Man. For some reason, the dreams of fairness and equality that had so stirred French and English breasts for centuries had found no echo in Brazilian hearts.

If they had, then maybe Virgulino Ferreira da Silva, as Lampião was still called that day, would have taken his personal affront as general, looked beyond his family and seen that there were others up there, on both sides of the line, who were also if not murdered then at least routinely cheated out of their fair share of both crops and livestock, and maybe there would have been revolution then in the backlands of Brazil, given Lampião as a leader.

But he, being a Brazilian in the heartland of Brazil, had reacted in the traditional fashion. He changed his quest for justice to one for vengeance, and sent out word to the bandits already killing Carvalhos in the region that he would like to join their group.

They were led by Sinhô Pereira, who with his cousin had formed a band about a year earlier, when their own fathers were killed by the Carvalhos. They had about twenty men with them, and welcomed Lampião. He was good with horses, good at tracking, good at leatherwork—key, since their clothes were leather, plus their hats, their sandals, their gun belts, their knife sheaths, all leather, and all needing constant fixing, and even decoration, interweaving, which the young Lampião did well. And he danced well, too, and played the accordion, but the main thing was the way he shot.

They still had flintlock rifles, which meant a delay between rounds, but with Lampião's gun there was no delay. When he started shooting, the fire never stopped. It lit up the night, like one of those lanterns, a *lampião*, which was what Sinhô Pereira called him. He was the best shot out there, even though he was blind in one eye—one of those injuries not uncommon among men who spend their lives riding through thorns and cactus.

He took to the bandit life right away, the nomadic camp life, he was the one who was up before dawn in the mornings, and last by the fire at night. He didn't say much at first, as they sat around roasting goat meat at night, or drinking coffee under the morning star. He let Sinhô Pereira do the talking, since he wasn't sure yet how much he had to learn.

It turned out to be not much. Everything he'd done till then had trained him for the bandit life. All that horse-breaking and goat-tracking—goat paths, goat trails, goats that he'd lost as a boy and followed down the wrong gully, that kept him from supper that night and taught him the value of a sharper eye. And of the other senses, too, when the eyes don't help, when the goats are out of sight. He told a reporter he'd learned to track from an old man in the bush who, when his goats wandered off, would lie down in the dust and sniff.

"Not for goat," the old man had told him, they all smell of goat, but for the *favela* leaves that they'd have brushed up against, or the scent of *jurubeba* they'd been nibbling as they wandered past. And Lampião learned his lesson well, and was first the best goat boy and later the best tracker in the region, and by the time he came to fight beside Sinhô Pereira, all he really had to learn was the cool eye.

The waiting eye, that knows there's always a way to win, or at least escape, and has the presence to watch and wait for it. For the *jeitinho*, the sweet little way it's going to work out in the end, even if things look bad in the beginning. Lampião saw that in action, in his first real skirmish, when they found themselves surrounded by a hundred and twenty soldiers and Sinhô Pereira had only nine men with him at the time.

Lampião's first thought, he said later, was an overwhelming remorse. He would die that day for nothing, with all his father's killers still sleeping sound in their beds. He'd been scared, too, and almost ready to run, when he glanced at Sinhô Pereira's eyes.

Calm eyes, steady eyes—Sinhô was rich, he was proud and brave, and a hundred and twenty soldiers to him were all the more to shoot. His eyes remained fixed on them, and when he saw a small break, some shifting among the soldiers—they were changing positions, turning their backs—Sinhô Pereira led his men straight for them, shouting like crazy men, but shooting cool and straight, so they hit a few of the soldiers right away.

Which led to panic in the ranks and scattered the rest, who fell back, passing the word that there were hundreds of bandits, wild men, bandits in front, bandits behind, nothing to do but run for it—and who could blame them? "Better to escape with a stinking foot than die perfumed," was the proverb, and what was it, really, to these soldiers if they shot Sinhô Pereira that day, or let him escape with his men, out into the backlands?

Which was where Lampião learned his next big lesson—who his friends were, or had to be, if he was going to survive. He rode with Sinhô Pereira through the whole state of Pernambuco, from one relative's ranch to the next one, never once touching down, so to speak, on unfriendly territory. Always managing to stay on land belonging to what you might call the rich "opposition," those on the wrong side of official power, but strong enough to maintain their own personal boundaries, with their own personal bands of armed ranch hands that the government's police and soldiers didn't care to take on.

Lampião said he was surprised at first, even in awe, at who was both powerful enough to offer protection and at war with the same forces as he and Sinhô. Who was locked in a blood feud with the governor, or whose father, brother, or second cousin had been rashly, and with official impunity, shot down. Who woke every morning wanting the same eye, the same tooth that the bandits did, and who was willing to pay for it, with money, weapons, salt, food, and a safe place to hide. That was the key to Sinhô Pereira's survival, the tacit support from this shadow government—or shadow banditry, depending on how you saw it.

All this must have been key to the making of Lampião, his training, but how long did it last? Probably not long. Lampião and his comrade Sinhô Pereira probably didn't do much more than pass in the night. Fought together a few times, laughed, danced, listened to music, drank coffee, and then after about a year Sinhô got lucky, he got out. He was connected, and his family put together a shaky truce so that he could "disappear" out onto a ranch they owned, at the far end of the state of Minas Gerais.

And Bezerra had heard that he'd invited Lampião to come with him, and Lampião almost did. That would have been around 1921, 1922, when no one knew his name yet, and he still could have brushed off his hands and ridden west.

But Sinhô Pereira's band had grown to fifty men by then, and they were looking more and more to Lampião. And, thinking of all his enemies still left to kill, he decided not to quit just yet. Instead, he led his men over to Água Branca—which was where he and Bezerra first crossed paths.

Sixteen years ago—just after Lampião took over Sinhô's band. His first act was to invade the house of the old Baronesa of Água Branca, whose sons were connected to the men who'd shot his father.

No one was home but a few ancient servants and the old Baronesa, and when Lampião burst into her bedroom before dawn, guns drawn, she mistook him for a priest who'd come for matins.

"You're late!" she accused him, and Lampião had apologized and led her in prayers as he looted the place. "Bless you, my child," as he lifted the necklaces over her head. "Forgive us our trespasses," as he slipped the diamond bracelets from her wrists. "May we be truly grateful," as he tossed stack after stack of folded banknotes into his pack, along with her father's gold watches and her mother's diamonds and pearls.

"Don't be late for Vespers!" people heard her calling after him, as the bandits thundered out of town.

AFTERWARD, HER SONS had demanded action, and the Alagoas state forces, led by Lucena with young Bezerra in the ranks, had marched out of Águas Belas ten days later, two hundred strong, prepared to make mincemeat of these upshot bandits, whose names no one even knew.

"No mercy at all!" Lucena had bellowed to his men, and they'd boomed it back at him, why not? There were only fifty bandits at most, and they'd been on the run for ten days by then, so fifty tired and hungry bandits as opposed to two hundred fresh well-armed, well-fed state troops.

The only problem was that by the time the fighting started the bandits had taken the high ground, and all they had to do then was sit up there shooting down on the soldiers till they'd killed enough to get the rest of them asking what would turn out to be the pertinent questions for the next twenty years: that is, "What am I doing here?" and, "Am I really supposed to die out here today? For what, in fact? To stop bandits from robbing the rich?"

And once they looked at it that way, any sensible men, even policemen or soldiers, would turn and run—which was exactly what happened that day, sixteen years ago, in their first real battle, both his and Lampião's. Bezerra didn't know at the time what he was up against, or that he had met for the first but not the last time the man who would define both the police and the bandits for a whole generation.

He didn't even know his name until he read it in the papers. "Lampião," read the headlines in the *Diário de Pernambuco*, "One of the Worst Bandits in Brazil"—an exaggeration, Bezerra had thought at the time.

XI

Sereno had run down, guns drawn, when he heard someone approaching, but it was only Pedro Candido and his brother, bringing in some more supplies. And the truth was he had half a thought to shoot them right then anyway and call it a mistake, say he'd mistook them for the police. There was something about Pedro Candido he didn't like, something that didn't sit well with him—the guy was too familiar, made himself too cozy with them. Half the time he'd stay for supper, sometimes even to sleep—and who was Pedro Candido to be sleeping beside one of the boys, on the river? Aside from being just one of the countless guys who supplied them—and profited mightily. Pedro Candido was getting rich off them, for Christ's sake—but who the hell was he? Someone they could trust? How far?

Although everyone else was glad enough to see him, and they were all crowding around to see what he'd brought, which Sereno could see was plenty, but wasn't that something to think about, too? Hadn't Erasmo Felix been out yesterday with nothing but a few bars of soap and a couple of packs of needles? Said that was all he could buy without attracting attention. Said that even the market was crawling with police.

Especially the market. They'd asked him to buy them some salt, but he didn't dare. Someone might have noticed Erasmo Felix buying extra salt and said something. And then he would have been caught. Questioned at least, beaten maybe. So he'd bought his soap and left.

But here was Pedro Candido, back again—that was another thing. He'd just been in the day before. And here he was again—wasn't that dangerous? Something to call attention? And loaded down this time, with salt and bottles of whiskey, meat, tobacco—how could he buy all that, and Erasmo Felix, an old-time supplier, someone who'd been true over the years, couldn't?

Sereno walked down the steep little ridge to where they were gathered. It looked good, Sereno had to admit. A big piece of meat—"*Bem bonitinho,*" the girls were saying, really nice, and it was. And there were more needles, which they really needed, and a good supply of salt, some more cloth, always good. A watermelon, which would make Cila happy, and even some cheese, which no one had managed to bring them for a while. Sereno had to admit that just the sight of it made his mouth water.

"*Oi, Pedro*"—he walked over. There was the little brother—what was his name? He lived over here, on this side, in the house with his mother, a little bit downriver. A kid, fifteen, sixteen—still blushed. Some of the girls were teasing him.

"Who's your girlfriend, Durval? Can it be me?"

"No, me!"

"Both of them," called Pedro Candido.

"Both?" said Durval, blushing. Everyone laughed, except Sereno. Durval had come, he told the girls, to take back his mother's sewing machine, which they'd borrowed.

But they weren't done. "Tomorrow," they told him.

"You're leaving tomorrow?" Pedro Candido asked.

"Maybe—" one of the girls began.

"What's it to you?" Sereno cut in.

"No, nothing to me," said Pedro Candido quickly, "I was just wondering if you needed a boat or anything—"

"You don't need to wonder," Sereno said, who was wondering himself. Wishing he'd just shot the guy. Not the brother, just Pedro. He'd say he was sorry, and it would pass.

But it would have been better for them, better for the group. When in doubt, take no chances. Next time, he told himself.

"Pedro!" Maria was calling. Smiling at Pedro Candido, hoping for cigarettes—that was another thing. He always knew what to bring her to keep her on his side. Sereno had seen them in the hamper, the Jockey Clubs, those deep red boxes marked with the little gold hat and whip. Who wouldn't like that? Twenty smooth white ovals lying all in a row, untouched, clean, like a row of white babies. As opposed to the thick brown corn husks they rolled themselves.

Not that they didn't both get you to the same place.

"O, *Pedro!*"

Good, Lampião.

"O, *Capitão!*" Pedro Candido turned and smiled.

"Look at all that Pedro has brought us," Maria Bonita said to him. Lampião looked through the hamper, nodded.

"You didn't have trouble with the police? No one saw you?"

"Nah, I bought it at different places, here and there, so no one noticed."

We hope, thought Sereno. And pray—he would pray for that himself.

Lampião thanked Pedro, paid him twice what he asked, in gold coins, and invited him to stay for dinner. Good, thought Sereno. Because if he stayed, Sereno swore to God that he would find a way, a pretext, to kill him.

Although he could see that Lampião liked him. And Lampião always knew. So maybe Sereno was off here, unfair. Still, would it hurt to rid the world of one more question mark? Why was he, Sereno, standing here, off to the side, at odds with every one of his comrades and brothers, feeling something was not right with Pedro Candido? He, too, had been right in the past. He, too, knew something, and if Pedro Candido stayed, he would find a way, that very night. So what if he was wrong? What would they lose? They had plenty of suppliers around here, and so what if he was the only one to bring fancy liquor and smooth white cigarettes?

But Pedro Candido didn't stay—lucky for him. Sereno went with Lampião down the draw to see him off. As soon as Pedro was gone, Sereno began. "Captain, we've got to leave here—today."

Lampião looked at him.

"Now," said Sereno, "unless you want to get shot out of here!"

Lampião took a breath—he looked tired. How tired? What would happen if Sereno left him, struck out on his own?

Lampião started in on his arguments—they were safe here, the place was remote and back from the river, in the midst of wild *caatinga*, "impossible to find—"

"Hard, but not impossible!" Sereno countered, and too close to Piranhas for comfort, with too many police around. Too many people, too, what with Pedro Candido and his brother coming and going, "practically carving a path through the briars, straight to us!"

From Lampião, nothing. Then, finally, "Tomorrow."

Sereno was ready to say good-bye, take his own band, the guys he'd been leading for a while, and the women, head off, and arrange to meet Lampião in a few days, somewhere to the west, off the river.

But then Lampião looked up and met his eye. Half-smiled, and Sereno found he couldn't say it. Couldn't bring himself to defy—because that's what it would be—the man who'd brought him in, made him, given him everything.

Because was it that bad? He looked around—the sun was out, it was quiet. The last news they'd got was that the police were looking for them up at Moxotó. If they left tomorrow, that should be all right.

"Pedro Candido brought a watermelon, but it's not enough for everyone," Lampião was saying. "Why don't you take it off to the side and cut it for Cila and Dulce?"

Cila's favorite—she'd like that.

"Get Maria, too. And then tonight we'll roast the meat and have some music."

That would be good. They hadn't had meat or music all month, it being July. The month of penitence, of fasts.

So was July over? Sereno tried to figure. He'd put it at the twenty-seventh or maybe twenty-eighth, but had he lost count? Had they got through it, one more July?

"And leave at dawn?" he said to Lampião.

"Before dawn," Lampião answered.

XII

"Have a look." Bezerra offered his field glasses to Aniceto. Not that there was anything to see on the other side of the river, just that it was something to do. To look active—the whiskey was going around, and the men were restless, wanting action. Men he'd seen run from action in the past.

"No, more that way." Bezerra moved the field glasses downriver. That's where the bandits had to be, the more he thought about it—downriver from the town. Around bends they couldn't see from where they were, not yet. And when they could see them, it would be too dark.

Not that there would be much to see, anyway. It was all the same, from here all the way to the sea, on that side of the river. Nothing, no one. One little settlement with a cashew plantation downriver, where Lampião had once given a dance. A young man there told him that he'd gotten drunk, for the first time, on Lampião's whiskey—so drunk that he'd danced into Lampião's dog.

The dog had yelped, the bandits pulled their guns,

and the guy figured he was dead, but then Maria Bonita stepped in front of him and told them to leave it, he was just a boy, a drunk country boy, nothing to worry about, and then she even danced with him. He was seventeen, and "very cute," she told him.

"What was she like?" Bezerra had asked him.

"Not so beautiful—" one of the women there had answered.

"Beautiful!" All the men had smiled.

"She looks like the postmistress, in Pedra—" said the woman.

Snorts from the men. "And her legs, so well formed, so smooth—"

"That's just her silk stockings."

Silk stockings. Bezerra would have liked to dance with her himself. He'd seen pictures—in some she was beautiful, if you liked that type, and he did. A beautiful girl from the backlands, or woman now—how old would she be? It must have been about eight or nine years since she'd run off with Lampião, and how old had she been then? Not a kid, anyway. She'd been married for years before that.

To a shoemaker, and who could blame her for leaving? A beautiful young woman like her with an old man like him, it was almost inconceivable—Maria Bonita as the shoemaker's wife. Not that she was Maria Bonita then, just another Maria. One more Maria, married to a man she couldn't stand.

Still, she must be pushing thirty now. Not young. People died old at thirty. But even in the bad photos she still looked good, nothing like most thirty-year-old women in the backlands.

But then her life had been nothing like theirs, either. No nine or ten babies, no hauling water, no long hours bent over a hoe in the sun, hacking at weeds in the hardest dirt in the country.

She'd got herself free from all that, though there'd be a price to pay for it in the end. If not tonight, then some other night. Lampião, too—how old would he be? He'd been a bandit for more than twenty years, so forty? Was that possible?

But Lampião being forty didn't make sense. There was no such thing as old age for bandits.

Which was the best reason for Bezerra to be sitting in this cornfield. Since there would have to come a time when Lampião got tired, and it might be today.

Though maybe it wouldn't—not quite yet. That was fine with Bezerra, too. Let life go on as it always had. Because, in fact, what would they do without the bandits?

And not just the police—what about the street singers and the poets, what about the old ladies in their dark parlors? His own mother had died not long ago, and they'd found, among her letters and things, some old clippings from the papers about Lampião, some from ten, twelve years back. They'd crumbled in his hand when he read them, but they were like a history lesson, better than what they put in books. A real look at what went on up there, in a way that you could almost see it before your eyes, like you never could in the history books.

"You remember the Communists?" Bezerra asked Aniceto.

"I was just a kid," said Aniceto, and so was Bezerra, but he remembered being scared, or, more, his parents being scared. The Communists were on the march, everyone was saying, and they were going to kill all the priests and mayors, even the town clerks, and take everyone's houses.

That was in 1926. And everyone who could took off, disappeared, including all the police and soldiers who were supposed to be protecting them. All the priests, too—especially the priests, but up in Juazeiro do Norte, Padre Cícero couldn't flee. He was what you would have called the Pope of Brazil.

The most important priest of all, especially in the Sertão. He had been a living saint among them, a miracle worker, ever since the 1880s, when the Communion wine had turned to blood under his hands. It happened again more than once, was confirmed, reconfirmed, and people started hanging his picture on their walls for protection and flocking to Juazeiro, in Ceará, where he lived. They carried medals, relics, beads, and ribbons that had been blessed in Juazeiro, and all true souls out there called him their godfather, their *padím*.

Which made him much more of a target for the revolutionary Prestes and his Communist "columns," as they were called, who were reported to be heading toward Juazeiro. Padre Cícero sent desperate pleas for help to the capitals Fortaleza and Recife, but there was no one there to even receive them. The governors had fled, the whole government had fled—even the army had fled. All the big houses were locked and barred.

Padre Cícero was old by then—in his eighties, too old for running, plus he had a whole city of faithful at his feet, among them Lampião's sisters, to whom he'd given refuge from police persecution. They had lived protected in his town for years, and now he turned to them. He asked if they could possibly get a message to their brother, urging him to come to Juazeiro at once to protect him.

Padre Cícero was loved by his people, revered, a living saint. When Lampião got the summons, he rushed the hundred miles up to Juazeiro, barely stopping to eat or sleep along the way. He entered the holy city one evening with forty-nine of his men, and the whole town, four thousand strong, turned out to greet him. They set off fireworks in his honor and paraded after him through the streets, cheering and throwing flowers.

The clippings seemed to have fallen in love with Lampião. They went on and on, about his manner—"calm and deliberate"; his speech—"thoughtful, and serious"; even his appearance—"of medium height, thin and well proportioned, with dark skin and thick black hair." Around his neck he wore a green silk scarf, secured by a diamond ring, and on his fingers six more rings including "a ruby, a topaz, an emerald, and three more diamonds, all big." The cartridge belts across his chest were "two palms wide, with four rows of bullets, and lined with coins of silver and gold."

He had proceeded, fully armed, straight to Padre Cícero in the main church, where he fell to his knees and laid an enormous offering at his feet—paper money, shaken from one end of the Sertão to the other. This the old priest had accepted.

Then he put his holy hand on the bandit's bowed head, and it occurred to Bezerra that in that one moment, the two native responses to God and the devil in the backlands—the popular church, offering the poor their miracles, and the indigenous banditry, bringing them at least one version of justice—had touched.

THE NEXT DAY, Padre Cícero ordered the only government official left in town, a junior assistant inspector of agriculture, to draw up an official "patent," designating Lampião a captain in the Brazilian army. He then pardoned all past offenses, swore him in as leader of the town's "Patriotic Battalions," and issued to him and his men the bolt-action Mausers that the government had sent out for the defense of the city.

Lampião would leave the next morning before dawn to join forces with the regular army and take on Prestes, but that afternoon he strolled the streets with his men and his sisters, sitting for photos, conversing with one and all, distributing alms to the poor. He visited all the churches in the town, and funded masses of thanksgiving, in gold, in honor of his visit to Padre Cícero. He heard mass and wept tears of joy. He had left the past behind. He was in a state of grace. He had come in from the cold.

He granted an interview to the local paper, which

was continually interrupted, the reporter noted, by well-wishers. One old woman brought him a small metal cross which she'd made herself. He kissed it with much reverence, and paid her three times what it was worth.

"Are you rich?" the reporter asked him.

"Rich enough to support my whole band—which isn't nothing, feeding and clothing all those men—and to keep us well armed, and give to the poor."

"How do you get your money?"

"From the rich. I ask first, and take by force only from those too miserly to help me freely."

"How do you escape from the police so often?"

"By fighting like a madman, and running like the wind when I see I can't win. Aside from this, I'm extremely vigilant, and even when I trust, I trust mistrusting. Plus, I'd like to note that I have good friends throughout the region, who keep me advised of police movements. Not to mention my spies—another expense, but extremely useful."

"Do you have any regrets?"

"I've committed violence and depredations, by resolving to take vengeance first on my enemies, and then on those who persecute me. Even so, it's my way to respect families, no matter how humble, and if I hear that one of my men has disrespected a woman, I punish him severely."

"Have you been wounded?"

"Four times, even once in the head that I survived only by a miracle. My men, too, have been badly wounded, but we have people in the group who know how to treat us, so we're always well taken care of. Because of this, as you can see, I'm strong and in perfect health"—at this he leapt into the air, right over the reporter, with the lightness of a cat, though carrying at least forty pounds of guns and knives and ammunition.

"Why did you come here?"

"To lead Padre Cícero's Patriotic Forces of Juazeiro, and take on the rebels. I am also offering strategic advice to the government. I think if they accept my service and follow my plans, there's much we can accomplish."

"Who do you like best? What profession of people?"

"I like farmers," he said, "and ranchers, men of the land, and salesmen, because they know how to work hard. I respect and venerate priests, because I'm Catholic. I'm a friend of telegraph men, because more than a few have saved me from grave danger. Judges, because they are men of the law."

"What would you do if you stopped being a bandit?"

"Maybe I'll become a businessman," he said, and then got up, and continued on his way through the streets to his sisters' house, where for the first time in nine years he slept in a bed.

CAPTAIN VIRGULINO—though that was never to be. Especially since by the time he marched out from Juazeiro the next day the Communists were no longer a threat, nor were they even Communists. They were just dreamers, ill-prepared young officers, seeking, ironically, the same kind of justice as Lampião.

But the masses of people they'd expected to flock to them when they'd marched out from São Paulo, banners high, never materialized, and their young leader, Luís Carlos Prestes, had already fled to Argentina by the time Lampião and his men took to the field. The threat was now over, and the first government troops they encountered opened fire on them, despite their flag of truce.

Once word got out that Padre Cícero had not only received Lampião but armed him, a firestorm broke over his white head. There was talk of retribution, talk of prosecution, but the old priest was also an old politician; he hadn't maintained power in a tough state for fifty years for nothing. He knew that this, too, would pass, but on the other hand, when Lampião came riding back to him, distraught at the government's refusal to recognize him as rehabilitated, a captain now, the priest could no longer receive him.

He sent out a messenger with a statement that was also given to the press: "Padre Cícero begs Lampião to give up his life of crime, and ride away from Juazeiro at once."

LAMPIÃO APPARENTLY held no grudge there. He continued to venerate Padre Cícero, wear his medal, call him godfather. But shortly after that, when a reporter asked him if he ever thought about quitting, "Who thinks about quitting when things are going well?" he'd replied.

Though he had, Bezerra realized, reading the clippings, not only thought about it, but had quit, or thought he had. He'd ridden out of Juazeiro with an "open heart," as he put it, that day in 1926, straight into the soldiers' bullets.

But once he was disabused of those springtime hopes and dreams—impossible, he must have seen, in retrospect—he also would have seen that his Juazeiro sojourn hadn't been all bad. He'd left there with the best guns in the region, plus all the blessings, special medals, and powerful amulets, the strongest there were, straight from the hand of Padre Cícero himself. With resources like those, there wasn't a troop in Brazil who could touch him, and later that month he announced that he was renewing his struggle against the government "without quarter."

As it proved to be. Bezerra's mother had kept another clipping, the official tally of the eight months immediately following Lampião's visit to Padre Cícero in 1926:

APRIL 16: Lampião's band invades the town of Algodões. Peaceful sacking; take what they need, move on. No one shot.
MAY 7: They invade the town of Triunfo, in Pernambuco. No resistance, so no one hurt.
AUGUST 14: Lampião cuts off all communication to the town of Vila Bela, cutting the telegraph lines and burning the train station. No one hurt.
AUGUST 18: Gunfight between Lampião's men and the Pernambuco troops, on the Fazenda Favela, outside of Floresta, resulting in ten soldiers killed and seven wounded. No bandit fatalities.
AUGUST 26: Lampião attacks the village of Tapera, killing thirteen people. Circumstances unclear.

SEPTEMBER 2: Lampião invades the town of Cabrobó, at the head of a hundred and fifty men, in perfect military formation, marching to a bugle. No one hurt.
SEPTEMBER 6: Lampião invades the village of Leopoldina, shooting four residents, sacking the businesses and the tax collector's office, and cutting the telegraph lines.
OCTOBER 1: Near Floresta, Lampião meets a Pernambuco troop of a hundred and twenty-six men, and puts them to flight.
NOVEMBER 25: Lampião takes hostage American representatives from Standard Oil, demanding ransom. When they explain they have to type the demand in triplicate, he smashes their typewriter, burns their car, and takes them hostage.
NOVEMBER 26: Violent skirmish outside of Morada, with Pernambuco troops, attempting to rescue the hostages. The fight lasts all day and all night, until Lampião, with a hundred and twenty men, puts the troops to flight. Ransom is then paid, and the hostages set free.
DECEMBER 12: On the Fazenda Juá, outside of Floresta, the bandits shoot a hundred and twenty-seven cows belonging to Joaquim Jardim, who had murdered the father of one of the bandits.
DECEMBER 14: Shoot-out in Serra Grande, in which Lampião, with ninety men, takes on two hundred and sixty soldiers. The soldiers lose twenty men, and retreat.

And how many since then, how many hundreds, all of them avoidable? And all the deaths still to come, his own perhaps among them—why not? It was as likely as Lampião's, more likely, statistically. How many police had Lampião killed since he'd attempted to leave his bandit life under the holy hands of Padre Cícero? And didn't those deaths belong not on his head, but on the heads of the government, who refused his truce?

Anyway, the article ended by referring to the general feeling throughout the region that "*you can't talk about the Sertão without talking about the three great forces: the drought, Padre Cícero, and Lampião.*"

Bezerra turned back to Aniceto. "See anything?"

But Aniceto didn't. As Bezerra had said, there was nothing to see.

XIII

Cila passed the sewing machine to Dulce and got to her feet and stretched. Everyone was in one of those moods, but she didn't see what was so bad about the place. It was quiet, and seemed protected enough to her, in the middle of all these thorns, a regular briar patch. She'd gone out a little ways, off trail, earlier in the day, and was pretty much stopped by the tangle. She almost gave up, plus it was the wrong time of year for her cactus fruits, but she knew how to look, and sure enough, she found one last one, deep purple and full of juice.

Even Sereno was nervous as a cat. He was thinking of taking them off, he told her, of leaving Lampião. He didn't like Pedro Candido, didn't trust him anymore or his brother, either, and their other supplier, Erasmo, had come out empty-handed, with just a bar of soap, saying the police were watching, and he didn't dare buy more.

"This river is nothing but police!" Sereno was saying.

But then Pedro Candido had come in with what even

Sereno had to admit was a beautiful load of stuff for them. A side of beef and plenty of salt and manioc, and Lampião's whiskey, his Cavalinho, and even some Cinzano, which all the girls loved, mixed with whiskey. And the sun was out, and Sereno told her that Lampião said they would leave tomorrow, which was fine with her. She was glad for another day here.

It was land she knew—not far from the village where she'd grown up. Which was good and bad—good in that she knew the purple cactus fruit, bad in that it set her thinking, not that she was one for looking back.

Though when she was in this part of the country she couldn't help missing her mother a little bit, and her sisters, and the mud walls that used to stand around her. Funny, that was what she missed the most, being back inside that little house, even in that small, cramped bedroom, crowded in with everyone else, three, four to a bed, but with four walls around her and a roof overhead.

Actually, she didn't even need the roof, just the walls. Then let them shoot—the walls were thick mud. Shoot all you want, police from this state, police from that state, cousins or no cousins, just give her some mud walls and they could shoot all they wanted. She, Cila, would be sound asleep and snoring.

She imagined going back for everyone to see her. She knew just what it would be like, since she knew how it had been for her, when the bandits had come through and she'd been on the other side, watching. Her brother had joined up when she was about fourteen, and whenever they were traveling through, they'd come by the village, not to take anything—it was too poor there—but to see everyone. And the people would all turn out, to talk to them, bring them food and flowers, and just stand there and be around them, these bandits who were somehow them, but a different them, them touched with a magic wand.

Because they, the locals, were the ones who'd stayed at home, standing on the side of the road in homespun and rotting leather, mostly brown—not even brown. Dust-colored, gray, no matter how it started, even the ones who'd gone up to Juazeiro to see Padre Cícero and came back in blue. But nothing stayed blue out here. It all turned to that gray-brown, slowly, though, so you mostly didn't notice. She remembered her old aunt telling her to go into the house and fetch her "blue scarf," and she knew what she meant, since the old woman had only one scarf, but it hadn't been blue for Cila's whole lifetime, for twenty years.

But then the bandits would come through, and there they would be, themselves but transformed, their brothers and sisters, dressed not in homespun but silks, green and red, and decked in gold and jewels, like they'd come down from some enchanted kingdom, and not just in out of the same thornbush and cactus that they themselves walked through with their goats every day.

It seemed half-miraculous to them, at home, and after the bandits left, disappeared into the wild the same way they'd come, people would stand for a while, talking low, still moved, touched, by the visitation.

And she decided one day, as she stood there looking

after them long after there was anything to see, that if any of them asked her, she'd go—though, thinking back, it wasn't quite like that. Life didn't quite work that way. You didn't exactly decide—any more than you'd decide to marry a local boy and grow old before your time, having ten, twelve children, and watching them live or die, while scrubbing clothes and scratching up grain from land that didn't want to give it. It just happened, like being born poor and here, instead of rich and on the coast.

But she remembered thinking that day that if her chance ever came, she'd be ready and grab it. And the next day, she traded her best lace to a woman for some medals of the Virgin with special powers, and sure enough, a few months later the bandits came back.

And that time Lampião gave a dance, and she was lined up across from Sereno, because she was short and he was short—and that was her medal working that night. Because none of the other girls were asked, but Sereno—she could feel his eyes on her before he ever said a word. She and her sister were wearing the striped skirts her mother had finished stitching for them that afternoon, full skirts that whirled, twirled, way out, more than anyone else's.

She'd never been to a dance before—they were too poor in her village, and everyone was excited, even the old ones, and everyone lined up to dance. And people she could never have imagined dancing, mean old women, scrawny old men, started moving with a sort of grace you'd have never known if Lampião hadn't given them a dance that night, and she and her sisters, too, were swirling back and forth with the rest of them, and every time she looked up, there was Sereno, looking back.

And when the music stopped, he asked her if she wanted some punch, and she said yes, and that was all she ever said to him after that—yes. And when she left with him, it didn't seem that strange, because of her brother being already out there and one of them, and she didn't even have to blame herself for the police harassing her family, since it was already happening.

And she could hardly believe her luck at first. Sereno was smart, good-hearted, always smiling. His eye was scarred, too, like Lampião's, from an injury in the bush, but it hadn't blinded him, like Lampião. It had happened just after he'd joined, he told her—they'd been on the run, moving fast and silent, and he was last in the line, and the guy in front of him had let a branch fly, and it had caught him full in the face and knocked him out.

And no one had noticed for a while, but when they stopped to eat, Lampião saw he was missing and allowed that he'd probably gotten scared and run away.

But Sereno was Zé Bahiano's cousin, one of Lampião's main men, and Bahiano insisted there'd never been a coward in his family, so he went back to have a look, and found Sereno still unconscious, lying in the dirt, with the buzzards already circling.

So the first thing Sereno taught her was to take care on the trail, and then how to shoot, but everything else was just more of what she already knew. They'd wake in the morning and pray on their knees—Lampião always leading. Then they'd wash up and the men would make coffee, and if they weren't on the run they'd talk a bit and then see what had to be done. But what had to be done, really? There was nothing much to clean, nothing to sweep, and the main thing was they didn't have to raise their own food. It came to them, as it did to the rich, brought out to their camps by loyal suppliers whom no degree of police brutality could suppress.

And when one of them came out, with their salt and their sides of beef and a barrel of whiskey, then it would turn into a party. They would roast the meat, have a great dinner, a feast, and afterward someone would play a guitar or accordion and they would dance, when Lampião was in a good mood, which was most of the time, especially in the early days. At night the single men slept out, and the couples in their tents, four-points on the ground, as good as a house, she used to think, and she never once saw a snake.

Though the first time she was in a shoot-out—well, she'd thought she was prepared, thought she'd be brave, and she was brave, grabbed her gun, ran to her place, and didn't cry or make a scene, none of them did. They were all girls who weren't surprised by trouble, but what she hadn't been expecting was the way it would envelop you, all that smoke and fire, that there'd be smoke all around, and you'd be breathing it, hot smoke, which made a person almost desperate for a drink.

"Were you scared, Cila?" Sereno had asked her afterward.

"No, just thirsty," she said, and that had become a sort of joke, how brave she was. But it wasn't that she wasn't scared, it was more that she was so thirsty. Now she kept water in a canteen beside her all the time, plus all her charms, all her special prayers, dipped in holy water and purchased with gold and jewels.

And people laughed at her, too, for that, but they had them, too, especially in July, when Lampião said he was going to die, and if he died, what about the rest of them?

Though maybe if the police were from Sergipe, her cousins—

"Cila!"

"I'm coming," she called. It was Sereno—maybe he'd changed his mind, maybe they were leaving. The sun was still high enough for that, on this side of the river, though they'd be caught out in the dark and have to sleep in the cold, though not for the first time. Or the last, she hoped. She walked back through the underbrush to him.

"We're leaving?"

"Tomorrow," said Sereno.

He was holding a watermelon—how nice! Thinking about how thirsty she'd been that time had made her suddenly thirst now.

"Watermelon!" Pedro Candido must have brought it out, which was one more reason to like him. Along with the cigarettes, which Maria sometimes shared with her.

Sereno said that Lampião had sent her the watermelon, knew it was her favorite. One more reason to love Lampião. Love and honor and obey, now that she thought about it. Look what it got them. Watermelon in dry country.

They walked back down to where Dulce was finishing

the sewing—finally. It had taken forever, mostly because the needles were so dull, till Erasmo brought them some new ones yesterday, and now Sereno waited while Cila helped her put away the machine. It belonged to Pedro Candido's mother, and his little brother Durval had sneaked it out of the house for them, and made them swear on their souls to take special care of it. His mother would kill him, he said, if she knew.

Though of course she'd know—any woman would know. No matter how careful they were, there'd be some sign. But it was a good machine, and they'd used it with a light hand, and were leaving it with a new needle, and now they wrapped it in cloth and stowed it safely under the rocks, in the grove of *macambeira* trees where he told them to leave it. Since they'd be gone before he came back to get it in the morning.

As for her, she was glad they weren't leaving now, glad for one more evening here. Who knew the future? No one, ever. You could sneeze in your bed and die, or fall off your horse. One of her little sisters had fallen down a well, and her grandfather had been mistaken for someone else and shot. The guy who did it was sorry, her grandmother always told everyone, as if this would make any difference, would bring him back.

But nothing brought anyone back.

She was glad of the sun, glad for the watermelon. "Go get Maria," she said to Dulce, and then walked off with Sereno to cut the watermelon.

XIV

The sun must have stopped moving. At least it was afternoon, but it had been afternoon for a long time now, Bezerra found himself thinking, and wishing, too, that he had a map. Not for information—he knew the place well enough. The points in question were the river ports of Piranhas, and Entremontes, about ten miles downriver, and then the bandits' hideout, somewhere across the river, presumably close.

He knew them all. He'd lived in Piranhas for years, and had been down the river countless times to Entremontes, where Pedro Candido lived, it was a piece of the river he knew, but still felt it would be helpful right then to have a map.

Reassuring, just to be sitting there putting pins in a map. Something to do, not that there were any good maps of the region. He remembered reading as a schoolboy that even the best maps conveyed "scant information," showing instead "an expressive blank, a hiatus, labeled

Terra Ignota, a mere scrawl indicating a problematic river or an idealized mountain range."

No one knew the place, the writer, Euclides da Cunha, had complained—but it wasn't quite like that. It was more that the ones who knew it weren't making maps, not that that stopped them from knowing the place. Those rivers weren't "problematic" to the soldiers out here, or any of the trackers, to say nothing of the bandits. Lampião could fill in that "expressive blank" rock by rock, cactus by cactus. He could sketch in every curve of every river and even creek, from his own red hills of Pernambuco to the green waters of the São Francisco, dotting in the native palms and bromeliads around Monte Santo, and the falls at Paulo Afonso, where the bandits filled their canteens when they emerged, parched, from the Raso.

With no maps, though he'd seen one once, years ago, in Glória, that Lampião himself had drawn, or rather annotated, that belonged to the priest there. It was leather, and a full meter square, all Brazil, and apparently the priest had brought it out, along with a thick blue pencil, and asked Lampião to mark out the extent of his "kingdom."

"Since you are a sort of king," the priest had said—this was after Lampião had come into the church for mass and left a donation. And he'd been intrigued, and worked on it hard, all afternoon, drawing out the territory where he could roam freely, either welcome or stronger than the police. In the end, it extended throughout the entire Sertão, including parts of seven states, the hard parts, from Mossoró in Rio Grande do Norte, down through

Ceará, Paraíba, Pernambuco, Alagoas, Sergipe, and into Bahia—"Bigger than Spain!" said the clerk who showed it to Bezerra. He'd done the math, measured it out. "Almost as big as France," he said.

Lampião. The King of the Sertão. Not that his life had been easy—he knew both, he always said, good times and bad. "And if I've suffered, then in compensation, I've had a very good time."

Bezerra had always liked that, it made him feel better when things weren't going his way, either. And sometimes he felt he had more in common with Lampião than with any of the men on his side of the river. What he wanted, in truth, this afternoon was less to kill him than to sit with him under the trees and talk—like Nunes had, why not? If Lampião had talked to Nunes that time, why not him?

Since Nunes had been not just an enemy but an archenemy, commander of the Pernambuco forces, a man whom Lampião managed to take prisoner and planned to kill.

That had been something—Bezerra still remembered the shock that went through the troops when they heard that Lampião had Nunes. Nunes was retired from active service by then, but he was still one of their commanders, one of their top men, and they couldn't understand how he could have gone out alone to his ranch, near Águas Belas, without even a small detachment of bodyguards. Maybe he thought that his fight with the bandits was over, but they didn't see it that way, and when someone tipped them off that he was out there on his own, they moved quickly and surrounded his house.

And waited till dawn, till Nunes came out alone, with a basin. They watched in silence as he walked over to the cistern to wash his face. Then Lampião approached, still silent, still waiting, gun drawn. When Nunes looked up and saw him, "I'm dead!" he cried.

"Who are you?" Lampião asked him, as a formality.

A breath. "Colonel João Nunes."

"Good, then, because it's you I've come for."

And then it was Nunes's turn to give that Sertão half-smile, which he himself had drawn so many times from bandits or even just their supporters right before he shot them, when a man is lost and knows it. "I'm in your hands," he said.

"Tie him up." One of the boys moved forward with a rope.

"We'll pay," Nunes began, "any ransom—"

Of course he'd pay—he'd love to pay! Money was no object to Nunes, but Lampião said he wasn't sure in this case if it was an object to him, either. He'd never killed a man who'd paid his ransom, and sometimes didn't kill men even if they didn't. Not too long ago, he'd let a boy go whose father had refused to pay any ransom.

"You'll kill him even with the money, so kill him without it, and my loss will be less," said the father.

And Lampião had turned the boy loose in disgust. "No son deserves to die for such a father," he said.

But Nunes's case was different. How many bandits

had he killed, either by his own hand or by his command, men already tied up, shot point-blank? And how many of Lampião's suppliers had he terrorized, peaceable farmers, just making their way in the world? What he wanted from Nunes first and foremost was blood, but maybe he'd take some retribution as well.

"Fifteen *contos*," he said to Nunes. The price of two hundred cows.

Fine, said Nunes, they'd get it right out, from the bank in Recife, the capital city, on the coast—

"Recife?" Lampião spat on the ground. "Recife's too far."

"But I don't keep that kind of money at the ranch, only in the bank—"

"Then die."

"Then *patiencia*," said Nunes. But even if they killed him, he said, he still didn't have the money here. Though if they let him, he could send his man Old Tó running to the nearby village of Águas Belas to wire for the money, and his family would get it out to them in a day, or two "at most!" Nunes swore.

Maybe yes, maybe no. Lampião knew better than Nunes the permutations and combinations of that one. Every one of the steps along the way was likely to misfire—Old Tó might not get to town, or he might go to the police instead of the telegraph office. And Nunes's family might send soldiers instead of the cash, and so on, and even if none of these things happened, still the chances of the bandits both getting the money and not having to fight off the armed forces of Pernambuco for it were slim to none, and the only real question in his mind was whether to kill Nunes then or later.

Because kill him he would, and he didn't believe in drawing these things out. But on the other hand, he wasn't averse to the idea of crossing the countryside with the former commander-in-chief of the state of Pernambuco tied behind one of his mules. He decided to take Nunes with them for a while and see how it went. He could kill him anywhere.

They headed for Alagoas, with Nunes on foot, tied to the tail of Zé Bahiano's horse. Nunes had gotten older, but proved surprisingly *disposta*, willing. Brave, uncomplaining, walking along like the soldier he was. He'd pursued them for years, he'd been one of the worst ones, and if Lampião had shot him at any moment in the back of the head, none of his men would have wondered why. Still, when they set off again after lunch, they weren't really surprised when Lampião told them to hoist his old enemy up onto a horse.

They were moving south, fast. They knew the news would have gone out by then from Águas Belas; though they didn't expect real fighting from the Pernambuco police, with their former chief as hostage. But as soon as they crossed into the state of Alagoas they found themselves surrounded by troops in a cow pasture, just before dusk.

Nunes said afterward that it had been a bizarre incident for him, everything upside down, white, black, and black, white. He was terrified of the police, terrified that their bungling would cause his death. On the other hand, he found himself trusting in Lampião, praying even, that his tactics would save them all, himself included. And sure enough, once darkness fell, Lampião had cowbells distributed among his men, and led them slowly, at the pace of the cattle, out through the police lines, ringing the bells.

With Nunes at the front, gun at his head, though this was unnecessary. He knew where his chances lay, and maintained rigid discipline, then and on the fast march that followed. He was silent when silence was called for, helped as he could, cutting branches and walking backward to cover their tracks, eating and drinking little so as not to burden them, and when they made camp the next night, Lampião had him untied, "just for dinner."

They'd given the forces the slip, so they took off their gear and sat under the trees, Nunes among them, talking about battles and strategy, women, and the virtues and drawbacks of various guns. And a little later, someone pulled out a guitar and they sang into the night, the old songs, and Nunes sang with them, even the bandits' marching songs, "*You teach me to make lace, and I'll teach you to make love*"—he knew them all. And when they went to sleep under the stars, the bandit Zé Bahiano gave Nunes his own blankets.

The next day, though, when they crossed into Sergipe and found themselves facing more police and either some real fighting or a serious march, Nunes became a luxury they could no longer afford. His ransom hadn't arrived yet, but Lampião wasn't thinking about killing him anymore.

He set him free under a flowering *umbu* tree outside Bom Sucesso, and Nunes shook each bandit's hand in turn, almost regretfully. Said he wouldn't have minded another night with them, under the stars. He hadn't slept out in a while, and had forgotten how nice it could be. He embraced Zé Bahiano, who'd taken care of him "like a son," and told him he would never forget him.

Zé Bahiano asked the colonel if he had any money with him, "to get home."

Nunes, embarrassed, turned out his pockets. "As you see"—nothing but a pencil and a pocket handkerchief.

So Lampião ended up giving him thirty *mil réis* for passage back across the river, and that turned out to be all the money that ever passed between them. So much for the fifteen *contos*—all those cows.

Though Nunes did repay him in a fashion. All Brazil saw the headlines the next week: "A Bandit, Yes, But with a Good Heart and Brilliant Strategy!" In the article that followed, Nunes praised Lampião's "lack of malice. Otherwise, how could I, his worst enemy, still be among the living?"

He went on about his "great tactics"—though what Bezerra remembered best was the photo: Nunes and his daughter, Abigail, "an American name," the newspaper said. This Abigail had rushed out from Recife with the ransom money, in a car, with only her sister's husband. No one else would come, she said. Not her father's "so-called friends," not even her own fiancé, "or rather, *ex*-fiancé," said Abigail Nunes.

Bezerra had studied the picture closely. Abigail Nunes

wore a new-style dress and had her hair cut short. She was a girl who could toss her hair and walk into a bank in Recife and out again with a fortune in banknotes, and then drive in a car all the way from her world to theirs, dressed in what looked to be light-colored silks.

A girl who could change her mind when she felt like it, a girl with an "ex-fiancé"—a man she could dismiss when she no longer wanted to marry him. Bezerra felt sorry for the guy, but could see that a man like that, a guy with no guts, no spine, would never have done for Abigail Nunes. That had been when? Eight, nine years ago. Bezerra wondered if she'd married—though of course she'd have married, a girl like that. With money to boot.

But he wondered what kind of man she'd chosen, and if their paths might not cross someday. Especially now, if—But Bezerra didn't want to say it, didn't even want to think it. Just some day if.

XV

Maria Bonita woke up on the rock, coughing. She'd been lying too long—the sun was lower, and a chill had come up. She tried to take a deep breath, but slowly, with caution. She didn't want it to turn into one of those fits, with blood.

She'd been dreaming, something, couldn't quite remember. Something bad, though, slaughter, loss. And regret, infinite, lingering.

The baby would be a little over three years old by now. Expedita—"Tita." That was Lampião's doing, the name. She'd wanted to call her Rosa, after her grandmother, if it was a girl, or João, after her father, if it was a boy. But "Tita"—she'd never much liked the name, though it grew on her, it was sweet, she'd come to like it. To love it. "Little Tita," she'd whispered into her hair.

Though now, three years later, the girl didn't even know her. The last time they'd gone over to see her, she'd clung to the ranch woman who was raising her. Her "mother."

"Go, little Tita, give Auntie a hug," the woman had urged her.

But Tita hadn't wanted to give "Auntie" a hug. All she wanted to do was to run and play with the others—"Auntie" understood, she told the woman, and she did, she understood. Just couldn't help the tears.

And when they gave her the doll they'd managed to get for her—paying a spy, and then rejecting the first one and the second as not sufficiently wonderful—when they gave her the doll with glass eyes that opened and closed, which had come first all the way from Recife, and then out over dusty trail, first by truck, then cart, and finally donkey, instead of the happy smiles, the clapping of hands that they'd anticipated, the child had held back and asked if there was one for her sister. The ranch woman's daughter—the girls thought they were sisters, twins.

Which was absolutely right, perfect, the way it had to be. And she knew that, and knew, too, how good it was for the child, for little Tita, to love her foster mother and care more for her so-called sister than the true parents who stood there, mute with pain and longing, bearing elaborate gifts, but not the right ones, she understood that. They should have brought any two dolls rather than one special one, and now she knew, and the next time—although maybe better still would be to just leave it, not go down there again. What was the good in it, mixing all that grief in her heart again with some crazy hope? Of what though? Recognition?

The girl kissing her and smelling something she knew and whispering, *Mommy?*

But that would be fatal to the child. Better to leave it. For her sake, too, and his, because every time they said good-bye and walked away, it was always the first time, the day she'd handed the child over to the woman and walked away from her, sobbing, first to the cactus and then to the stars, her breasts pounding with milk.

A LIZARD RAN up on the rock, saw her, and froze, surprised. This must be his rock most of the time, his home. Maybe she'd get Lampião to go back by her old house, Caysara Malhada, which wasn't too far from here. If they left this afternoon, they could camp near there tonight, and then, depending on how far they got now, maybe she could just slip in there after dark for a visit.

Spend a few hours inside, in a house, sitting around the table, in a chair, drinking coffee, eating cheese, and talking about nothing. The neighbors, the price of goats, the eternal rain or no rain—anything except the police or the government.

She lit a quick cigarette. Pedro Candido said that Odilon Flor was creeping around after them across the river—that same Odilon who had recently mowed down a whole camp of pilgrims, four hundred unarmed men, women, and children in Curral Novo.

Followers of a sacred bull, another one of those cults that comes up every now and then. One of those preachers who emerges out of the dust and is always able to stir up a few followers, no matter what he's preaching. And these so-called pilgrims were half-crazy, no doubt, prophesying the end of the world and dancing around a bull god, but was that any reason to kill them? Any reason for Odilon Flor to march in there with his big guns and open fire in a hot sandy square under the blazing sun, just because some mayor wanted his town cleared out? Shoot them all, and then walk among the bodies, kicking, turning, putting bullets in the heads of anyone still moving?

But how many times had this same Flor run from Lampião? And everyone knew it, everyone in the Sertão knew that, despite all that murder, Flor was an essential coward, thanks to Lampião.

Maybe she'd been half-crazy herself, to run off with him, maybe she'd die sooner rather than later because of it, at the mouth of a rifle, but didn't women die young at home, too, from a jealous husband and a bullet to the head? That happened even to women who woke at dawn, scrubbed the clothes, cooked the food, swept and sewed and fell into bed at dusk, too exhausted to dream of betrayal, and still their husbands came home and shot them, and nothing was ever done about it. "A crime of passion," it was called.

But where was the passion in that?

"Maria!"

It was Dulce, come for her—so they must be leaving? Good. "Over here," she called out, but it set her off coughing, so hard she couldn't get her breath and knocked the cigarettes to the ground.

She clutched at the rock, trying to stop, trying to breathe.

Dulce scrambled up. "Are you all right?" Dulce poured a little water from her canteen into a cup, and finally she got a half-breath and could take a sip.

She pulled out her handkerchief, red silk which didn't show the blood, and took another breath.

"*Calma*, Maria," said Dulce. But she was calm now, it was all right. She wiped the tears from her eyes.

"Are we leaving?" she whispered.

"Tomorrow, early."

"Not now?"

"No, I guess they thought tomorrow would be better."

So they wouldn't be camping by her mother's house that evening.

Although the truth was she was never going to sit at that table with her mother again anyway. She'd heard that her mother had been bitten by a rattlesnake and died last year.

"Lampião said we should cut the watermelon, just for us girls," Dulce was saying.

"Is he down there?"

"No, but he said to cut it."

She got carefully to her feet. Watermelon—perfect. Just the thing for her throat. She climbed down from the rock, and stepped over the cigarettes that had fallen. Leave them. Good. She wasn't going to smoke anymore, she couldn't.

She started after Dulce, then turned back. They were expensive and hard to get, it would be stupid to leave them. She grabbed the cigarettes and stuffed them in her pack.

XVI

Aniceto had come up to him twice already—"*Vamos!*"—and twice Bezerra'd had to say, "Not yet."

Wednesday was market day in Piranhas, and there would be men there, no doubt, buying supplies for Lampião. Bezerra pretty much knew who they were, just couldn't do anything about it. If you stopped one, killed him even, and ran his family off their land, reduced them, starved them, in his place there would be another. It wasn't as if Lampião himself would starve, or even feel it. It was the local people who would suffer, people Bezerra knew. They were his friends, his wife's cousins, her mother's. Just on the other side of the fence, that's all, and it wasn't as if the twain never met. They met all the time.

Hadn't he seen Erasmo Felix at the market in Pão de Açucar the other day, buying three times as much cheese and five times the salt as usual? Plus six liters of Cavalinho whiskey—Bezerra might have asked, *Who for?* if he didn't already know. Though knowing that Erasmo Felix was buying supplies for Lampião was less to the point than knowing that Erasmo Felix lived and worked on the ranch of Antonio Caixeiro, whose son was governor of Sergipe, and that whatever action he was taking in support of Lampião was under the protection of the governor's father, which was to say, the governor himself.

So was Bezerra supposed to take him on? When not even Lucena dared move against him? And even if he did, even if he threw Erasmo Felix behind bars for a few days, then he'd see someone else buying too much salt, plus five watermelons—so what was he going to do? Arrest the whole town? Stop the market?

Not that that approach hadn't been tried, by the federal government, men in Rio or São Paulo, men too far away to understand the consequences or care. Though they had been right in their analysis. Lampião was so interwoven into the fabric of life in the Sertão that to destroy him you'd have to destroy that fabric. Shoot the men, empty the villages, burn the fields, scatter the flocks—but wasn't it better his way, in the end?

His way maybe no one would even get hurt. As long as they were patient and waited until it was dark—"really dark," Bezerra repeated to Aniceto—waited till Lampião's spies in Piranhas were all home in their beds, then all they'd have to do was slip back into Piranhas, down to the riverfront, and get a boat to take them down the river.

XVII

The River of Disorder

Lampião thought that Sereno seemed all right now, and probably wouldn't leave him. He knew what he was thinking, though, what they were all thinking, knew there was a desperation running through them that they'd never known before. No one had ever thought of walking on him. Now the possibility was there, in everyone's mind.

Even hers. He'd seen her looking at Corisco the other day with something like longing. It was funny—they were hardly talking to each other these days, and he hadn't even known he still loved her, till he stood there watching her as closely as he'd ever watched anything, measuring the flickering light in her eyes, hearing the words behind her words, smelling her hope and then her hopelessness.

He could hear the river from here—couldn't not hear it. He was a man of the dry backlands, of rivers that dried up come summer, and this constant running, all this water, made him uneasy. *The River of Disorder*, he couldn't help thinking—he'd heard of it first from his grandmother, all those years ago, in 1902 or '03, during one of the really bad droughts, when they were standing in the doorway watching another group of men, women, and children come up out of the dust.

Shimmering in the distance, like ghosts at first, but then as they came closer you could see they were real from the dirt on their faces and the rags on their backs. They never had any horses, or even goats—they never left till after the goats died, his grandmother said.

She told him they were the Retirantes, the "leaving ones," driven from the land by the drought that was tormenting the whole region, turning every leaf, every crop, every stalk of grass from green to gray. His grandmother had called to his father, who was standing by the well with his machete. They'd given water to the first ones, but now there were too many, and not enough water. Hardly any water left.

"Forgive me," his father would murmur as they trudged past, and one or two had nodded, but most of them didn't even spare the strength to look over, just kept walking past, one foot in front of the other, until they shimmered and then turned back to dust.

"Have mercy!" his grandmother had whispered. She herself had been one of them when she was a girl, during the Drought of the Two Sixes, 1866, the worst anyone could remember. Though no one knew, she said, how bad it was going to get—if it would rain in time to save them, or just keep getting worse. So her people had tried to wait it out, thinking that maybe they'd get through, since most times they did, but that year, 1866, all the early signs were bad.

On Santa Luzia's Day, they put out the salt—six big lumps, just before dark. If it melted or came apart, there would be rain. And they'd prayed all night, but when they went out to look in the morning, the salt hadn't changed at all.

And then the *caruaru* birds weren't singing, and the frogs disappeared, and the worker ants—"and do the ants ever lie?"

No, the old people knew, never.

The priest came out to the village right before São José's Day in March with special prayers, and everyone fasted and beat their backs, tied thorns underneath their shirts, and walked to church on their knees, over the dry rocky ground, seeking forgiveness for whatever had brought this down upon their heads. But still the sky was cloudless, and that's when their neighbors started leaving, since if it didn't rain on São José's Day, it wouldn't rain all winter.

And it didn't, just kept getting drier, and one day Lampião's future grandmother, then about ten, walked out to the pasture with her father. The few cows still standing had moved into the dark circle of dust that used to be their water hole, and when her father came near, they turned those gentle brown eyes to him and asked, *Why?* just as clearly as if they'd said it.

And he told them about the River of Disorder, which was always underneath them, always flowing, but mostly stayed underground, where it did no harm, but left men like him and beasts like them to live out their natural lives.

"But once in while," he said to the cows who stood there, the old woman swore, listening, "it breaks out and comes up to earth and wreaks havoc"—he pointed to the withered trees, the parched fields, the dust blowing across the water hole—"and you die of thirst, and I lose everything."

She helped her father set fire to the *macambeira* thicket then, to burn off the thorns, so the cows could eat what little was left. But they died anyway, dried up and keeled over, and not even the buzzards could peck through their skins. They'd turned to leather on their feet.

And the family had held out a little while longer, eating the harsh and bitter roots of the wild bromeliads, which made them sick but kept them alive, but then the baby died and one of her little sisters. And that's when they left. Her father nailed shut the door and windows, they shouldered their cooking pot and some hammocks, and turned their backs and walked away.

"Where are we going?" she'd asked him.

"Away," was all he said, away from the sun that was doing the devil's work now, and the pitiless blue sky that had forgotten how to rain.

They headed east, across Pernambuco, hoping first that the Moxotó River would have water. When it didn't, she feared they'd all die—plenty had, they'd seen bones, bleaching in the sun, all along the way. Proof of their sin and the end of the world, said the wandering preachers.

But when they got to the Ipanema River there was still a trickle of water, and her father had some cousins there—otherwise they wouldn't let you stay. They'd drive you on, and you couldn't blame them. No one had enough food or water.

But one of her father's cousins had made room for them on his place, and her father had worked for him, humbly, like a slave, like the dependent that he was, for a full year or so, until one day they heard thunder.

Everyone stopped and stood stock-still, listening. "It's just the heat," they said to each other, not daring to believe, not wanting to jinx.

But then came another rumble, louder and closer, and they all ran up onto a little rise, even the old women, to get a better look at the sky. There were rain clouds, no doubt, but still they doubted until the rain actually started falling, and when it rained again the next day, rained more, and the day after, too, they went into the village for a mass of thanksgiving. The rains had come back to the Sertão.

People embraced each other in the street, rejoicing in the transformation of the land around them. "You go to sleep gray and wake up green," Lampião's grandmother told him, and your wasteland is once again a garden, and proof that you'd returned to favor in God's eyes.

And soon after that, her father started tying up their bundles.

"Stay," his cousin urged him, "why go back? It's easier here," and her father didn't deny it, didn't argue or even explain. Just smiled a little smile—for the first time since they'd left home, she realized—and shortly after that they set out again, only toward the sun this time, not away, and once they were on the road home, he started singing.

A kind of walking song, with verses that they made up as they went along, to keep themselves going. And his grandmother had taught it to him, and he'd changed the words a bit and turned it into his own song, "Mulher Rendeira."

You teach me to make lace,
and I'll teach you to make love

HE'D WALKED BACK and forth across the whole Sertão for twenty years now, singing that song, and everyone who heard him, every soldier and policeman, farmer and merchant, man, woman, and child, rich, poor, or in between, knew he meant it, or at least, what he meant.

That his heart was light, open, free, and that he was winning, would always win. Every time they heard that song, it meant that he was happy—in love with life, his own and theirs, too, their Sertão that he loved with such passion that it in turn had given itself to him like a lover, and then it had been easy.

He'd dream his campaigns at night, and then wake up in the morning, taking in the sky avidly, a lover, and that's when he'd notice birds flying where they shouldn't be, which meant they'd been scared up somewhere—by the police who never were lovers and so didn't even notice they'd sent up flares for you.

And they called it luck, "the luck of Lampião," but what happens to your luck if you're not making love anymore? If you wake up one day no longer caring what's down the next draw, or which colonel might be wanting to give you dinner or sell you bullets—not quite believing in it anymore? Is that what they mean when they say your luck's run out?

He'd been thinking back to their early days together, his and hers, when they seemed to be wandering carefree under a good star that never seemed to change, through a life filled with camaraderie, music, laughter, high spirits. All of them young and brave, some smart, some beautiful, and all cut loose, as if by magic, from the worries of the rest of the world. For them there were no crops, no drought, or goats, or chickens, no bad neighbors, or even birth or death, for a while.

And then, from one day to the next, it had reversed. He'd found himself standing over the graves of first one and then another of his brothers. Both all wrong—first Antonio, killed by accident, when Luis Pedro fell asleep and dropped his gun and it misfired and hit Antonio in the stomach, killed him on the spot.

Luis Pedro had cried and begged Lampião to kill him, too, and he'd thought about it, but ended up forgiving him—told him he'd have to stand in as a brother, then, and Luis Pedro did, or tried. As much as anyone can stand in for a brother.

He knew this, though there's knowing and knowing, and when he really knew it, knew it to the depths, was when his other brother, Ezekiel, called Ponto Fino, was killed, the best shot among them. Not that that was the point—they could all shoot, but he and Ezekiel were so close in age neither of them remembered a day alive without the other, and when Lampião had become a bandit, Ezekiel took that as his fate, too, no questions asked. Just questions answered, every day—they worked together, always, side by side, looking into the sun, backward into the thornbush and cactus, judging, figuring, mapping, and then drawing up their plans together with a stick in the dust.

And it shouldn't have happened, it was just a scuffle with some police they'd caught off guard and run off from an encampment, with hardly any fire exchanged. But one of them took a potshot back over his shoulder as they fled, which by chance—by all the bad luck in the Sertão that day—happened to catch Ezekiel in the leg.

There was hardly any blood, and it hadn't hit the bone, so they thought it was all right at first. Lampião bandaged it, and left Ezekiel to rest a bit underneath some mimosa trees, and turned his attention to what the police had left behind—some machine guns and a cache of hand grenades, which they'd never seen before. They fiddled with one a bit and got nowhere, until one of the boys tossed it into the fire. The explosion knocked them all back, off their feet.

They were picking themselves up, getting their breath, starting to joke—"Popcorn that knows how to pop!"—when Maria ran up. "Lampião, Ezekiel is dying!"

He ran over, shouting, "Ezekiel!" and lifted his brother's head, but his eyes had already rolled back. He tore the bandage off the wound—it looked clean, looked fine. What had happened? Had the bullet somehow got into his stomach?

"Don't die!" He kissed him. Pushed the long hair from his light brown face. "Don't die, Zeke!"

"*Adeus, Virgulino,*" Ezekiel whispered.

"No, Ezekiel, you'll get better, this is nothing—" he cried. And silently, *Don't leave me*, since he never had, not in this life. But Ezekiel was gone, and Lampião had to fight off real despair then. They lit candles around the body, dug the grave deep enough so the buzzards wouldn't come in and bring the police—so deep they could hardly get him in, could hardly keep him wrapped in his hammock. So deep that when they started to fill it, he'd had to turn away in tears.

HE'D WALKED AWAY from that, whispered one last prayer and left his last brother far from home in an unmarked grave, and right after that, if he recalled it right, she got pregnant, and none of the remedies worked, and as her belly started growing, she was reduced from a girl whose world was a garden to the kind of woman you'd see sometimes outside a church, sewing beautiful little clothes for a baby she'd never see grow to wear them.

She was still brave, though—tossed her head and called it a nuisance, refused to slow down or feel the kicks. He, too, though when she was born, ten little fingers, ten little toes, he found himself overcome, weeping. "Tita," he'd sobbed into the little head, despite having vowed to keep his distance. Determined not to even look at the girl—or the mother. Temporary mother. Maria Bonita was nobody's mother, couldn't be.

AND WHEN THAT was over and done with, it wasn't long after that they'd ridden into Serrinha and she'd been shot.

She got over that, too, but do you, ever? He had, but he'd been young then. Just starting out, still with that high good humor that comes from just being alive. She'd been through too much by then, and came back not really wanting to make it all work again. What she wanted—who knew? Wanted to leave, but there was no leaving. She knew that, sometimes.

"YOU'LL BE SAFE as long as you don't have a woman"—Padre Cícero had said in his blessing, and Lampião was thinking then that he probably should have stuck to that, especially when he saw her moping around, dark and gloomy, like a blackbird with a broken wing.

Then she cut her hair, and all the smoking—where was the blue-eyed girl he'd kissed that day in her father's pasture, under the giant flowering *ipê* tree? The girl who'd looked just right and smelled so good that he couldn't stay away from her after that, he had to get back there and get her, risk his luck, stretch his blessing, to grab at the happiness, the wild, triple, ten-times happiness that he hadn't felt since he was a boy.

And they'd been happy—really happy, and if he tried, he could still see her smiling somewhere back there, and that's what he wanted now, her smile. Not to be alone again, but to be with her smiling. If she would ever smile again.

But would she? He rustled in his pack, pulled out his cardboard, with his clippings. There she was—smiling, her famous "Garbo shot." Taken by the Turk, who'd come out from Vila Bela with one of their suppliers to make a movie of their lives, "a real cowboy movie," he told them, and begged to be allowed to follow them around for a while and film them as they went about their daily lives.

They'd been suspicious at first—even checked the movie camera for guns, but there were no guns, just a sort of party spirit that took hold, starting with the Turk himself. He loved them, loved everything about them—the way they dressed, the way they walked though the bush, the way they made coffee, the way they combed each other's hair. And he filmed it all, and let them look through the camera, and they started to see themselves through his eyes.

And it started feeling like the old days, like earlier days when there hadn't been so much to weigh so heavily, though Maria had held off for a while. But then the Turk asked her to pose for a picture, with her guns and the dogs, "like Garbo," he said, the great movie star. And then a small smile started turning up the corners of her mouth, and one evening, when the dancing started, the Turk directed her to dance.

She hadn't danced since the shooting—but the Turk didn't know about that, so finally she'd turned, almost hesitantly, to Lampião, and they'd got to their feet, shy at first, stiff, but then she, too, let it all go, all of it, the baby, the shot, the never-ending fear, now that she knew it, and started dancing like the girl he'd run off with, and their life became, like magic, their life again.

The Turk was going to show his movie in Rio, and America, and people would line up to see it, people had never seen anything like it before, the real thing. All he needed now was a fight scene with the police. But he also needed more film, and went back to Vila Bela to get it. They'd set a place to meet the next day, but the Turk didn't show up. And a few days later, one of their suppliers came out with the news that he'd been shot dead.

They'd all stood stunned, as if they'd never known anyone to have been shot before.

"The Turk?" they'd repeated.

Yeah, said the supplier, it was one of those things. His girlfriend's husband, or his wife's boyfriend, one or the other, but anyway, in his underwear. In a bedroom.

What about his cameras? he'd asked.

The supplier didn't know about that, but he'd brought them out a copy of the paper from Salvador. There on the front page was the Turk's "Garbo" shot of her. He must have sent it out just before he died.

They crowded around—it was a beautiful picture. She'd looked at it a long time, with tears rolling down her face. But that night she'd held him close, and turned to him with passion, and soon after that, in a small town where the people had turned out to greet them, a newsman asked him if he'd ever surrender.

Questions like that didn't deserve real answers, and he'd usually just jibe something back, like, "Why would I surrender?" or "Surrender to who?"

But that day, a silence had fallen, and he saw that she had turned to him, and so he spoke, not to the reporter, but to her.

"No," he said, "they'll never take me. I'll die, but I won't give up. And if that's hard, if I suffer, I live a great life. And what else is there?"

They held each other's gaze. And then she turned to the reporter—she had a message, she said, for the Pernambuco police who'd tried to kill her. She'd give it to them in rhyme, so they could remember:

I'm in love and having fun,
And I'm not afraid of anyone!

"SIGNED," SHE SAID, "*The Bandita, Maria Bonita.*"

The bandit—Maria Bonita.

Lampião got to his feet. A woman like that, whom they'd shot and chased and kept from her own child. They'd done their worst, and what does she say to them?

"I'm in love"—which was to say alive, and so was he, alive that day, despite it all, the worst of a whole sovereign nation, they were still alive.

" . . . and having fun"—he'd almost forgotten that.

How much a part of them that was, or had to be. Because without it, they were nothing but grim-faced gunmen who'd armed and organized themselves to the point where they could kill some of those who did them wrong. But not all, evil was infinite—that was something he could say he'd learned, something he hadn't known when he'd walked out of the courtroom almost twenty years ago, thinking he'd kill the devils who'd killed his father and be done with it.

But there is no end, and if he had to sum it up now, he'd have to admit that he hadn't even gotten those individuals. He'd gotten close to them, gotten their relatives, and their men, their allies, but his primary enemies had died in their beds, just as they would have had he, Virgulino Ferreira da Silva, lowered his head that day and exited the courtroom, leaving justice to God after all.

As it is anyway—justice is with God. He knew that, too, now, this day, on his knees, by this River of Disorder, whispering Maria Bonita's little taunt to the police. In the end, despite the ones you catch and the ones who get away, real justice is still with God—which meant that what he'd really done with his life, in the end, was to have fun.

Which was saying something in this hard world and this hard place—to be a man whose life was more than chasing goats and waiting for rain, more than a nod from a colonel when he was in the mood. He, Lampião, was the one among them whose pleasure extended beyond his own pipe and hammock to the far fields of the biggest landowners in all seven states of their own Sertão—and he could see now that this was what he gave the people, as much as the gold he put in their hands or left in their village churches. He gave them his own happiness, and hers, too, as they walked down dusty village streets in their silks and their jewels, and danced with the people into the night, the only time the people danced.

And the women would crowd around her, and pick up her smile, the toss of her head, the way she'd dared to walk away from her own dreary life. And the dances would get more animated, laughter would start, people who didn't dance would line up, there would be twirling and stamping of old boots and worn sandals, and the baker would forget to leave early to make his dough, and the mothers would let their children run wild—since there were no demons walking the land when Lampião was in town.

Maria Bonita. He'd been hanging his head since she'd been shot, he could see it now. They'd had good times, the two of them, and the band, and he'd had his strategic successes. Otherwise he wouldn't be kneeling by this river. But he hadn't let himself have that fun, felt somehow undeserving, as a man who couldn't stop them from shooting his woman.

But he was wrong there—not wrong in feeling bad, who wouldn't? Not wrong in screaming it to the stars, in crying it in his heart every night—that would always be there. That shot in the dark in Serrinha would always be ringing in his ears. But he'd been wrong to let it get between them.

And wrong to pine, wrong to let bitterness engulf him,

even if he called it "fasting." Because in the end it was a failure of spirit, which was also, in his case, a betrayal, he could see that now.

Because his whole life, his mission, was high spirits, and if the world around him had changed, passed him by in some ways, he'd have to change, too, so that he could keep his spirits high. That was his job. And it wasn't as if he still didn't love the smell of the dust before the rain, even in the worst drought, when it was mixed with the last desperate leaves the goats had nibbled.

" . . . *I'm not afraid of anyone.*" That's how she'd ended it. Not: *I'm safe*, or *You can't get me.*

"*I'm not afraid.*" Though she was afraid—she had those bad dreams, and "walked scared," as they said, but she could toss her head and tell the village people that she was never afraid, and shoot her gun for them. Hit a cup in the air.

She was a bandit, she said—"*The Bandita, Maria Bonita.*" And if that's how she'd die, that's how she'd live as well.

JULY WAS NEARLY over. He'd been praying long enough. He got to his feet. He'd got word that Bezerra had gone up to Moxotó and Odilon Flor was creeping around on the wrong side of the river. There was no one else over there to give him any trouble, which meant that the River of Disorder was receding.

Pedro Candido had brought them out a whole side of beef and two barrels of whiskey. The thing now was to eat a good dinner, eat meat again, with all of them, drink his Cavalinho, and laugh a bit, sing, and then take her in his arms. Smile at her, get her to laugh, hear her laugh—when had he last heard her laugh? And then they'd get up early, before dawn, and move on, away from the river. And in three days it'd be August, and they'd have another year.

The sun was getting low. He walked back into the camp.

XVIII

Bezerra was scanning the other side of the river with his field glasses when Chico Ferreira came up to him again. The boys were ready to roll, said Chico, though what he meant was that they were drunk.

"Sit down," he said to Chico, but Chico wouldn't sit. His grudge with Lampião was an old one, personal. His cousin had been one of the policemen the bandits had shot in Queimadas, years ago—it was one of those stories. The police had mistaken the bandits for troops from the next town and saluted instead of shooting. Lampião had locked them in their own jail and taken over the town.

Not some tiny backwater, but Queimadas, a railroad town. Then they'd not so much looted the place as collected tribute—got the local judge to draw up a list of who had money in Queimadas and how much they could give "without feeling it," as Lampião always said. The town fathers actually went out with them to collect—

there wasn't any shooting, any violence. It was so "calm" there that Lampião even gave a dance.

Afterward, they interviewed the boy who'd played for them. He was just seventeen, and had never had a drink till then, or a smoke. But Lampião gave him some of his own Cavalinho, and asked him to play his favorite song, "Never Love Without Being Loved." The boy was shy at first, but Lampião seemed to like his music, though he didn't dance, just stood by the boy, watching the door. People were having a good time, but Lampião wasn't smiling.

"You know why I live this life?" Lampião turned to the boy, when he finished a song.

"Yes, Captain," the boy said, though he didn't.

"They killed my father—did you know that?"

"Yes, Captain," though he didn't, but what else was there but "yes" with Lampião?

"Shot him down in cold blood. Did they show him any mercy that day?"

Yes, Captain, or no—whatever it was. Lampião gave him another drink.

"Where was the mercy the day the police shot my father?"

The boy didn't know.

"There was no mercy, in the whole Sertão." Now it was Lampião who was drinking. "Or justice, either."

And then he said there was something he had to see to personally, but he'd be back soon. He told the boy to keep singing and wait for him.

And the boy meant to do just that. He heard the first

shot just as he was ending a *baião*, "*Eu sei que eu morro de bala . . . ,*" "I know that I'll die by the bullet," and then *bang*. Perfect. *Bang* again a little later, and then again, and again. Six times, like drums, the boy was thinking, not scared—nothing scared him anymore. He was going to run off with the bandits that night, he'd already decided. Wouldn't tell his mother till he'd gone.

Though suddenly, out of nowhere, there was his father, looking scared, his face the color of the bread they baked every morning. He pulled him over to one side by the arm and whispered hoarsely that Lampião had killed every policeman in town—took them out of the station one by one and shot them on the steps. Some of them begging, some crying for their children, one fighting—anyway, they were all dead, and the steps of the station were running with blood.

And Chico Ferreira's cousin had been among them, not that you needed a cousin to feel it. Every policeman and soldier out there felt Queimadas, and Bezerra always thought it was one of Lampião's rare mistakes. Not that he couldn't understand wanting vengeance—for his father, and now his brother. But no one knew better than Lampião how impossible that really was, how elusive—what you want to kill is an idea, but what you're killing is a man, and those policemen in Queimadas weren't The Police, they were the same backwoods boys as the bandits, just with different hats, and Lampião usually knew this.

Bezerra always considered Queimadas a tactical error, and Lampião must have, too, since he hadn't done anything like it since. And the funny thing was that if they killed him tonight, you could say that it came, like an arrow, straight from that.

"You see that chapel?" Bezerra turned to Chico Ferreira, pointing to the little silver-blue hut across the river, on the Sergipe side. His boys were restless, wanting to move, but it was too early. They'd spoil it if they moved now, out of restlessness, drunkenness—like all the other grand plans to get Lampião.

Chico nodded.

"Well, come back to me when you don't."

XIX

The sun was getting low as Sereno cut the watermelon. The women, Cila, Dulce, Maria, were talking softly. They'd laid out the boy's uniform and were figuring how much was still left to be done—not much. A little hand work was all. The Kid—that's what they'd decided to call him—could be parading around in it tomorrow afternoon. Or the next day, whenever they stopped.

Sereno remembered that thrill, when you first join up and put on your uniform, like the rest of the men. Join the brotherhood, smell the gunpowder, the bullets, the fire. You never think of death then, or even getting hurt. You love Lampião like your own father, or more.

The last of the sunlight was coming through the wispy trees, and the last big black birds flapped away. Funny, how the buzzards always took him back to Virginio, Lampião's brother-in-law. "Moderno," the Kid, they'd named him, too, when he joined them, but that name never stuck because Virginio was never a kid. He was a natural leader, just like Lampião.

The only one who had ever come close. Corisco was brave and fearless under fire, no one was better, whooping and shooting with both hands, and nothing scared him, but Corisco was violent, crazy violent. Once he hung a man from a pole, had him drawn and quartered, a mortal enemy, granted, the very one who'd driven him from his peaceful life to start with.

But it had made news, the brutality of it, and brought down one of those joint campaigns on their heads that had got two of the boys killed. Plus there were always those problems with Corisco's band, a couple of shootings over the women, and now these rumors that one of his boys was carrying on with the wife of a boatman. Christ, Lampião treated those people like gold, he depended on them, both to carry them across the river and to keep their mouths shut. He'd shoot any man who even thought of touching one of their wives.

But Corisco just let it roll—he was "fat where Lampião is thin," as Dadá once put it, and they'd laughed, but it wasn't all funny, since you needed someone in front of you who knew not only where to go but where to stop.

Like Lampião, and Virginio, too—he knew the land almost as well as Lampião, came to them already well trained for bandit life by everything honest he'd done till then. He was good with horses, good at leatherwork—key, since their clothes needed constant fixing, and even decoration, braiding, weaving, which Virginio did very well.

And he was good at tracking, but most of all, he understood Lampião's way. "We want to get along with the people, not offend them," he once told a reporter. "We might have to kill a man, but we'd never mistreat him."

But Virginio was always more backwoodsman than bandit. And one day, when he was pushing his way through the kind of closed bush that you can never quite see through, he came to one of those rocks a tracker dreams of, and climbed up to get a clear view out over the top.

Breaking the first rule of banditry—you never climb up where you can be seen. But Virginio thought it was all right, because there weren't any soldiers in the area.

Except that there were, five soldiers, half-lost, half-AWOL, stumbling randomly through the bush, and coming up on that same rock from the other side, and when Virginio loomed up there, right over them, one of them drew an easy bead and shot him through the heart.

From so close that he flew up in the air and landed with his arms crossed over his chest, "like a *beato*," a holy man, his boys told Lampião. But they didn't bury him, since the shooting had stampeded their horses, and they didn't know where it had come from or what they were up against, so they dragged his body into the bush and took off on foot, as did the soldiers who'd shot him—so scared they ran "the fastest footrace in the history of the Sertão," they told the papers.

It took the bandits a few days to get back for the body, and by the time they did, Virginio belonged to the buzzards—what was left of Virginio. They were flopping up and down his legs, and the women had screamed, and the men threw rocks, but Lampião said it wasn't the buzzards who were the problem. They were the solution, the traditional burial in the Sertão, the old Indian way. This digging of graves had come in from the coast, with the Portuguese, and what was the improvement there? How was it so much better? The Indians had wrapped their dead in hammocks and left them out for the birds—and since you were bound someday to become your own Last Supper, all it came down to was who you fed, buzzards or worms.

Funny, the other day they saw another one of those clippings—Lampião was dead again. From TB this time, he'd died in his bed—the bed, actually, of the father of the governor of Sergipe, the papers said. Not bad, as his deaths went, he'd said with a shrug, he'd died plenty of worse ones, shot by the police usually, how many times had they shot him? Mané Neto alone had killed him so many times that they didn't even print his claims anymore. And Lucena, a couple of times, too, monkeys all.

The sun was going down behind the hills, and the chill was descending on them. Another night of fog and mist. Sereno had had enough of this river.

"Chilly," said Maria Bonita.

"Yeah, let's go down to the fire," said Cila. They picked up, and then headed down, half-stumbling as they followed the streambed. Darkness had fallen as it did here, all at once.

XX

"It's time," said Bezerra.

The men, who'd been so restless till then, fell still and got to their feet almost reluctantly. Now that it was dark enough, the mist had come up and made it even darker.

"This way—" Bezerra led them down the hill from the cornfields, and took the first trail back to town. It wasn't far, just a half a league, but there were forty-six of them, all loaded down with rifles and ammunition, plus the three machine guns with two hundred rounds each.

Enough to kill all the bandits in Brazil and more, no question, though it made for slow going. "Quiet!" he had to hiss more than once, and they'd stopped a couple of times to change hands, take turns with the machine guns.

When they finally got back to town and down to the dock, the place was just as silent and deserted as Bezerra had hoped, as it had to be. But when he looked around at the boats tied up at the dock, there wasn't one big enough to take them down the river.

There were usually big boats there at the dock on any given evening, but nothing tonight, except the wooden dories that the fishermen used. Fine for twelve, even fifteen fishermen, but no good at all to forty-six fully loaded soldiers, one stool pigeon, and the three heavyweight machine guns on which the whole equation was based.

So that was it. "The luck of Lampião," one more time. It wasn't as if Bezerra was really surprised, or even entirely disappointed. He peered out into the fog, the mist, the blackness rising from the river—the whole thing was just as well left alone. On a night like this, the devil would take care of his own. Better to let Lampião sleep in peace tonight and live to fight another day, while he, Bezerra, would go home to his own warm bed, from which he, too, would rise in the morning.

Bezerra was just starting to say as much to Aniceto, and pull rank if he had to, since Aniceto had been hitting the bottle and getting braver all afternoon, when an old boatman approached him.

"Maybe I can resolve a problem for you, Lieutenant."

One of Lampião's spies? Bezerra turned to him. "Do I have a problem, my man?"

"If you did—"

Aniceto came forward. "How?"

"I could tie the boats together for you, and that way you could load up and get across."

Or drown trying, thought Bezerra. "And will that work, friend? Have you done it before?"

"Plenty of times, but it all depends on the rope. If the rope's strong, it works."

"Have you got the right rope?"

Not enough, he said, but since it was market day, there was a chance that a shop would still be open for the stragglers, selling the last necessities, whiskey, cigarettes, and, with luck, good rope. The old man offered to walk up into town to see.

Bezerra gave the money to Aniceto and sent him along. The funny thing was, Bezerra was thinking, as he looked out over the black river, that his own luck now probably lay with Lampião's. It would be better for them both if there was no rope in Piranhas tonight.

But Aniceto and the boatman came back with good strong *caroá*, local rope made from native bushes, as tough as you could get. And then, more luck—though good or bad, Bezerra no longer knew—someone was raising a roof in Piranhas, and the beams had just come in and were still on the dock, precisely what was needed to hold the boats together. The old man went to get another boatman to help him, who turned out to be the brother of one of Bezerra's soldiers—another good sign?—and together they lay the beams across three of the boats and tied them securely bow and stern, asking no questions, so Bezerra was telling no lies. Still, there were the machine guns, speaking for themselves. These they loaded onto the beams.

It was around seven or eight at night by then. Bezerra didn't know for sure, and didn't want to know. What was happening now was happening on its own time, like birth or death.

The boatmen threw a heavy canvas tarp over the

machine guns, and then there was no more reason to hang around on the dock, even if it was the last time they'd ever stand there as live men. Bezerra ordered his soldiers into the boats. He hadn't told them exactly what they were up to, though they would have put it together by now. There was only one reason to be going out on the river with machine guns on a night like this one.

He climbed in. "*Vamos.*" The boats were loaded, overloaded, it felt to him, but the boatman seemed unconcerned, and the first part would be easy. All they had to do now was float a few leagues down, to Remanso, still on this side of the river, to talk to Lampião's supplier Pedro Candido, and with any luck, Pedro Candido wouldn't be home.

XXI

It was a beautiful evening. The mist had risen on the other side of the river, but this side was still clear. The last of the golden light had been beautiful in the treetops, and if you kept looking, you could still make out the glow.

Lampião was sitting among them, drinking his whiskey, laughing, teasing. He reached out and took her hand. She looked almost startled at first, but then he said something funny in her ear, and she laughed, and pushed him and said something back, and then they were both laughing, and everyone else was, too.

He was pouring his Cavalinho, and the beautiful side of beef that Pedro Candido had brought was roasting over the fire. Lampião had paid him enough for a whole cow, two, maybe, but what was money to them? Money was theirs for the taking, all over the Sertão, all the money in the world.

July was as good as over, and their spies had been consistent—Bezerra had gone with his forces up to

Moxotó. By the time he figured out his mistake, they'd be long gone from here. The first of August was New Year's Day for them. They'd have another year.

Lampião asked one of the boys to play, and then he stood up to dance. He asked one of the other girls first, to tease her, and she tossed her head, and took Luis Pedro by the hand. But that didn't last long, you couldn't keep them apart when they were smiling, that was all it ever took, just one smile from either one, and they were in each other's arms again.

The guitar played on, softly, and they were all up, all dancing. The girls, casting down glances and moving closer, always closer, and then, twirl, a turn, and back away, and the boys bowing and clowning, just like in the old days, all of them, *amando, gozando, e querendo bem*, alive, in love, and glad of both, on this, their last night on the river.

They were passing the bottle, the whiskey, the Cinzano, both together—it didn't matter. There were no goats to be brought in, no chickens to feed. No children to wash and change or cook for, nothing but this dance tonight.

She caught Lampião's eye, and then looked away again. There are knots you don't untie. She'd been thinking about leaving, but that was just play, it didn't exist—to leave a man like Lampião? Never. Not when there was the chance of his smile, or one more night in his arms.

There was much to cry for, but here they were dancing under the stars, before the mist moved in. People were handing around slices of meat, and there was plenty of salt, plenty of whiskey, plenty of everything, and Lampião was smiling and dancing like no one else.

XXII

It was worse than it had looked on the river, as bad a night as Bezerra had ever seen. The mist was so heavy it might as well have been rain, which meant hardly any visibility—hard for the boatmen, and dangerous for them all. Though from another perspective it was just what they needed. It would be impossible for anyone on the other shore to see them on the river. Therefore, the best of all nights.

To die, though? Bezerra was starting to wonder. Because that's how it was starting to feel to him—if this went much further, it would go all the way. It wouldn't be another one of those *fracasos*, a pathetic half-effort where the police look like fools, but live to be laughed at. This one would be live or die: either win so big his heart leapt at the possibility, or turn to food for the buzzards. Fish food, if they died on the river.

The mist was so heavy that his men had taken off their uniforms to keep them dry, and stowed them under the tarps.

"Dressed like Adam," one of them joked.

"Seeking salvation," said another.

Ship of fools, thought Bezerra. Naked and damned.

"Shut up," he commanded, "and no smoking, that's an order." But he pulled out a bottle of whiskey and sent it around, "to heat up the angel." Keep them from thinking too much.

The boatman hugged the near shore as close as he dared, to avoid the sandbanks that would have caught them in the middle. Not that that would have been fatal—nothing would be fatal yet. If the boats didn't make it downriver, if Pedro Candido wasn't home, if the bandits had already got wind, sensed it the way they always did and decamped in time, well, *tudo bem*. It had happened before, all the law's elaborate preparations gone for nothing. You live to try another day, and what was so bad about that, in the end?

Then, sooner than Bezerra expected, and just as he was getting used to the chill, thinking that he wouldn't mind floating down the São Francisco River with this boatload of naked souls forever, they turned toward the shore.

He scanned. "This isn't Entremontes," he said to the boatman.

No, but it was better to dock here in Remanso, the old man said, and go the rest of the way by foot. The river got tricky farther down, and you couldn't always tie up at night.

Fine with Bezerra. His men scrambled out of the boat, and grabbed their clothes and turned from lost souls back into soldiers even before they were in uniform, just by virtue of their activity. Action, that was the thing now, no more thinking. Pedro Candido's house was only a quarter league away. Bezerra motioned to Bida, his foster son, a boy he'd taken in off the streets. He was nearly eighteen now, and a distant cousin of Pedro Candido.

Bezerra put his hand on Bida's shoulder and said, "You know the way to Pedro Candido's?"

"Yes, sir."

"Go get him for me. Bring him back here as fast as you can."

And Bida was off.

THE REST OF THEM crowded into a couple of small huts by the water and waited. No one had told the men what was going on, not in so many words, but everyone pretty much knew by now. There was Joca, off to the side—and they all knew Pedro Candido was Lampião's man. The soldiers checked and rechecked their guns, their ammunition. Now that they could talk, there seemed to be nothing to say, except for an occasional, "Cold tonight," and "Damned cold," and "Cold as it gets!"

Bezerra was just standing in the doorway, watching for Bida. It would be about a fifteen-minute run over there, he figured, though it could take longer coming back, if Pedro Candido resisted.

So—maybe half an hour, maybe more. He pulled out his own bottle, a good one, Cavalinho, what Lampião drank. Better than the rotgut the men were guzzling. He took a swig, another, and then Bida came running back, out of breath, alone.

Bezerra suddenly felt the warmth, the fire of the whiskey. So there it was—Pedro Candido wasn't home after all. He'd been warned, or simply gone away, just by coincidence. "The luck of Lampião!" Fine. It was over.

"He wasn't there?" he said to Bida.

"No, he was there, but he's sick—"

"What?"

"He has a fever, plus his wife is about to have a baby—"

Bezerra grabbed the boy. Slapped him across the face, twice, forward and backward. "Go back there and get him, or I'll kill you as a traitor, do you hear me?"

Old Mané got to his feet. He was a seasoned soldier, one of Bezerra's best, not a kid like Bida. "I'll go with him," he said.

And they were off, faster this time, though not fast enough, no chance of that now. Pedro Candido would be long gone by the time they got back there, as far away as a man running for his life could get.

"The luck of Lampião." Well, they'd come close this time, gone to plenty of trouble, what with the boats, and the truck earlier, the raw corn in the field, the secret trek back to town on a dark, cold night. All water under the bridge now, along with their chance to make their names and fortunes tonight by killing Lampião.

And still, none of it fatal. Bezerra took out his cards and sat down for a game with Chico Ferreira and Aniceto. He threw out a little more money this time. He didn't mind using up his luck now. He wouldn't need it for the easy trip back up the river.

OLD MANÉ—not that he was old. He was still in his twenties then, but he'd been a soldier for almost ten years. He knew he should have gone with Bida the first time—Bezerra should have sent him. Bida had wrecked it now for them, not that it was his fault, more Bezerra's. Mané had sensed some ambiguity there. Bezerra was scared—Mané could smell it, plus everyone knew he sold Lampião bullets. Maybe he didn't want to lose that steady stream of gold.

Mané picked up the pace, though he didn't think there was a chance in the world that Pedro Candido would still be there. He had his warning, probably took his wife—even if his story was true. Was she having a baby? If she was, he'd have carried her to her mother's, or to anyone's, some neighbor with a sensible woman in the house, and then lit out for somewhere dark and hidden to pass the night, and then get as far away as he could until Lampião was well off the river.

Which would be tomorrow if it wasn't tonight, and all this would be a very short verse in a long song. How the police in Piranhas almost got Lampião one night.

Still, Mané was all for covering the distance as fast as they could, and he took out his flask and passed it to Bida. Let the kid grow up a bit tonight. And when they got to Pedro Candido's house, instead of knocking, Mané pounded on the door with his rifle, more for Bida, since he wasn't expecting an answer—but to his own amazement, there came a whine from inside: "Leave us alone, for the love of God!"

"Open up, Pedro!" Bida shouted. "Open the door, or we'll break it down!"

The door opened a crack. Even at that, Mané could see that Bida hadn't been lying. Pedro Candido was sick, he was trembling and probably feverish. Still, why hadn't he run? Mané wondered that night and for the rest of his life. They learned later that another one of Lampião's suppliers had been there visiting the first time Bida came, but he'd dived out the back window while Bida was standing at the front door.

And why hadn't Pedro Candido followed him? Old Mané wondered. Life is a mystery, he came to think.

He dragged Pedro Candido out of the house. Bida took one more swig at the flask and then pulled his knife on his friend and cousin, and held it to his throat. "He told me to bring you back or kill you!"

Pedro Candido looked at him. "And would you, Bida?"

"Try not coming!" Bida shouted. A new Bida—one part nice normal Bida, to whom three parts sugarcane whiskey had been added. He punched Pedro Candido on the side of his face. "Try it and see!"

Pedro Candido held his face and looked at Bida, and then called inside, "I'll be back," and turned and followed the soldiers down the path.

XXIII

The bandits were kneeling under the trees. "*Nossa Senhora, full of grace . . .*"

Cila looked around the circle at the faces, and for some reason, started whispering the names. "*Vila Nova, Quinta Feira, Amoroso, Moeda. Cajarana, Matchbox, Elétrico, Paturí.*" A prayer in itself, those names, warrior names. Brave boys who could have stayed home, all of them. Could have lowered their heads and lived safe lives, full of children and goats, but here they all were, under the trees, brave and free instead.

"*Blessed is the fruit of thy womb.*" Blessed. "*Zé Julião*"—he never got a bandit name. She wondered why. Maybe because his name had a ring to it already, Zé Ju-li-ão. And next to him, *Criança*, Little Child, not that he was one, with Dulce by his side—sweet Dulce, from right nearby here; Poço, a nice girl, who could be anyone, anyone's sister or wife, until you gave her a Mauser. She had the head for it, too, would stand there, draw her bead, and shoot. Never faltered, just stood and shot, though afterward sometimes you'd find her crying, softly, hidden. Why? you'd ask, and she'd say, for her sister, back home, or something like that.

"*Santa Maria, Mother of God*"—beside Dulce knelt Cajazeira with Enedina, with her curly hair and the biggest smile of all. Then Candeiro, Mangueira, and young José, Lampião's nephew. They were going to call him the Kid, she'd heard, as soon as he got his uniform, so he could stand there like a bandit instead of a farm boy. Since his mother had died, he'd been living near Propriá with his uncle, trying to live, but the police wouldn't leave him alone. They threw him in jail every time he brought his uncle's goats to town.

So what else could he do but come out and join them, and Lampião had welcomed the boy, but she'd seen the look that had crossed his face. Part despair, part just plain exhaustion—this boy was only seventeen, he had his whole life ahead of him. And how much longer did they think Lampião could keep at this?

"*Pray for us poor sinners*"—Lampião was leading the prayer. But Cila had a prayer of her own, an incantation that she'd bought from a woman near Monte Santo, and paid high for it, traded her best gold necklace in exchange for the direct protection of Saint John the Baptist, as well as his assistance against her enemies, "*Be they man or woman*," the prayer promised, "*still will they be caught under my left foot*."

And Cila believed it, believed without question that Saint John the Baptist would turn from his own stated mission by the River Jordan, from his infinite work of baptism among the world's infidels, the thousands, maybe millions still innocent of his holy water, lay aside his staff, and direct instead his wrath on the enemies of Cila Ribeira da Souza, here in this particular corner of Brazil. Nor did it stop with that: he would also be standing by, when the time came, to "*open the gates of heaven*" for her, and "*close the gates of hell, forever and ever*"—not a bad trade for a gold chain.

Lampião was closing. "*Now and at the hour of our death.*" They'd had a nice dinner, the nicest one all month. Lots of them didn't like Pedro Candido, and Sereno had come close to shooting him earlier this afternoon, said he didn't trust him. But the meat he'd brought them was the best they'd had in a long time, plus the whiskey. And Lampião had sat among them and eaten, even the meat, and then danced with them all, her too. And they were leaving before dawn the next morning, and that was that.

"*Amen*," she said with the rest in unison, kissed her little paper incantation, safe in a gold locket she wore around her neck, and got to her feet.

XXIV

"They're coming!"

Bezerra threw down a good hand of cards. He ran outside, and strained his eyes. "How many?"

"Two—no, three—"

Two or three? They couldn't make out. He stood there with Aniceto and Chico Ferreira, who were next in command. It was hard to see until there he was—Pedro Candido, the key to it all, or so Joca the Cuckold was claiming.

Bida and Old Mané brought him up to the shack. He was protesting his innocence, though when he saw Joca he fell silent.

Bezerra grabbed him. "Where is he?"

"I don't know—I never knew!"

"Can you take us there?"

"No, it's impossible, there are too many—"

At that, Aniceto sprang across the room, threw Pedro Candido down on the wet ground, and punched him in the face. Kicked him—"Stop, please, for the love of God!"—started pulling out his nails—"I don't know anything! I don't know anything!" But when Aniceto broke one of his ribs, Pedro Candido stopped protesting and started to cry.

"He always said we weren't supposed to die for him!"

Bezerra pulled off Aniceto. "Now it's with me," he said, not unkindly, and helped Pedro Candido to his feet.

"No more games," said Bezerra.

Some sniffles and a nod from Pedro Candido.

"He's nearby here, isn't he?"

"There're too many of them—"

"Where?"

"There—just across the river. In Angicos—"

"You know the place?"

"It's my mother's ranch—"

"When did you last see them?"

"Today."

"Are they still there?"

"Yeah. They're leaving in the morning."

So. There it was. The right man, in the right place, and that's what turns out to be fatal.

"How many?" asked Bezerra.

"I don't know"—a knife again, on his broken rib—"sixty, seventy."

Seventy! So, a hundred and forty, each bandit being worth two. At least two.

"Well situated?"

"Of course. They've all got their positions."

Seventy bandits, worth a hundred and forty men

entrenched—fatal. He had forty-five men. He'd be leading them to slaughter.

Bezerra pushed Pedro Candido away and motioned Chico Ferreira and Aniceto off to the side.

"We should rethink," Bezerra began, "call for reinforcements, we need more men—"

Chico Ferreira didn't let him finish. "I'm going," he shouted, "and so are my men!"

"Wait a minute, let's talk—"

But Chico Ferreira was already drunk. Bezerra should have stopped the liquor. Should have waited. Should have done a lot of things.

"Men from Mata Grande!" Chico Ferreira was yelling. "Step forward if you're going!" They did—all sixteen of them. "Men from Mata Grande can die, but we can't run from a chance to fight Lampião!"

"Calm down!" said Bezerra.

"No, Lieutenant! No more calm! Action, but no calm! You come or you don't come, but we're going!" He went over and grabbed Pedro Candido, twisted his arm. "You're going to take us in there, you son of the plague! You filthy collaborator!"

Bezerra took a breath. It couldn't go like this. He couldn't let Chico take command—though in truth, he already had. Forced his hand. Nothing he could do about it now, except die at the head of the pack instead of behind it. If Chico went and he didn't, he could be demoted, disgraced. Investigated, even. He ordered Chico away from Pedro Candido, pulled out his own knife, and held it to Pedro's throat.

"No, please, no, don't kill me!"

And Bezerra didn't want to. He'd always liked Pedro Candido, they'd done business together. When Bezerra sold bullets to Lampião, he went through Pedro Candido. He'd just never caught him with the bandits on his land before.

Maybe they'd never been there before. A damned bad place to stop, so close to town. Lampião usually did better.

"I'll kill you now if I have to—you know that?"

From Pedro Candido, a very miserable nod. Bezerra understood. Pedro Candido had helped Lampião—supplied him for years—but Lampião had helped him more. Gave him enough money to buy a store—who else out here could buy a store? And who else had ever given any help to Pedro Candido? It wasn't something a man forgot.

Plus there would have been all the days and nights they'd spent together, over the fire, laughing and eating, dancing and drinking—probably the best times Pedro Candido had ever had. Lampião had been the shining star on Pedro Candido's horizon, and Bezerra felt for him. He took out his bottle and gave Pedro Candido a drink.

"Didn't he always tell you not to die for him?"

From Pedro Candido, another nod. It was over.

"You don't want to die for the bandits tonight, do you?"

A pause. Another drink. Finally, from Pedro Candido, "You're the ones who will die, without me."

"How do we get in there?"

"By Forquilha, a little upriver from Angicos. It's safer,

and from there we go over the *Morro dos Perdidos*, and then down on them."

The *Morro dos Perdidos*, the Hill of the Damned, or the Lost, could be either. Or both, for that matter. A bad name, either way.

"Into the boats," he commanded. The mist was no longer rising, but had settled on the river. The men could keep their clothes on this time. No longer Adams dreaming of salvation, they pushed out into the dark.

THERE WAS SOMETHING strange, almost unnatural, in the darkness in the middle of the river. They'd all heard stories about people who'd set off from one shore and never reached the other, fishermen who'd got sucked into the whirlpools and never even floated to the surface again.

Bezerra realized that drowning was a fate he'd never considered. People didn't drown much in this river. It wasn't deep enough near the shores, and most of the children could swim enough to stay alive, except the odd one now and again who got swept off. "Taken," people said, as if the river had done it on purpose, an evil spirit that lived in the whirlpools. Bezerra took a deep breath, another. Gulped air—he wasn't the only one. They were all doing it.

But then Pedro Candido touched the boatman's arm, and he turned the rudder, took down the sails, and they put in to shore.

The boats pulled up at what they could just make out

to be a dry streambed, a small pebbly landing on the riverbank. It was called Forquilha, and according to Pedro Candido, the bandits were up the next one, Tamanduá, Anteater.

So Lampião's camp was on a stream called Anteater—it came to Bezerra that he hadn't seen one for a while. What had they done with all the anteaters? Strange little beasts that scuttled up the streambeds when you went after them. Not bad to eat, if you were hungry.

The soldiers climbed ashore in silence. Bezerra had warned them earlier that he'd turn the machine guns on anyone who made the slightest noise, but what really kept them dead silent was the proximity of Lampião.

The possible proximity. Even if Pedro Candido wasn't lying, the chances were good that the bandits had already left. That was the way it usually worked with Lampião—no, always worked. The reason why he was alive to be killed that day.

The plan now was for Pedro Candido to take him and Chico Ferreira up the rocky creek bed, Forquilha, to his mother's house, to get his younger brother, who knew the paths better. He would be the one to guide them in.

With Chico Ferreira's men hauling two of the machine guns and Bezerra the other, they started up. It was misting again on this side, and so dark you couldn't see in front of you. Bezerra held Pedro Candido tightly by the arm, gun at his back. He wasn't about to take any chances on him running or even making any noise. Plus, how else could he follow him, in all this darkness? He stumbled—

they both stumbled. All they needed now was to alert the bandits by falling over some rocks and shooting off one of the guns.

"Can they see us from there?" Bezerra whispered.

Pedro Candido said they couldn't, the camp was enclosed by big rocks. Bezerra lit his little lantern. Even that bit of light made him feel less like a man stepping into the abyss.

"This way," said Pedro Candido. The path got steep here. The Hill of the Damned? Bezerra wondered.

They climbed on.

XXV

The fire was low now, and Lampião was conferring with Sereno, planning their departure, before dawn. They wouldn't cross the river, but instead head south and then west, and meet up with Corisco before they got to the Raso.

Maria Bonita picked up the box of cigarettes. "Come on," she whispered to Cila.

Cila put down her cup—she'd been drinking too much, she realized when she got to her feet. It was the Cinzano that Pedro Candido had brought, along with the whiskey, and they'd been mixing it. Bad but good. She nearly fell over when she took her first step.

But then she found her legs, and followed Maria to the edge of the hideout, farthest from Lampião's tent. A couple of truants—that's how Maria liked to smoke, as far away from Lampião as possible.

The two women climbed up on a high rock, facing out, toward the river. They sat down close together and Maria struck a match. In the flash of light, they caught each other's eye, and smiled. "Just one," Maria whispered.

Cila nodded, happy, too. Happy that Maria was happy. Because if she was happy, then Lampião was happy, and if Lampião was happy, it was like a warm soft blanket over them all.

Which was how it used to be, and how it could be—she had almost forgotten, how good it was when it was good.

And what could be better? Sitting with friends who were almost brothers and sisters, and a fire and meat and salt and drink, music even, and dancing. Stars or no stars, moon or no moon. Another night there'd be stars again, and a good moon. And they would eat without working and then rise to the music and bow to each other and dance into the night.

And then later they'd go into tents with men they'd chosen for themselves—how many women in the Sertão could say that? How many fell into arms they loved to have around them, how many ever made love in their lives, despite their strong safe houses?

Or maybe because of them, Maria was saying. Maybe what it took for love was no house, no safety—

"What's that?" Cila interrupted.

"What?"

"Over there." She pointed down to the Hill of Perdidos.

"Where?"

"Must be coming up from the river."

"What?"

"Lights, I saw them—"

"What lights?"

Cila got to her feet, a frown on her face—a nice enough face, Maria was thinking, but annoying, too, the way she broke into a person's thoughts like that. Cila, with all her prayers and amulets and special chants.

"Have another cigarette"—she held them out to her, just to shut her up, so she herself could sit there quietly with the last of her own cigarette.

Cila took it, and sat back down. "It was probably nothing."

Then, a minute later, "Look! There they are again!"

Maria didn't see anything, and she was suddenly sick of Cila. She was a fool, a stranger who would never be her sister, never know the blue mountain or the rise and fall of the land outside their house like her sister did.

"Fireflies," she said to her.

"Are you sure?"

Yeah, she was sure.

"Those aren't lanterns?" Cila was peering into the darkness.

"No, just fireflies." She stubbed out her cigarette and got to her feet. Why was she out here smoking tonight anyway, when Lampião was going to be in the tent? Maybe he was there already, waiting to take down her dress, over her shoulders, the way he liked it, and kiss her neck. Start with her neck.

"We should probably go to sleep now, since we're leaving early." She kissed Cila on both cheeks and walked off.

Cila hesitated, looking still at the point down the hill where she'd seen the flickering lights. If the police were coming up from the river, wouldn't they have lanterns?

She was trying to remember if she'd seen any fireflies here before, at this time of year, in the dark and the damp.

On the other hand, Maria Bonita was older and smarter than she was. She'd been around, and now that Cila looked again, she didn't see them anymore, whatever they were.

She walked back up the streambed a bit, up above, to where she and Zé Sereno had pitched their tent. She'd tell him about the lights anyway, and he could go have a look, see if they were fireflies or not.

But when she crawled into their tent, Sereno was already dead asleep—all that liquor. She shook him gently. "Zé," she whispered, but he didn't even grunt, didn't even turn over. If she wanted to ask him now about what she'd seen on the Hill of the Lost, she'd have to shake him hard, and maybe even throw some cold water on his face.

And was it worth it, to make him lose the little bit of sleep that was all he'd get that night, since they were leaving before daybreak? Especially if it turned out that all she'd woken him for was to look at some fireflies.

And then in the morning Maria would laugh at her and say that she'd told her so. And she'd be right. She had—told her so.

Cila crawled in next to Sereno. It wasn't like she wasn't tipsy herself, maybe even seeing things. It was all that mixing, the whiskey and Cinzano, though no one could say it hadn't been fun.

She said her prayers, kissed Sereno, and climbed in beside him, and slept "with the angels" that night.

XXVI

It occurred to Bezerra that if Pedro Candido ran now, into the darkness, he could probably get over to the bandits and bring them down on the police, and Bezerra wouldn't even know which way to point the machine gun. He tightened his hold on Pedro, but all it would take was one good twist for Pedro to get away.

But Pedro didn't run, and then, there in the light of the lantern, they could make out his mother's house, sleeping, locked and barred, darker than the darkness, hemmed in by a stand of *quixabeira* trees, all of them dripping wet from the fog.

Pedro Candido stopped suddenly and turned to them. "What if they're in there?"

"What?"

"They could be inside. Sometimes they come down, the whole band, all of them . . ."

Bezerra had to keep himself from reeling. Was it possible? Not that the bandits could be there—of course that was possible, probable even, on a night like this, now that he thought about it.

But possible that this quivering wretch of a sneak Pedro Candido, who'd been trembling like a schoolgirl all night, had, with one stroke, turned the tables? Had he been leading them into the mouth of the wolf the whole time?

"Why didn't you tell me? So I could have brought the rest of the troops?" Bezerra stammered, just to say something. To live a moment longer.

"I forgot," Pedro Candido answered. He was still trembling, though with fear or laughter, Bezerra didn't know.

He took a breath and told himself that he, like all men, had been born to die. He sent Chico Ferreira around to cover the back of the house, and loaded a clip of fifty shots into his machine gun. If he was going, at least he'd take some of them for company.

He said one last prayer, commended himself to his saints, and gave Pedro Candido a shove—why drag it out? "Go call your brother."

Pedro Candido walked up to the front of the house. The place was as dark as a tomb, not a flicker of lights from behind the shutters. Either your run-of-the-mill country house with people who'd gone to sleep with the sun, or a nest of bandits, watching him scratch his nose through the sights of their guns.

Pedro Candido stooped down—Bezerra almost shot him—and picked up some pebbles from under the trees. He threw them lightly at one of the windows.

He whispered hoarsely, "Durval!"

From inside came an answering whisper, "Already?"

Bezerra's heart leapt at that. Did the boy think they were the bandits? If so, then they weren't inside—unless he was deceiving them, too?

"Come outside!" Pedro Candido whispered.

"I'm coming, I'm coming," and the door opened. Pedro Candido's seventeen-year-old brother stepped out, with a small lantern in his hand.

It took all of Bezerra's years of discipline to keep from blasting him to kingdom come as he stood in the doorway of his mother's house, squinting into the darkness.

"Did you bring it?" the boy asked.

Bring what? Bezerra wondered, suddenly a little less terrified. This kid apparently thought they were the bandits, bringing him something. They were therefore not inside, nor was this to be the exact spot and hour of Bezerra's death, though he kept the machine gun trained on the door.

Durval came out the door, then stopped, sensing something.

"Listen, Durval," whispered Pedro Candido, "it's Lieutenant Bezerra who's with me."

It was too dark to see the boy's mouth drop open, but Bezerra swore he could hear it. Durval stood there with his hand on the door, trying to grasp the notion that the stars had changed places in the sky. He looked back toward the house, which wouldn't do him any good now, unless it was crawling with bandits—but Bezerra would almost bet his life now, had bet his life, that it wasn't.

Finally Durval found his voice. "Cold tonight," he stammered.

Now Bezerra stepped forward. "At this time of year, it usually is. Cold, this time of year."

The boy nodded.

"Tell me something. You were just there, in the hideout"—not a question.

Durval nodded.

"Are they still there?"

No answer. Chico Ferreira came forward with Pedro Candido, who didn't lift his head. Spoke to the ground: "Remember how he said we weren't supposed to die for him?"

Bezerra lowered his gun and put his hand on the boy's arm.

"Who's there?"

A pause. A breath. "The captain and his men."

Bezerra's heart skipped. He'd known, but now he knew. "What were you doing up there?"

"I went to pick up my mother's sewing machine—I lent it without asking her, and they promised they'd give it back today. But when I got there, they were still sewing, so they told me to come back in the morning and they'd leave it at the foot of the *macambeira* trees."

"So now we'll go back and get your mother's sewing machine together," said Bezerra.

The boy laughed. "Virgin Maria! No way I'm going with you!"

Bezerra took his arm—Durval was young, a baby,

in fact. But key, at the moment, a key baby. "Of course you're going—how could you not go?"

He led Durval away from the house. "You take the other one," he said to Chico Ferreira, and they made their way back down the path, to the troops by the river.

PEDRO CANDIDO AND his brother were now in the hands of their enemies, who were not at this point nearly so dangerous as their friends. The soldiers might shoot them, but if the bandits caught them now, they'd skin them alive. And worse than that would be having to look them in the face. Just this afternoon, Lampião had paid him so well, so beautifully, for the supplies he'd brought, and with such an open hand—Christ, everything Pedro Candido had, his house, his shop, his horse, his cart, was thanks to Lampião's generosity. Which extended not only to him, but to his brother, too, his whole family.

"They're divided into groups," Pedro Candido started explaining to Bezerra. "Lampião and his little group are in the curve by the riverbed; Zé Sereno and his group are above, under some *quixabeira* trees. Luis Pedro's group is under the *umbu* tree, by the big rocks." Pedro Candido and Durval would show them the way when they got closer.

Fine, Bezerra was thinking. Not thinking, actually—this thing was now rolling, and it would work out how it worked out. They took Durval and rejoined the rest by the river, and he divided his men into four groups: one under Chico Ferreira, who would go in below; one under Aniceto, who would come in from the top; one with Old Mané; and another with him, who together with Mané would take the center. He cleared his throat—probably couldn't have uttered a word half an hour earlier, but now he was nothing but calm.

He addressed his men, in a whisper but clear: "We go in absolute silence, you all know that. We'll have to crawl in, but with no noise. No missteps, no backfires this time. If you do it right, you'll be rich men in the morning, rich and famous, but it has to be right, which means everything right. No one shoots until I do. That will be your signal to start and never stop shooting. Understand?"

They understood.

"No one shoots lying down—anyone who does gets shot by me. Crouching, yes, but lying down, no. You've got to be able to move fast. And one last thing," said Bezerra, with a silent nod to the bandit Volta Seca, "no one shoots high. Only cowards shoot high, but you're the bravest men in Brazil tonight. So shoot low and hit your mark! Afterwards, I'm going to look around, and if I see any bullets in the trees, I swear to you I'll hold an inquest and hang someone—you know I will, don't you?"

More nods. You could still smell the fear, but it was mixed now with excitement. They were starting to feel it, that there actually was a chance here, that maybe they'd be the ones to do it.

"So now we're going to see who's more man—Lampião or me!" Bezerra held out his hand—the men grabbed it, one by one. Hoarse whispers: "Or me!" "Or me!" "Or me!"

"God be with us!"

"God be with us!" echoed Pedro Candido, the most passionate among them. Having, Bezerra congratulated himself, the most to lose.

"Let's go," said Bezerra, for the last time that night. Pedro Candido started leading them up the nearest hill, the Morro dos Perdidos, whose name had scared Bezerra earlier. But Bezerra wouldn't think of that again until it was over, and by then it wouldn't matter anymore.

XXVII

Zé Sereno stirred, turned back over. Stirred again, sat up. Thought he'd heard a donkey.

He listened. Nothing. His head was pounding—Christ, he shouldn't have had that Cinzano, not on top of the whiskey.

There it was—more braying. Sereno sat up, listening for the dogs. If there was anything amiss, they'd bark, his dog and Lampião's, and then he'd have to go out there with his gun.

But the dogs didn't bark—maybe they were the ones teasing the donkeys. Sereno listened, but didn't hear anything more.

He wouldn't mind a little more sleep before they headed off—soon. Couldn't be more than an hour or two. Wasn't someone on watch anyway? Wouldn't they pick it up, if something was going on with the donkeys? Unless they'd fallen asleep with the same bad head that he had.

Still, it had been fun, all that drinking, and the carrying on. Just what they needed, and good to see Lampião again with some light in his eye. Good to talk to him about where they were going, like old times.

It'd be good to move on, too, but till then, till it was time to pull down the tents, pack up the gear, load the donkeys, and strike out again, Sereno would be damned if he wouldn't grab a few more winks.

He put his hand under Cila's shirt and closed his eyes again.

XXVIII

It was around four o'clock in the morning, maybe later. Still silent. Pedro Candido's brother had led the police up over the hill, instead of bringing them in from the side near the river. "It's safer this way, less chance they'll see us."

The bandits were still sleeping. Not a sound from the camp. Chico Ferreira was drunk and threatening trouble—"Let me at them! I'm through waiting!"

Bezerra turned the machine gun on him—"Silence, or you're the first to die!"

Pedro Candido had already explained about the three small creeks that led into the main stream, and now Bezerra slightly changed the plan. He himself, with one of the machine guns and ten men, would come down above the stream, where Lampião was sleeping; Aniceto with his ten would close in from the top; and Chico Ferreira and Old Mané would flank the bandits with the other twenty-six, divided in two groups, from the other side. Which should work, if all went well. Everything.

They crouched down and started moving in. Just above, they'd practically tripped over three donkeys that were tied outside the camp. One of the donkeys brayed— "We're dead!" the soldiers whispered, which was true, figured Bezerra. They'd have to fight now, before they were in position, and the bandits would kill half of them and the rest would live to have been "betrayed by a donkey," a good joke—but he'd rushed to the animals and managed to quiet them, and to his amazement, the bandits didn't respond.

Were they still sleeping? Hadn't they heard the donkeys? And then it came to him that maybe they'd already left, gotten wind and lit out, leaving their donkeys. They'd done it before and would probably do it again, and all this was for nothing—but then he heard something. Not much—a match striking, he realized. And then a candle was lit, in one of the tents.

Holy Christ. Jesus Maria! Someone came out—and there he was, Lampião in the flesh. Lampião! Five meters away.

"Don't shoot!" Bezerra rasped.

Lampião got down on his knees—they could hear him praying. Bezerra almost forgot what he was doing. Just crouched there, fascinated, listening, watching. "*With the light of day, I see my Lord, Jesus Christ, and the Virgin Maria. I walk with the Lord and nothing can touch me . . .*"

Was it true, Bezerra wondered, even now? Lampião— Bezerra wouldn't kill him. Just take him in, and get him a pardon, once the dust cleared, and then they could sit and talk for the rest of their years.

Lampião was his hero. He'd admit it now. Lampião had

been the man in all their lives—for all their lives. It was over for him now, but that was just a law of nature, just the end of everything that starts, and nothing to do with Lampião himself. It wasn't as if he would lose a battle—would never lose a fight with the police. He was betrayed, finally, that was all. Nothing to do with his strategy.

And he would end unbeaten—taken but never beaten. There was still no better fighter than Lampião. What Bezerra would have given to fight under a man like that. They'd been on opposing sides, but it could have been different. One small twist of fate, and they'd have been colleagues. Friends.

A woman came out of the tent, and kissed him lightly, behind the ear, on the neck. Ran her fingers through his long hair. He smiled at her. Maria Bonita! She had a basin in her hand, an old cheese tin, it looked like. For water—to wash her face. He would watch Maria Bonita wash her face!

Someone came up to them, one of the bandits, with a cup of water. He handed it to Lampião, who took it and raised it to his lips.

And then a shot rang out, and another, a third, a fourth—Bezerra watched almost uncomprehending as Lampião fell to the ground.

"Don't shoot!" he shouted, but it was too late. There was chaos all around him. Lampião was down. Bezerra opened fire with his machine gun and let it roar.

XXIX

What amazed her most was how it had come out of nowhere. She'd always thought that it would happen in a gunfight, and there'd be a moment between them, one last look. But there was no look, just a terrible thunder, and one moment, he'd been there, cup at his lips, and the next, he was lying in the dirt, the cup on the ground beside him.

He was dead. She knew it the second she saw him, even before she saw him, even before he was hit. She'd recognized the shot. She was just about to start down to the pools in the rocks just below, to get some water, when she heard that shot, then a long silence, and knew it was the end of the world, in smoke and fire.

She saw him fall. It took a long time—he went up and then he went down, slowly, soft. Cup still at his lips—that was good. There was something good about it, a good death, holy even. Prayers in the air, and a cup at his lip. Holy water. Lampião. She was running to him when it hit her, too, whatever it was. The end of the world. Another shot in the back.

Wham—she felt it, but not like the last one. She'd felt that one because Lampião was there beside her, but now that he was gone, and she was alone and beyond all help, she didn't feel a thing. She, too, was untouchable. The shot slammed her down, doubled her up, but she didn't really feel it. Nor did it stop her moving toward Lampião.

Her life had become clear and simple, with only one thing to do now—to close his eyes. Touch his hand. Whisper good-bye. He'd died just like he'd said, "at the mouth of a rifle." Which was good, because it was one thing to say it and another to do it, and now that he'd done it, they could all see that he'd meant what he'd said. He was brave, and he'd died brave—no prison cell for him, no new life or second thoughts. Just Lampião through and through, in life and now in death.

"Lampião!" she was crying. Though what she'd whisper in his ear, when she got there, was, "Virgulino." His Christian name, her husband, her love, just as if they were two old people, dying in their beds.

Another shot—from the front this time, into her stomach. Now it was harder to move, and it occurred to her that she, too, was dying at the mouth of a gun. She hadn't been sure she'd be brave enough to do it, but here she was—shot and down, and brave enough to die this morning.

So that's how it would be—"Lampião and Maria Bonita." The headlines all over the country. They'd finally done it, the monkeys—but which ones? Didn't matter, just so long as it wasn't Mané Neto, just so that laugh stayed with Lampião. Not that he cared anymore, but still, just for the record. But who was it? Whose men? And who had led them in here? Pedro Candido? Had to be.

But why? Only yesterday he'd brought them more supplies, and Lampião had paid him well, and they'd shaken hands. He'd wanted to spend another night with them, but he'd told them his wife was about to have a baby, and so he went off.

"*Até logo*," Pedro Candido had said. Until the next time.

She got to Lampião and grabbed his wrist—still warm! Last night he'd taken her in his arms again, for the first time in almost a month. July—his month of renunciation, when he renounced everything, even her. But last night, he'd gone into the tent with her instead of out to the rocks to pray. Took her in his arms, and they were Lampião and Maria Bonita again.

But July hadn't been over, and he was right. He did die in July. She wanted to kiss his lips, but someone grabbed her, one of the police or soldiers, whatever they were—"Where's your money, bandit?"

"Don't kill me!" she screamed, or someone did. If it was her, she didn't mean it. She was dead already. She lifted her head a bit—there was so much shooting she couldn't see much through the smoke and fire, but there was Pedro Candido, running off into the bush, and Durval, too, crouched behind a rock, tears streaming down his face.

So even if Pedro Candido had done it, maybe it hadn't been by choice? Maybe someone had betrayed him first, gone to the police and talked, but who?

And then she saw him, off to the side—Joca the Cuckold! A born betrayer, and the worst part of it was that he wasn't even one of Lampião's guys, he was Corisco's. Lampião had never trusted Joca, didn't like the shift in his eyes, but Corisco didn't worry about it. Not even when he heard that one of his boys was fooling around with Joca's wife.

Lampião wouldn't have stood for anything like that. His allies' women were strictly off-limits, and if one of his boys had even looked twice at anyone's wife, he'd have kicked him out, or shot him if he had to, knowing that something like that led straight to something like this.

But Corisco had let it go, and now he was drinking coffee across the river, while Lampião was lying dead in the dust. And no wonder he saw the place as a rat trap, since it was his rat running around on the opposite shore.

My God, my God! It didn't seem fair, didn't seem right—she saw Luis Pedro, running out, over the top of the rocks. "Luis Pedro!" she screamed. "Lampião's dead!"

He stopped, turned. "Where are you, Maria?" He came running back toward her, but there was another burst of the machine guns, and then she never saw him again.

A soldier yanked her hair back and held a knife to her throat.

"Don't kill me!" she cried to him, and "I surrender!" and "Please!"—words somehow coming out on their own. She'd already died, just hadn't stopped talking. This pleading for her life was like a chicken running around with its head cut off.

So Cila had been right, then—about the lights? She must have seen them coming, seen their lights, and she, Maria, in her impatience, her disregard, had lost the chance to save them all. If she'd even mentioned it to Lampião, he'd have decamped right then and there.

Why hadn't she mentioned it to Lampião? But if she'd told him, he would have run out of the tent, and what she wanted was for him to stay, to take her in his arms. And hadn't that been the bargain—death in the morning for one more night of love in the tent?

But she should have told him—how could she not have told him? And even if he'd been unable to resist, too, even if he'd have been willing to risk much for those few hours last night together, at least if she'd mentioned the lights he'd have been alerted and ready to fight, instead of standing still, cup at lips, a perfect target, to be shot to pieces.

And who was on guard, and what about the dog? Why hadn't the dog barked? Lampião's dog, Guaraní, which he'd raised from a pup and fed by hand. Why hadn't he barked? Was it the mist? It was wet last night, such thick fog that it was almost rain—had the dog taken shelter over by the rocks, on the other side?

Or was it destiny after all? That falling star? "*No one escapes his destiny.*" Was that how life worked? Was it written?

And had they been written, too, then? Her and him, her and the shoemaker, all of it?

"Lampião!" They'd been together eight years—a lifetime, in retrospect. So one more miracle. Did people know that—how a day could be a year when you're on the run?

"Where's your money, you pestilent bandit?"

"I don't have any—I don't know . . ." They wanted her money, but she couldn't remember where it was. She had her gold, her necklaces, her rings—theirs, now. Even if she was alive and walking away, they could have it all.

"For the love of God—don't kill me!" What Lampião had feared most was betrayal—"*If I lay down my arms, they'll shoot me like a dog.*" But he hadn't died like a dog, even though they'd shot him. He'd been a man, drinking his morning water, saying his morning prayers. A man who'd lived and now died, and made his name in the stars.

"Lampião." She called him Virgulino, but his name was Lampião.

And her name was Maria Bonita. That had always meant that she would die like this someday. *Yes!* she'd still say to him that first day, with her smile. It was still *Yes*, even now with this soldier's knife at her throat.

And the truth was, he never went down in battle. They'd tricked him, betrayed him, found a betrayer of a dog so low that he'd bite the hand that fed him, and then they finally managed to pull off an ambush and shoot him from behind a rock—which was something else entirely from beating him in battle. Lampião was dead, but he'd never been beaten.

And now he never would be. They'd never beat him.

She saw Sereno run by, with some of the soldiers—he'd picked up one of their hats and put it on his head.

"I'm with you!" he was shouting, as he ran among them and escaped—how clever, how lucky! "I'm with you!" he shouted to the soldiers, and they let him go by. And then—she saw it!—when he got to the top, he turned and fired a whole clip at them, then jumped down into the draw and disappeared.

Sereno! She could hear some of the soldiers shouting for Cila—"Come to me, Cila!"

"No, come to me!"

Don't go to any of them, Cila! she was trying to shout now. *Run up, over the top, and follow Sereno, and get away. Carry it on*—not that they could, without Lampião. Even when the men took groups of their own and went off, it was always to come back and tell Lampião. What they'd done, how they'd done it, and get his laugh, his nod, that eye. One eye.

"What's your name, bandit?"

They weren't talking to her, they were talking to Elétrico, who was hit, but not dead. Maybe they'd take him alive.

"Tell me your name," one of the soldiers was saying.

"Ask your wife!" Elétrico spit out. "She knows my name!"

Maria Bonita laughed. Elétrico! He'd always sworn, too, that he'd die with Lampião.

"I'm giving you a chance, bandit! I'll guarantee your life, take you in myself!"

"You think a cuckold like you takes a man like me?" returned Elétrico. His last words. The guy shot him.

She laughed again. Someone pulled her hair. "Are you laughing at me, you bandit whore?"

Of course she was laughing at them, Elétrico was laughing, they were bandits who lived and died laughing at the police. And it was funny, too, that they'd never beaten Lampião, and now they never would, the cowards, the monkeys! They could sneak up on him in the night, but they could never beat him.

"A bandit'll die, but he won't run," Lampião had said, and now, she could say it, too. "She." *A bandit will die, but she won't run.* Her life was over, but looking back, she couldn't have wished for even another day. She'd had so many—so many days.

All those days in the beginning, as a girl with her sister, dancing with cowboys and dreaming over Lampião's picture in the paper—she could still smell that dust! The dust of home, and then those bitter days with the shoemaker, when she lay in the hammock and thought she was wasting away, but what she was really doing was slowly building up the courage, night by night, to turn her back and leave.

Six years, it had taken—nothing, in the end. And then came the shining days when she rode off with Lampião, and couldn't believe her luck, couldn't believe what life had brought her, and what, she could say it now, she'd been bold enough to take.

Because it isn't everyone who does it. Most people

don't—most people live long lives wishing, but when they get their one chance, they turn away.

But she'd said yes to Lampião—"Yes!" Always yes, and if she hadn't, she'd be alive tomorrow, sweeping the shoemaker's floor.

Suffering and happiness. "And if we suffer, in return, we have such good times." Such good times—and such bad times, but none of them sweeping the shoemaker's floor.

Not that that wasn't good, too. Calm. Quiet. Safe. Good, too.

But not grandeur, not passion, not Lampião. And not Maria Bonita. He'd named her that, Maria the Beautiful, he'd loved her, she'd loved him, and they'd lived a thousand years. And they were dying together, so she wouldn't have to bury him. That would have been worse than dying—watching the clods of dirt fall on his body.

Dying turned out to be easy. She looked up to see if the black sisters knew yet. But of course they knew, they must have known even as the soldiers were creeping in over the hills. They were already circling and soon would be down, once the smoke cleared and the soldiers went away, they'd fly in from all over, maybe from her own backyard. Wouldn't even have to cross the river—just swoop down, in those big circles, and carry her home. Him, too. Mix their flesh together, a bite from her, one from him, and they'd be together again.

She'd been horrified by buzzards, but she was glad of them now, glad they were coming to take care of them.

Bury them their own way, like the Indians, the first ones out here. Though there was no one to wrap her in a hammock, which would be nice now. Soft, and kind.

The soldier was pulling his knife out. "Save me, Nossa Senhora!" she cried. How many times had she called on Her, and how many times had She answered? *How do I thank Her?* wondered Maria Bonita. But now she couldn't even lift her hand to make the sign of the cross.

Still she could pray. *Now and at the hour of our death*—she'd been saying those words all her life, but they had never been her words, always words for something far in the distance. Stretching out like the sands in the Raso, the beautiful sands, those vistas that had no end. Like her life, till this morning.

She was almost thirty, Lampião was forty-one, the Bible said, "Threescore and ten," which they were—together. More proof, another sign. Their mystical connection.

The hour of our death. She tried to picture the Virgin Mary, or the kind face of Jesus on the cross, but what came to her was the bleeding heart of Jesus, pierced with daggers. As in the pictures, on every wall in the whole Sertão, where it hung beside the picture of Padre Cícero.

The Sacred Heart, pierced and bleeding—how beautiful it was. Did other people love it, too? The way they did in the Sertão? It spoke so true, so clearly to them, showed them what had been asked before, told of a martyrdom not so different from their own. A martyrdom that gave them hope, every time they fell to their knees to pray for rains that didn't come.

Though they always did come, the rains, now that she thought about it. Maybe not in time, not when people wanted or needed them, but they always came, in the end. That was what she was just realizing, that the rains always come in the end—when a soldier in Chico Ferreira's troop, from across the river, pulled his knife and cut her throat.

Epilogue

Cila was still in her tent when the shooting started, and her first thought was, *So! Fireflies nothing!* It *had* been the police, she'd been right, Maria was wrong—she grabbed what she could, two canteens, one filled with water and one with jewels, couldn't find her shoes, and ran out into the smoke and chaos. Her brother lay dead, right at the door of her tent. She took his gun from his hand and looked around, desperate.

She couldn't see through the fog and the smoke from all the shooting, didn't know which way to run. She gathered from the shouting that Lampião was dead, but what about Sereno? Was he lying there dead, too, beside Lampião? He'd gone down there to pray with him—had they shot him? She was alive because she'd been groggy and stayed in their tent, but what about Sereno? And which way should she run?

She took cover behind a nearby rock, but some soldiers were nearby and saw her. "Come to me, Cila!" they shouted.

"No, to me!"

Would they kill her? She'd heard their songs—"*From Sereno I'll take Cila, / From Lampião, Maria Bonita . . .*" but she knew from the screaming down below that they'd killed Maria. She'd be next.

But how to get away from them? She couldn't see her way out, and they were calling to her, her brother was dead, Lampião was dead, Sereno was probably dead, and she was about to give herself up when Criança, Dulce, and Enedina came running past her—"Up this way, Cila!" and she went.

She followed them, up through the rocks and cactus, barefoot, but she would only realize that afterward. At that point, all she knew was that she was half-crawling, half-running for her life, with Enedina right behind her.

Enedina tripped once—"Save me, Nossa Senhora!"—but Cila picked her up and they kept running, they were almost to the top of the hill, and then they'd be over and away, when there was a shot, and a scream from Enedina, and then something warm and terrible splattered onto Cila's back.

She didn't looked back, didn't turn, she knew what was running down her back. But she kept running—there was nothing else to do. Another one of the boys, Candieiro, was up ahead, shot, too, but just in the arm.

"I'm dying, Cila!"

"Get up!" She pulled him to his feet, grabbed his gun,

and kept running. She put her canteen to her lips, for a gulp of water—her throat had never been so parched. But it turned out that she'd grabbed the wrong canteen, the sugar instead of the water, and when she swallowed some of that, it made it worse.

She gagged, but kept running with the others who'd made it—she heard later that Aniceto hadn't come in to flank like he was supposed to, had turned tail and crept back down to the river instead. This saved her life, and the twenty others' who escaped that way that day.

But Cila didn't know that at the time. She just ran with the few who were with her, until they were out of earshot of the shooting, until there was silence all around them, and then crawled into the underbrush and collapsed. There were four of them together—*The last ones left alive*, they thought, and didn't have words for it yet, or even tears. They just lay there, breathing in and out.

But a little later they heard a distinctive series of shots—Sereno's signals, calling them together, was it possible? So he was alive? And that's when Cila started to cry. She ran, sobbing, all the way to meet him, and he told them about the soft hat, how he'd traded his hat for one of the soldiers', and then had run right through them and lived to tell the tale.

Cila, too—lived long, too long, long enough to forswear her past and fall into that vast, sad migration down to São Paulo, the dank metropolis that had no beginning and no end, that first doubled and then tripled in size as displaced country folk like them flooded in, no longer cowboys and bandits who could smell the rain, but maids and street guards, working for people who understood nothing of their lives.

That was after Sereno was captured, and Corisco killed. And that was pretty much the end, for the bandits, for the culture, for the whole time and place. It's still there, in that you can fly, then drive, to see the village where Lampião was born, the town where Maria Bonita lived with the shoemaker, her house, even, and the little clearing—surprisingly small—by the river where they were killed.

But as far as the Sertão they loved so much, with its vast emptiness, its colonels and bandits and police, intertwined forever, that pretty much ended when Lampião was shot.

AS FOR THE POLICE, when the smoke cleared that day in the grotto of Angicos, where the streambed curved around and leveled out a bit, eleven bandits lay dead in twenty-five square meters of blood-soaked dust, and the soldiers were already coming to blows over the spoils. Old Mané, who had killed Luis Pedro, was cutting off his hands, to get at his rings. When Chico Ferreira commanded him to stop, Mané leveled his gun at his officer. That's when Bida advised Durval to run home to his mother's, to be out of range of "the devil's own fight" that would start now that the soldiers were going at it over the gold.

Durval testified afterward that he picked up the last of Lampião's watermelon and walked home slurping it, half-dazed. His mother and sisters had heard the shots and were already crying. Pedro Candido had come back, and had told them he was dead. When he walked in, they fell to their knees, screaming. They took him for a ghost.

Which he wasn't, he said afterward, only thanks to Bezerra, who'd managed, on the strength of his machine gun, to maintain a rough discipline. Bezerra himself had been shot in the thigh in the first round of fire, by one of his own men, in fact, but he'd tied up the wound and kept going, particularly once he saw that Lampião was down.

He was almost overcome, Bezerra would write later, by a euphoria that came in waves and kept swelling. He'd killed Lampião; he was the man who'd led the forces who had killed Lampião. He had brought down the giant. That made him, Lieutenant João Bezerra of the Piranhas police force, a hero, the bravest, strongest, toughest policeman and soldier in all of Brazil.

He took Lampião's pack for himself, and then turned his guns on his own men. The rest of the loot was "official," he declared, and he would kill any man who tried to keep it, hang any man who shot one of his colleagues, and swore on his soul to divide it among them, fair and square, once they got back to Piranhas.

But he was talking to soldiers, not schoolboys, and though they lowered their guns, they continued to stuff jewels, gold, silver, knives, and guns in their boots, down their pants, and under rocks and trees, well marked, so they could sneak back later and get them.

Not that any of it mattered in the end. Even the one

who got Maria Bonita's pack, filled with enough gold and jewels to change a man's fate, bought himself a farm, but didn't know how to run it, and lost it before the year was up. Sold it for nothing, and found himself, despite having cut the throat of Maria Bonita, just as poor as he'd been before.

They all were, except for Old Mané. When he killed Luis Pedro, he was so astounded by the amount of loot in his pack that he took him for Lampião at first. He cut off his hands when he couldn't pull off the rings, stuffed them in the pack. And when Bezerra demanded they throw the bandits' packs onto the common pile, he threw in his own khaki pack instead, which still sits in a museum in Salvador, along with Lampião's.

But Luis Pedro's pack Old Mané kept, with its kilos of gold, pounds of sterling, thirty-one wedding rings, a gold watch on the wrist he'd severed, and all those jeweled rings, still on the fingers. He wired his father as soon as he got back to Piranhas: *Buy a ranch*. His father did, and they lived out their lives in prosperity.

Relative prosperity. All it meant out here was that they were no longer dirt-poor.

"CUT OFF THEIR heads," Bezerra ordered that day at the hideout in Angicos. They needed proof—how many times had Lampião been killed before? The soldiers pulled out their machetes and worked in teams—one held up a head by the hair, and the other hacked. It took both hands. Some of the bandits were still moving, and thirty years later, Old Mané could still shake his head and remark on "how hard it is to kill a man."

Bezerra's leg was hurting, and he limped among the soldiers, trying not to slip on the blood. "Which one is this?" he asked one of the men, who was holding up a head.

"Him," the soldier answered. That is to say, Lampião.

Unrecognizable. Distorted. "No, it isn't," said Bezerra.

"Put horns on my head, then!" the soldier answered. "Wouldn't I know? I was one of his suppliers! I served him faithfully for two years!"

Bezerra made no reply. He'd opened the gates of hell, as he said later—what did he expect? The smell was already coming up, and the buzzards weighing down the trees, "like black fruit," someone said. They put the heads in some empty kerosene cans they found there, threw in the bandits' salt, and then staggered back across the river. People were lining the banks. They'd heard the shots all up and down the river and were waiting to see who'd killed whom.

The news beat Bezerra down the river, and he and his men were greeted in Piranhas with fireworks. His first telegram was to Lucena, who telegraphed to the president, Vargas, and after a bit of recuperation from his leg wound, Bezerra led his men on a triumphal march with the heads to the coast. The initial disbelief—"Comrade Lampião is accustomed to dying," was Corisco's initial reaction—gave way in the face of this graphic proof, but even so there were soon reports of sightings, of his ghost, if not himself.

Because it wasn't as if the loss wasn't felt. The Sertão without Lampião seemed a smaller place. As the street minstrels sang:

> The guitar is crying,
> crying with reason!
> He was betrayed, sold,
> the Giant of the Sertão!

A NEWSPAPER IN Rio regretted that "there's no place for roving bandits in a Brazil of schools, airplanes and Fords." A poet sold handmade books in village squares:

> He was dangerous and deadly,
> Virgulino, Lampião,
> But he was—we don't deny it,
> In our hearts, the truth lives on—
> The most perfect portrait
> Of our wild land, our Sertão.

Less wild, now, and less, somehow, their land. It was easier now for the "foreigners" to come in, Brazilians from the coast, from the south, with their roads which opened the place to their land grabs and their "secret ballots," which meant only that the crooks were no longer local, but strangers from afar. Lampião had stood against all that. But Lampião was dead.

And so was the Cangaço, the homegrown nomadic banditry. Corisco fought on for a year or so, but no one mistook him for Lampião. He was a bandit, not a culture, fighting for himself, not for a way of life. Once he was killed, whoever was still alive, Sereno, Labareda, a few of the women, turned themselves in, served their time, and came out dazed and reduced, looking small without their hats and gun belts, like the Indians in their first set of cast-off white men's clothes.

As for the rest of them, it went the way these things usually do. Bezerra was promoted, made captain, and wrote a book filled with tall tales—him smelling the bandits' coffee, Lampião falling into Maria Bonita's arms, Luis Pedro closing his eyes. He went back and put up a cross at the site of the killings.

Though after that, life didn't go quite as he'd expected. He got restless in Piranhas—without Lampião, there was nothing much for him to do there anymore. He moved back to Pernambuco, where he and Lampião had come from, and spent the rest of his life telling everyone who would listen how much they had in common, he and Lampião. Now and then he was invited to march in a parade.

As for the traitors—traitor, really, for Pedro Candido was only a pawn in the game. And though one might wish he'd done something different—most of all, run when he had that chance, the first time the police came around—still, it's hard to blame him. As it was, his life was completely disrupted. He had to flee his house, his store, his family, and go underground as long as Corisco was alive.

But Joca the Cuckold is another story. The active traitor, who rode into town on a mule with one spur on his boot, to tell the world that he was not the little man he looked to be, but "the cause of Lampião's death"—if there was any justice, any vengeance to be hoped for, one might seek it here.

In vain. Because when Corisco got his hands on Joca, a few days later, Joca not only denied his own role but blamed a farmer down the road, and Corisco went over there like a madman and took the unsuspecting family by storm. Refused to listen to their pleas for justice or even mercy, killed them all, men, women, and children, and left the place running with blood.

"You'll have to leave justice to God," a judge in rural Pernambuco had advised Lampião, twenty years earlier. Joca the Cuckold had eluded retribution from the bandits, but a strange thing happened after the massacre of those innocents he'd falsely accused. First he stopped showing up at any of his old haunts, and then people starting hearing that he couldn't talk anymore. Something was wrong with his tongue, and he died soon after, of a terrible cancer of the mouth.

AND AS FOR Pedro Candido, once Corisco was killed he'd ventured back to Remanso, back to the shop and house that he'd bought with Lampião's money. And as one year followed another, he came to feel that life had carried him along, too, to a certain safety.

But one dark night, when the moon was "sad," weak, waning—unlucky, people called it, like the bandits' last moon—Pedro Candido was out late, drinking, drunk, and decided to have a little fun with the half-witted boy he heard coming along the path. He hid behind a bush, and when the boy passed, he jumped out, hooting, "I'm the *lobishomem*!," the werewolf, just to scare him a little, but the kid pulled a knife and stabbed him to death.

The boy ran home elated—"I killed the werewolf!" he told everyone. But at daybreak, when they ventured back to see the body, he was horrified to find Pedro Candido instead.

Still, no one blamed him. These things happen out here.